HENRY GREEN was the pen name for Henry Vincent Yorke, the son of a prosperous Midlands industrialist. He was born near Tewkesbury in 1905 and was educated at Eton and Oxford, where he wrote his first novel, *Blindness*, published in 1926. He entered the family business on the factory floor, and went on to run the firm while writing eight other novels. For Angus Wilson, he "was one of the few really considerable novelists of our time", while W. H. Auden considered him to be "the finest living English novelist". Henry Green died in 1973.

JEREMY TREGLOWN is the author of *Romancing: the Life and Work of Henry Green*. He was educated at Oxford and was a lecturer there and at University College London before joining the staff of the *Times Literary Supplement*, of which he was editor from 1982 to 1990. He is now a professor of English at the University of Warwick. His other works include a biography of Roald Dahl.

Also by Henry Green

Fiction

BLINDNESS

LIVING

PARTY GOING

LOVING

BACK

CONCLUDING

NOTHING

DOTING

Uncollected Writings

SURVIVING

Memoir

PACK MY BAG

THE LONDON FICTION SERIES

Henry Green

CAUGHT

With an Introduction by
Jeremy Treglown

THE HARVILL PRESS
LONDON

First published in 1943 by The Hogarth Press

This paperback edition first published in 2001 by
The Harvill Press, 2 Aztec Row, Berners Road, London N1 0PW

www.harvill.com

1 3 5 7 9 8 6 4 2

A CIP catalogue record for this book is available from the British Library

ISBN 1 86046 831 4

Printed and bound in Great Britain by Mackays of Chatham

Photograph of Henry Green courtesy of the Imperial War Museum / *Observer to Sebastian*

INTRODUCTION

Caught is the most vivid and powerful novel set in the London Blitz, and among the most memorable fictions about any aspect of the Second World War. Henry Green inscribed the last page, "*London, June 1940 – Christmas 1942*" – a reminder not only of where and when he wrote the book but that, like all his work, it came directly out of personal experience. Contemporary propaganda, for good reasons, presented the city's inhabitants as responding to the Blitz not only with resilience but with communitarian generosity and, so far as the rescue services were concerned, with a high degree of organization and professional skill. *Caught* looks coolly at these still durable myths, while revealing with Green's inimitable clarity the emotional truth of each individual, "rolled", as he writes, "each in his or her deep mystery".

Brought up partly in central London and partly in the Gloucestershire countryside, Green – whose real name was Henry Yorke – spent his entire adult life, after university and a couple of years in industrial Birmingham, in the capital. He moved there permanently in 1929, when he married, and died there in 1973. When war threatened, he was among the earliest volunteers for the Auxiliary Fire Service, joining in October 1938. His base was Sub-station 34A5V "A" Division, at 79 Davies Street, W1, one of numerous fire stations responsible for the City of Westminster – roughly, the area bordered by Oxford Street, Fetter Lane, the River Thames and Kensington Gardens. To be a fireman there at that time was among the most dangerous and valuable tasks available to anyone.

Caught's main character, Richard Roe, in many ways closely resembles the novelist himself, but beyond Roe, the book, like all Green's novels, is intensely concerned to communicate the lives of "ordinary" people. Green was an exact contemporary of George Orwell, and his pioneering second novel, *Living* (1929), published four years before the latter's *Down and Out in Paris and London*, had been about factory workers in Birmingham. *Caught*, Green's fourth, is largely set in a wartime fire station. It concerns not only Richard, and the contrast between the fire service and the privileged country-house environment in which he was brought up and where his young son now lives, but also the people he gets to know in the AFS and the London worlds to which they belong. Green knows his characters extremely well: the over-promoted, insecure regular fireman, Pye; the ingenious old skiver, Piper; Piper's friend Mary, who becomes the cook. Individuals like these, however clumsy, inadequate and thwarted, are stubbornly presented as more important than their war-work, and often at odds with it. Piper is more concerned with his mother's bad leg than with listening to the fire service instructor. Mary Howells does her best at the cooking job but cares much more about what is happening to her maritally abused daughter, Brid, and her baby. Mary fails to help Brid and in the process gets into trouble at the fire station. Until near the end of the book these, and not the heroics of wartime propaganda, are the kinds of situation which Green wants to convey. If at times the novel reads like *EastEnders*, that is partly what he was aiming for.

He had other purposes, though. He was later to say that one of his major influences had been Céline, who had written in *Journey to the End of the Night* that recording the worst one has seen "without changing one word" is "work enough for a lifetime". Green's account of London in the Blitz has something in common with Céline's of Paris in 1914–18, with its focus on cowardice, looting and sexual licence. In *Caught*, Green came closer than any other English writer of the time to the shocked verisimilitude of poets of the First World War. There is none of the directness that this comparison implies. The book is wry and oblique, and part of its distinctiveness lies in the extent to which it isn't about the war at all, but about people conducting their muddled lives in much the same way as at any other time. But in the novel's stupendous last section we are at last given a full-scale account of Richard's role in the Blitz, and, through it, a bleak glimpse of the war as a whole.

Richard has been invalided home to the country, shocked by blast and exhausted by nine continuous weeks of fire-fighting. Wandering up and down the garden with his sister-in-law, Dy, while his son Christopher runs around playing, he gives a halting, obsessive account of the first big raid that he faced and in which it turns out that two of the firemen we have got to know were killed. This story – the first and only part of the book which describes military action – is intercut with a more full-blown third-person narrative descant, or Greek chorus, in which the more spectacular aspects are filled out. In this way, Richard's frustrated, dejected memories of general chaos and panic are qualified by another view, in which people – including, despite his self-castigation, Richard himself – are seen to have acted bravely in an uncontrollable situation: a massive dockland timberyard on fire, the flames spreading to ships moored in the Thames, scores of separate fire-fighting units racing around with no intercommunications and no effective overall command, enemy bombers still arriving in waves, water supplies cut off, hoses shredded, pigeons catching fire in the air. This agonizing double narrative – "simply repeatedly plain, the truth, over and over again", like the song heard in a nightclub by Richard and his fire service girlfriend Hilly – has to contend with a mixture on Dy's part of boredom, distraction and, despite her attempts at sympathy, her instinctive English resistance to any show of feeling. At one point she gives Richard a pat but when tears fill his eyes she briskly withdraws. Beside them, Christopher carries on his separate, but not unrelated, imaginative life of violent military fantasies, ironically imagining himself as the enemy from which his father has sought to protect him:

> "Look," his father interrupted, "haven't you knocked those branches about enough? There's hardly a bird left in the garden since you've been out. You'd do better to put food for them. They starve in this weather you know."
>
> "They're Polish people," Christopher said, "and I'm a German policeman, rootling them about."

This unnerving moment is one of few in the book when events outside England are mentioned. The firemen "hardly ever discussed the war", and Roe's superior Pye, in particular, is so caught up with his professional and psycho-sexual muddles that he is "too disturbed to notice the invasion of Norway". The war impinges on Pye's thoughts chiefly as an opportunity for social change. Characteristically, Green both satirizes his class resentments and sympathizes with them. Pye's strange, forced proximity to Roe is emphasized by the fact that their names are adjacent letters in the Greek alphabet – and together, of course, they mean fire. Yet there's no mistaking the contrasts between the two men, claustrophobically entangled while utterly separated by the kinds of determinant which not even war can change: luck, for example. So, Pye's tortured half-memories of an adolescent act of incest with his sister are set against the amiable tenderness between Richard and Dy. Pye is ditched by the girl with whom he has been having an affair, while Richard and Hilly have a more fulfilling, if temporary, relationship. And whereas the unmarried and childless Pye's kindness to a boy he finds in the street is fatally misinterpreted (this is one of the title's meanings), for Richard the end of the book means returning, complicatedly enough but far from unenviably, to his young son and the family home. There is a latent political theme, then, running alongside Green's less schematic absorption in how these very different men resemble each other in both rebelling against and being subdued by the relations and conventions of the work place. The latter is one of the issues which the book carries forward from *Living*.

Among its characters' longings, exaggerations, inventions and cover-ups, the narrative wanders in a fatalistic mood: "She was, of course, hopelessly wrong in this"; "But he was wrong"; "In this the men were wrong." Green later claimed to dislike too-knowing story-tellers, but what he really distrusted was omnipotence, not omniscience. He knows what his people are doing, but knows, too, that in an imaginatively truthful story they can't be saved from it. If few works of fiction are quicker than *Caught* to point out their own ironies, few, either, allow sympathetic characters to be simultaneously so craven. Richard buys favour with his fellow firemen. He pimps for them. He spreads gossip. He looks for his own immediate professional advantage even in his relationship with the WAFS girl, Hilly. Graham Greene did not admit so unheroic a hero into *Ministry of Fear*, his novel set in the Blitz and published at the same time as *Caught*, in June, 1943 – though the moral ambivalence of Maurice Bendrix, the protagonist of *The End of the Affair* (1951) may have owed something to Richard. Like Elizabeth Bowen in *The Heat of the Day* (largely written during the war, though not published until 1949), Graham Greene uses wartime London as a background for psycho-political melodrama, for treason and high speeches. When the main characters of these novelists behave badly, it is on a grand scale. No such indulgence is extended to Richard. Even his courage is largely motivated by fear of being thought incompetent, and what seems to stir him most is the opportunity for voyeurism afforded by a rapt couple he finds in an air-raid shelter.

Artistic honesty of this sort doesn't come without a struggle – one which Green didn't always win. Like Green's other novels, *Caught* involves experiments of style and handling which pose challenges to the reader, not least in the early flashback to the abduction of Richard's son in a department store, an episode which will link Richard with Pye. To a sympathetic reader, though, this and other inchoate-seeming elements come to seem part of the confusion of war itself. Unlike Bowen, with her deft but traditional narrative fluency, or Greene with his sensational sideshows, Henry Green refuses to let himself fall back on "artistry" or "effects". In this, the writer closest to him was his protégé James Hanley, whose *No Directions* was published in the same year as *Caught* and *Ministry of Fear*. *Caught*, though, is far the more complex book. It is also much more readable. It's often very funny – the firemen's cockroach race, the *Keystone Cops*-ish slapstick of Richard's first fire, when the two regular firemen charge up the stairs of the wrong house and the auxiliaries drive back without them. Such echoes of particular films are matched by a calculatedly cinematic vividness in the narrative cutting, especially in the central section with its interlaced duets – Pye and Prudence; Piper and Mary; Mary's daughter Brid and her husband; especially Richard and his girlfriend, Hilly.

While the book's title alludes to fire, as well as to being found out, in the slang of the time the word could also suggest romantic infatuation. The exhilaration of the wartime sexual freedom represented by Richard's affair with Hilly is one of *Caught*'s themes – exhilaration, but also what it half-concealed and what it could cost:

> . . . these women seemed already given up to the male in uniform so soon to go away, these girls, as they felt, soon to be killed themselves, so little time left, moth deathly gay, in a daze of giving.
>
> That same afternoon the train to Portsmouth had wives dragged along the platform hanging limp to door handles and snatched off by porters in the way a man, standing aside, will pick bulrushes out of a harvest waggon load of oats.

Caught is full of love and loss, not least in its vision of Roe's dead wife, recalled with longing tenderness, "now that he did not see her every evening, rather mocking, aloof, as gentle as he had been curt always, the touch of her white rose petal skin an unchanging part of what his life had been before". The novel is also permeated by a sense that things are going frighteningly out of control. For these and other reasons, it was controversial. Both the printers and the publisher, Leonard Woolf, were so anxious about the picture it gave of wartime London that, had it not been defended both by its editor, John Lehmann, and by another writer-fireman, Stephen Spender, it would not have appeared. As they and, later, some reviewers saw, the book's value lay precisely in its not being propagandist. *Caught* is simultaneously grim, tender, unexpected and true: the best tribute any artist could have paid to London and Londoners in the early 1940s.

JEREMY TREGLOWN

This book is about the Auxiliary Fire Service which saved London in her night blitzes, and bears no relation, or resemblance, to the National Fire Service, which took over when raids on London had ended.

The characters, while founded on the reality of that time, are not drawn from life. They are all imaginary men and women. In this book only 1940 in London is real. It is the effect of that time that I have written into the fiction of *Caught*.

H.G.

CAUGHT

WHEN WAR BROKE OUT in September we were told to expect air raids. Christopher, who was five, had been visiting his grandparents in the country. His father, a widower, decided that he must stay down there with his aunt, and not come back to London until the war was over.

The father, Richard Roe, had joined the Fire Service as an Auxiliary. He was allowed one day's leave in three. That is, throughout forty-eight hours he stood by in case there should be a fire, and then had twenty-four in which he could do as he pleased. There were no week-ends off. Public holidays were not recognised. The trains at once became so slow that there was no way he could get down to see Christopher in a day.

Christopher was like any other child of his age, not very interested or interesting, strident with health. He enjoyed teasing and was careful no one should know what he felt.

He was naturally, a responsibility but, with things as they were in the first few months, he was not too great a one, nevertheless rather irritating at a distance. War puts men in this position, however, that they can do little about their own affairs, they have no prospects, their incomes fluctuate wildly, heavier taxation is always threatened. As soon as Roe felt he could do no more for the boy than he had already done and by what he was still doing, dropping in to the office on leave days, Christopher grew very much closer to him.

After a time, when the turmoil of the first weeks of war subsided, conditions settled in the Service, and it became possible to do ninety-six on duty to get forty-eight hours off. In this way, after three months of war and no raids, that is of anticlimax, Roe worked four days to be two days on leave.

He took a train. It was raining. The carriages were full of young men uniformed. Soon they were in darkness. When, some time later, in considerable suspense, he stepped out at night into more cold rain, back into his old life, on to a platform shining as ink, like a dark picture done on glass framed to screen electric light, he told himself he had been wrong to expect so much of this meeting.

His aunt, Dy, had brought Christopher to meet the train with his cousin Rosemary. This child was three years older than Christopher who, at that time, would not be parted from her. But she was old enough to say some of the conventional things when they shook hands. Roe felt sorry she had not been left behind. It was too dark, the engine made much noise, and they had to see that Christopher was not bowled over, or did not get down on the line in his excitement, which, in part, was showing off. This tired Richard, and the boy had become over-excited. There was dark and hissing. In the car at last, Christopher talked incomprehensibly to Rosemary of some game or pretence of their own. With all this still between the three of them the child was put to bed by his nurse.

The next morning Roe went to fetch Christopher from day school. They were shy of each other. He wanted to buy him sweets but could not hear which shop the boy said was best, Christopher was so low off the ground, and he was rather deaf. It may have been politeness, but his son let him go by three which would have done, until, in the end, they came to almost the last shop in this small street, a stationer's. He took him in to look. There were no sweets, but he bought a children's paper Christopher wanted, then led him back to the shop he knew Dy liked, where she got her chocolate. It may now have been that the child's shyness of other school children, or the shyness of being alone with his father, was beginning to wear off, but when they got back to this particular shop Christopher said distinctly this was the best in town. It was the first thing Roe had really heard him say all morning, which was unusual because as a rule the child would shout the few things he wanted.

They bought a great deal, so much that Roe was afraid his son would only remember the leave by how ill he had been. The old man who served them was tiresome. Christopher said yes to whatever was offered. Roe began to feel the boy might not be having his own choice. He could pick nothing for himself. It is possible that he was confused by the amount he was getting. But he seemed satisfied, although he had not lost his reserve. He stayed silent until they had walked the few yards home, when he ran on ahead to shew some of the sweets to his cousin. Roe carried the rest to the nursery. Christopher asked if he could have lunch downstairs. Roe had not expected this. The house was full of people. He was relieved when the nanny had a good reason against.

After lunch father and son were to take a walk alone. When Christopher was punctually brought down ready to go out, Roe found that he himself was shy. The child seemed so unapproachably young.

There had, as yet, been no raids on London. Because this was his first leave, Roe felt that the moment he got back to the substation he might be in the thick of it, after the fruitless waiting.

Also this was to be their first walk alone together. Whereas in the old days he could have arranged it any afternoon.

By the time they started out the rain had stopped. Dy put the boy's hat in his pocket, and, with a pang Roe heard him angrily cry out that he did not want it. There was too much fuss before they were off.

He took his father up the garden by a back way. Roe had

never used this, and, to break the ice, tried to make something of its being so dark, for there was a high wall one side, thick shrubs on the other. But Christopher was definite. In a loud voice he told his father it was to hide all sight of the gardeners from the lawn, as these men went from kitchen to kitchen garden, and back again. From that moment he spoke up.

Separated by privet from the aspect of those lawns and borders familiar to him, Roe was brought to a red brick wall he knew, along which were trained pear trees, and to a door he had never seen, not the flamboyant wrought-iron gate which opened on to that cinder path between cabbages, which led to the peaches, but, when Christopher had turned a brass knob, one that let them into the glasshouse given over to palms, hot, with long dark flowing leaves perennially dark green. Christopher broke away. He ran on to be first so that he could open the door out, on a brass latch. Recognising, when they had gone through, what had last year been a bed of carrots, Roe asked whether he remembered how in the summer they had all gone to get something for his rabbit, that he had pulled one up, and eaten it raw. Christopher said he did not know, then added coldly that his rabbit was sent away.

It came on to rain as they went along, but gently, in a mist. Roe never thought to make him put on his hat.

By the time they had come to three gardeners in a fig house spraying the heart-shaped leaves from a portable tank, Christopher was quite wet. He insisted on working the handle, and Roe helped. Then he wanted to do it on his own. Then he went inside. He took the nozzle, sending the chemical solution where he pleased. Roe thought the boy might get some in his eyes, but did not like to forbid him.

Then Christopher took his father off. They went to the summer house beyond. They found a dead mouse.

They took a path up out of the gardens into the park. It was steep in places. Roe slipped and fell, full length.

Christopher was much amused. They both laughed. He kept on saying his father had looked so funny, too often. Roe noticed the wet had brought out a curl in the child's hair, which he had never seen anything but straight.

They climbed a gate into the park. Ordinarily there was a view, from the cart track they followed, out over country which stretched to the first Welsh hills. But this day a permanence of rain softened what was near, and half hid by catching the soft light all that was far, in the way a veil will obscure, yet enhance the beauty of a well-remembered face or, in a naked body so covered, sharpen the sight. In such a way this stretch of country he knew so well was made the nearer to him by rain.

They threw wet sticks to see who could send these amongst the deer that moved off faster than they came up, merging ahead until these heraldic cattle were a part of the mist, unidentifiable in rain. Christopher was light-hearted. His father had regrets. He wished it had all been less, as a man can search to find he knows not what behind a netted brilliant skin, the eyes of a veiled face, as he can also go with his young son parted from him by the years that are between, from her by the web of love and death, or from remembered country by the weather, in the sadness of not finding.

They were now on top of a hill which was not long. They came to where there was a hollow. Sunk in the middle of this, level with the turf, they found a big domed triangle of concrete. There was an iron door, padlocked fast. It might have been one of those houses in which ice used to be kept against the summer, when we had hard winters. In these days it was more probably a cistern to supply the manor house with water, but, speaking down to what he took to be his level of romance, Roe, in a roundabout way, said it was a secret, that he had never shewn anyone before, this was where the hob-goblins lived, no one had ever known this place but him. Christopher said, "but nanny knows, Rosemary knows, oh everybody knows." Roe said he'd had no idea of that. Christopher made out he was sorry but it was so, and he did not think fairies lived there. When he was asked how he could tell, all he would say was that he knew he did not think they did.

Christopher took hold of his father's hand. They went on with their walk, beneath bare oaks from which water dripped, watched by the deer, turned heads and pointed ears. Then, after a silence, Roe was surprised to be asked if he really thought fairies were people. He said he was not sure. He was told that his son knew they were. He asked why. He was answered that the nanny had met an old man from Wales who had seen one. Roe said if he should see one for himself then he would let Christopher know. The question next put to him was whether he would tell Christopher first. He told the boy he would let him know before anyone. He was then asked why. He said he supposed it would be because he was not sure that Dy would be interested, anyway that he had been talking about fairies to Christopher only, so it would be natural to tell Christopher first.

Christopher said, "Yes."

They came to the trap for rooks which stood in one corner of the park, a square space with walls of rabbit wire, now rotted. Christopher remembered, he said with satisfaction, how they used to caw in it, beating from side to side against the wire until the keeper came with his gun.

Then, as they turned to come back, going out of their way to climb along a fallen tree, another herd of deer moved off into the veil, heads up, one of them coughing. He wanted to know if it was going to die. Asking this he struck so close to the note this sad day played over and over, with the wet, the silence once broken, flying low over tops of trees, by a warplane which he did not even look up to watch, neither did the deer, and to the note repeated which was this separation that war had forced into their lives, all these sounded the closing phrase of a call to depart, and Roe said the deer would die, that it was sure to.

Roe had to go back that night. He said goodbye in the hall, the front door open on to the darkness and the journey. Standing there, awkwardly shaking hands, he wished, and he wished too late, that he had never made a point of not kissing Christopher. He was upset, at that moment no contact with his son could have been too close.

As he drove away he felt he had lost everything, and in particular the boy. Yet he had to admit that he could, at the time, feel nothing stronger than irritation when, some months earlier, as will appear, Christopher had really been lost in London.

ON THE JOURNEY BACK back he was alone in the carriage. He put his feet up and lay relaxed, his back to the whirling dark outside. He remembered how, from curiosity, he had been to look at the store out of which Christopher had been abducted. It was disastrous that the woman who took the boy away should be his Fireman Instructor's sister. Hardly less fatal that the store had been lit by stained glass windows in front of arc lamps which cast the violent colours of that glass over the goods laid out on counters.

He remembered, in the autumn, it was dusk as they used to arrive at the fire station to report, in dark blue overalls, rubber boots, and what looked like a chauffeur's cap with a white metal badge. The tower each station has in its yard, the five open platforms one above the other, each the height from ground level of the floor of a building, was partially visible by street lights, monstrous, overwhelming because there were no railings round its platforms.

When he was sixteen a friend of the family, a man who studied church windows, had taken them round just under those in the choir of Tewkesbury Abbey, on a ledge about forty feet from the ground. This step which ran along in the thickness of the walls was no more than a yard in width and had nothing to the side, no balustrade, no rail. Every so often they had to get by cords, cutting across from each window down to the floor that seemed so far beneath. These were the means by which panels in the glass could be opened to ventilate the choir. As they went round, each one in turn had to take hold of a cord with his right hand to step over left leg first, and then, in his own case, as he faced right to bring his right leg over, he had that terror of the urge to leap, his back to deep violet and yellow Bible stories on the glass, his eyes reluctant over the whole grey stretch of the Abbey until they were drawn, abruptly as to a chasm, inevitably, and so far beneath, down to that floor hemmed with pews, that height calling on the pulses and he did not know why to his ears, down to dropped stone flags over which sunlight had cast the colour in each window, the colour it seemed his blood had turned.

At the station they used to pitch the escape and climb up that sharply narrowing, rattling ladder, red, but it would by now be too dark to see, up to the head painted white for work at night with, in this dusk, a voice from the sea bellowing advice below, all of them getting out of breath, fumbling, some telling themselves, and even each other, not to look down. After the first few times they were handy at it, but in the beginning, and most of all before they had been sent up, he would get wet in the seat of his trousers as he walked past the half seen tower at six o'clock, unlike by more than the time of day that other under which, on sun-laden evenings, the windows for seven hundred years had stained the flags, as it might be with coward's blood.

As he lay in the carriage, he had to arch his back and twist to stub out his cigarette, in a tray fixed by the door.

When, from curiosity, he went to see for himself the store out of which Christopher had been abducted, he stopped, unknowing, by that very counter with the toy display which had so struck his son as to make him lost. Fire engines attracted the father, but deer, then sailboats, had bewitched the son. For both it was the deep colour spilled over these objects that, by evoking memories they would not name, and which they could not place, held them, and then led both to a loch-deep unconsciousness of all else.

The walls of this store being covered with stained glass windows which depicted trading scenes, that is of merchandise being loaded on to galleons, the leaving port, of incidents on the voyage, and then the unloading, all brilliantly lit from without, it follows that the body of the shop was inundated with colour, brimming, and this colour, as the sea was a predominant part of each window, was a permanence of sapphire in shopping hours. Pink neon lights on the high ceiling wore down this blue to some extent, made customers' faces less aggressively steeped in the body of the store, but enhanced, or deepened that fire brigade scarlet to carmine, and, in so doing, drugged Richard's consciousness.

He then saw the heraldic deer, the light that caught red in their bead eyes. And the sails, motionless, might have been stretched above a deeper patch of fathomless sea in the shade of foothills as though covered with hyacinths in that imagined light of evening, and round which, laden, was to come the wind that would give them power to move the purple shade they cast beside the painted boat they were to drive.

In remembering his stand at the counter he supposed he had been trying to see what his son had seen. He imagined that, his pink cheeks grape dark in the glow, Christopher had leant his face forward, held to ransom by the cupidity of boys, and had been lost in feelings that this colour, reflected in such a way on so much that he wanted, could not have failed to bring him who could have visited no flower-locked sea on the Aegean, and yet, with every other child, or boy at school, with any man in the mood, who knew and always would that stretch of water, those sails from the past, those boats fishing in the senses.

Christopher had been carrying one of these toy boats when he was brought back by the police.

(He had talked beneath his breath. "Not touch," the child said, "not touch." Looking straight in front he did not move his head. His feet, taking him sideways, let his eyes gather the hoard. At scarlet-painted fire engines, and he was so close that he saw them full size, he said "dad," and was satisfied. Until he came before the boats, "ships," he had said. He was done. He stood rooted, one finger up a nostril, his hot sloe mouth pressed against mahogany, before those sails the colour of his eyes.)

In the railway carriage, as he was being carried back, the father imagined his son must have pointed a finger and shouted, "I want, I want." He said to himself, it is not for us to measure the dark cupidity, the need.

(When the lady, who sidled by, talked to Christopher he did not answer, or try to break the spell which held his eyes. Words were no means of communication now. It was the same the second time she spoke. But when she pulled at his jacket, he did look up and saw nothing strange in how she was, caught full by the light from those windows, so that her skin was blue and her orbs, already sapphire, a sea flashing at hot sunset as, uneasy, she glanced left, then right. The illumination above, as it might be the late sun on bits of glass about the shores of Greece, stayed sharpened to points on her eyes as she turned these from person to person. She bent down to repeat what she had said. At the angle she now held herself she lost those rose diamonds in her eyes, these were shaded, and so had gone an even deeper blue. He became dazzled by the pink neon lights beyond her features. Caught in another patch of colour, some of her chin was pillar-box red, also a part of the silver fox she wore. Furtively she glanced right, then left, but when, to make him do as she wanted, she caught full at him with her eyes that, by the ocean in which they were steeped, were so much a part of the world his need had made, and so much more a part of it by being alive, then he felt anything must be natural, and was ready to do whatever she asked.)

(When, finally, she bought the boat his hunger took him close to until it was life size, and the saleswoman had engulfed it in a bag so that he could not see the glory, that is the transfiguration, die in those sails turned back to white canvas once out of the dominion of the glass, then he was finished as he clasped, within the paper that wrapped it, his ship, in his eyes wine coloured yet, still the colour his eyes had been and were now no longer, now that he had turned his back and was moving away, out of the store, led off by this stranger.)

(The moment they were outside, in the dull light of autumn when rain threatens at late afternoon, the instant the windows could no longer cast over him the storied sea he had never seen in the way a rose, held close, holds summer, sun-laden evenings at six o'clock, then he began to question his surroundings.)

(In the bus, whenever she caught a woman's eye, she smiled.)

(He sat, holding the bag on his knee, gradually losing what he held. The colour was gone out of those sails, although he would not look to make sure until he was back home. He held on to what he was losing by not allowing himself to find the glory had departed. Nevertheless, it made him critical of this lady and, because he had always had meals at regular hours and was now late for tea, he was hungry. "Where's Nan?" he asked as they went. He was thinking of food. She imagined he must mean a little sister.

If she had but known it, he was an only child. "She will be coming directly," was her answer and, as she did not reveal the mistake she had made, he was satisfied.)

(Then a short dark walk, and they had arrived.)

Lying on the carriage seat the father groaned in discomfort. Going over that store in memory, he had just told himself that the light was as though he had been seeing the toys through Christmas cracker paper.

(The lady took Christopher into a room. It was very hot. It had a coal fire. He was surprised that she did not take off his things. She crouched by the fire. Looking back over her shoulder, she poked it, saying, "the darling, the darling." She did not turn on the light, so that he could see her eyes only by their glitter, a sparkle by the fire, which, as it was disturbed to flame, sent her shadow reeling, gyrating round sprawling rosy walls. "I've done right haven't I, the darling," she murmured. "My tea," he announced, surprised to find none.)

(He imagined this was a party. He could not think where the other children could be playing. He began to unwrap the boat. She came across to unbutton his jacket. Her fingers trembled. She had difficulty. Her shoulder blotted out all direct light. The sails were now as dark as the shadows of her face. He had to bend his head down to his knees to see the hull. A movement of her arm and, in a flickering reddish light, as though in a show of dark rose petals, all his boat glowed at him for a moment, no longer blue, but as if revealed by a beacon afire on foothills above a dark ocean. Another movement of her body and he could no longer see the sails, or no more than a glint. She breathed quick. She muttered, "the darling." He was too hot. She went on at his coat. Then on a sudden he threw himself back. She had fumbled too much. "Don't," he cried out. Having voiced it he was very afraid. So much so that he did not at once begin to bawl and yell.)

(He screamed, "don't." She snatched away her hands

which, outspread before her face, wrists against mouth, fingers pointing at him, shook with urgency. "Hush dear," she said quiet, "oh hush." "Nan," he shouted out. "For Christ's sake," she said and gulped, "your little sister's coming, d'you hear." Then he saw. For he knew he had no sister.)

(He took a great breath. He opened his mouth wide. He yelled. In horror at the noise she leant back, letting the firelight full on to his face. This was now entirely round, red and so round that both eyes disappeared in his frown. His pointed tongue curled up, dull red. Bubbles were blown, then burst, then were blown again over his enamelled wet teeth. "Look," she said low, "your lovely boat." She held it up. He smashed, with one swipe of the wrist knocking it out of her hand. His ship fell mast first on to the carpet, and did not break. He did not watch. He drew another great breath. This time the yell was louder, higher. It cost him more effort, even made him twist his body. He lay sideways after. She put both hands over her mouth, which was wide open, and so left, in the shadow, a dark hole between firelit fingers over a dark face. He saw from her eyes, from a single, sly smirk, that she was looking at the door behind. Screwing up his eyes he took an even deeper breath, he swelled, he grew, bunched his hands up into fists, in his terror became years younger than his age, and, making an arch of his spine, he let out an astounding screech of hate and fright.)

(At that moment the door opened. Whoever it was came in, took the lady out. Christopher sobbed. Then, or almost at once, was quiet. Out of breath he sat up, gathered his vessel and, gasping, eyes floating with salt water which overflowed in huge tears, he fingered the bowsprit. He choked. He snivelled a bit. And then all was over, forgotten seemingly, done with.)

Roe leaned forward to scratch the calf of his right leg. Before he lay down once more, he blew his nose. He was smirking, that is to say embarrassed, because he did not know what Christopher had been through, the child was too young to be able to tell, because it was his Fireman Instructor, Pye's, sister of all people, and because, when the boy had been returned by the police, holding his boat tight, Roe was not in the house to put the questions expected.

He groaned as he remembered the upset. The police told Dy they had found Christopher seated comfortable in front of a fire. But if that were so, why was it that the boy could never play with a sailboat again? And why did Dy never refer to this, even when there was the scene with a tanker, painted tropic white, that Christopher simply hurled away from him not three weeks later? He groaned once more as he remembered the situation when at last he himself had returned that fatal afternoon.

"I do wish you had been here," she said, "so unlucky," and then went on that he would have thought of all kinds of things to ask. Then she told him the story as she knew it, but so brokenly, so interrupted by her imagination, by her feeling for the boy's feelings in surroundings she could not grasp that she was extremely vague, giving him no picture at all. On which he made her go over all the ground again. This time she had been more explicit, speaking something after this fashion:

"Well, when this man," she meant the fireman Pye, "came back from his work, they say he said he found my true darling absolutely all right, perfectly happy really, sitting there, you see, where she left him, good as gold. She went out to get some milk, or something. But I don't believe a word of it. I'm sure they were both of them preparing something awful, oh isn't it dreadful, the poor old chap. Oh yes, I forgot to tell you, that beast is a fireman. Richard," she had said, and this time he moaned where he lay at the recollection, "when are you going to finish with this Fire Service business?"

He had not known that Pye had a sister. For days after

he did not dare go to the station, telling himself there must be many of the same name in the Brigade, but experienced enough to know that there was no escape. The moment she told him he had known. Later he had asked if she were sure, and what station this Pye was supposed to come from? As he lay in the carriage he gave one short laugh at the thought of how he had tried to evade the inevitable so soon.

"How should I tell what station," she said, "darling? She's his sister or so he says. It's insane, the whole thing's mad. How can things like this happen nowadays? When you think of all the money that's spent on clinics and hospitals where people get treatment and still children are taken away, I'll never not believe any story like this again. But the darling's all right, the doctor is perfectly satisfied, isn't he Richard, he didn't tell you anything, did he, I mean when you were taking him to the door the last visit, and that you haven't told me, did he?"

She made him promise the doctor had not told him anything that he had not told her. And she had gone on about the fire station. Oh dear, and then she had gone on. But she had kept off Christopher's mother. And then the tears.

All this came to pass long before the war, in the days when he was still training to become an Auxiliary. Rolling uncomfortably on to his back, he turned Pye over, chewed the cud on Pye.

He called Pye to mind, the Pye of those days, the happy Pye on his pet subject. He was a small, dark, powerful man who, once each week, would make an address, it might be in the middle of a lecture on elementary hydraulics, but always in roughly the following muddled terms.

"I don't hold with the necessity of the AFS," he would say, "because I don't hold with the necessity for war. But our parents didn't ask us if we wanted to be born, they couldn't ask me or any of you. When I got to an age when I could use my mental processes, I found I had grown to be a man in a world other men had made to their own advantage.

Now, I have fought all my life to improve conditions in this job through the Fire Brigade's Union, though it's done me no good with what they once described to me here as 'the powers that be.' And what I'm getting at is this. We find ourselves in the condition that the right to live, or what is the same thing, the right to work, is put into the melting pot for the gain of a few. But if we do have a war, and mind you I'm not saying we shall 'ave, or that we ought to, because I don't think anything need be settled by killing innocent men, or their wives and families, then I say that there must be something like an AFS organisation. But I don't hold with it."

"No, that's right," an old recruit called Piper would say at this point, nodding his head. This man echoed, or put in a few words to shew that he agreed, whenever the instructor drew breath, or paused to disentangle the thoughts that rose like magic bean stalks in his head.

"Now there's many downstairs," Pye would go on, referring to his fellow firemen, "that don't like the idea of your coming into the Job. They think it may come to an attack on the conditions they exist under. Take a fireman's wage, it's not an abundance. But as I say to them in the messroom below, we can't expect to deal with the fires that may be started as a result of war action, not on our bloody own we can't. Yet some of them are like that, they'll hardly speak to a lad until he's three years out of the drill class, till he's been three years a fireman. And they're the kind who think this war, if there is one, will be like the last. I think they're mistaken. And I like to take an interest, I'm not afraid of new faces as some are, even educated men. My father could not give me a better or worse education than what many of you have, but I like to meet strangers, I take the position they may teach me something I don't know. Still there's a prejudice against you lads, you might as well know, it's only fair to you. And yet there's many like me have said right along that we in the Brigade must make the best of it with all of you which I'm bound to say I don't think necessary, because war is not an alternative, not with civilised human beings, or shouldn't be."

Then Piper would say, "of course it shouldn't."

This was before Christopher had been abducted, at a time when Pye could speak freely in Roe's presence, without ending almost every period, because he was always talking, by a dark reference to his sister's little trouble. Piper's echoes had been doubly embarrassing then.

Piper was older than the rest of the volunteers. He did say he was fifty-nine, but then he might well have been drawing his old age pension.

He had a narrow, dark face, not healthy, and coloured as is the sole of a shoe after walking dry streets in summer, whether by dirt, or ill-health, or both, it was hard to tell. Talking of the war that impended he would say if "this bit of trouble" came to anything, it would be his "fifth campaign." At lectures he dodged the instructors with approving comments. These men had learned by heart that which they had to give. Piper would hush any recruit who shuffled, and then would repeat the last few words of what he had just heard. At first he had been called on by Pye for confirmation, probably because he was so much older than the rest. Pye might be reciting:

"By virtue of the fact that you get gas before you know or you can realise, when I was out in France I have met lines of men coming back in single file, their hands on each other's shoulders, blinded. Is that right Piper?"

The old man would nod his head, which was newspaper white. He had thick dark eyebrows, with a yellow white moustache. His hair was short, so that the skin, dry and pied, and as though travel stained with dust, came through in places.

"That's right," he would say, "in file, caught before they rightly knew they 'ad it."

He was the prize bore. It was not long after that he was

repeating unasked. Worse, he began not to understand. He echoed wrong. So it came about, when they were doing "knots and lines," that Pye asked one of his long rhetorical questions, as follows:

"Now take a fire, you are in attendance, you've got inside, and there is a man flaked out at your feet, perhaps he's just by a window, it might be one of your own mates. You've got your lowering line handy, there may be no other means of getting him down, very likely the staircase will be burned out, well you would do the obvious, you will lower him away out of that window, or have a dab at it. Now then, what knot would you use?" "Why you would make a yachtsman's purchase," Piper put in too soon. For the first few times Pye kept his temper. He would say no more than, "No, you will use a chair knot, or the bowline on a bight, you all know what a yachtsman's purchase is for, or you should, to strengthen a ladder. But try and be a credit, don't speak out of turn." Piper said, "That's right." "When they come to give you the examination," Pye went on, "I shall get a bottle, they'll blame me if you pretend to more knowledge than you have required. Don't give them long answers if they should ask you. You can't know everything in this job. So don't get me a blister. For God's sake pipe down." At this the class would laugh dutifully, none louder than the ancient, his voice high and cracked. But, once started, nothing would stop Piper and before long he was saying "That's so," or "Of course," every five minutes, nodding his parched head in agreement, looking sideways.

"And how would you get a lowering line suppose you had gone in without? You can't send a message because your means of escape is cut off. Fire moves fast, as you'll find, it swirls and gets behind you. It makes a wind, that's a strange thing." "It would do," from Piper. Pye went on, "The man who loses his mental faculties is the one to get left. What's left of him will be his axe and spanner, and the buckle of his belt. I'm not telling you a story, there's the museum at Headquarters, you've only to ask the bastards there, and if you're lucky, very, they'll let you in. You'll find the label with his name on they got from the number stamped on 'is axe." "That's right," said Piper. "Well, all right," said Pye, and continued, "you don't want to fry, or do you? What would you do?" Piper said, "I would throw down me bobbin line." "Yes, your bobbin line, carried in a leather pouch on the belt, one hundred and twenty feet of the best unpolished sash cord wound round a reel. Now, when you go to drop this bobbin line, don't throw it out, or it will come back and smash the window directly below, and likely enough get caught up there. No, just drop it out quiet and easy, let the reel fall from your fingers, and you'll find it will unwind lovely. One of your mates on the ground will bend you the lowering line on the end. Now then, when you have raised the old lowering line, what would you make do? Remember, you're hot in where you are, you want to get out, you aren't an Indian, you daren't try the rope trick, though that's just superstition that story, my father only gave me what he could afford, namely a working man's ordinary education, but there's nothing that is heavier than air can manage. Well, what would you do?" He did not pause here, he went straight on, still, so it seemed to Roe at the time, concealing the question to which he had already demanded an answer. "You want to get out, this is not such a wonderful world for some of us, but the instinct in the 'uman animal to save itself is stronger than the ruling class can credit, now then, suppose you were up there and inside," then at last he brought his question out again, "what would you make fast to?" "Why, to the door, I don't doubt," Piper said, before anyone else had time to answer. "You would," Pye said, and fell silent. He looked at his shoes as he sat on the edge of the table. Then he went on, "a door swings, it's in the nature of them to swing, it's on 'inges, what's worse the landing outside is well alight, the door may be burned through, and Piper would go and make fast to the knob." Now it would be the turn of the whole class to laugh. "To the bloody knob," he continued, "with a lowering line an inch and an eighth in diameter made of best Manilla hemp and fourteen stone sliding down to the ground." "I get what you mean," the old man said. "You keep what you get to yourself," Pye replied. "You're dead, you're a smell, you've fried." Again they could all laugh. "Come on now, what is there in a bedroom?" After several suggestions he would get his answer. "Why yes, the bed. And round the middle part, bringing the bed up to the window, making fast to the middle where it will jam across the window frame. Not the foot, or the head, but the middle, the business part," he concluded and everyone, including Piper, laughed their appreciation again.

It had been very different after the abduction.

"Take a hospital," Pye might be saying, "you are called there, you arrive, and this lecture is called practical fire-fighting 'ints, but all this comes into the job, just as much as putting out the fire. Take an institution, even take what they call a place of public entertainment. Now what do you do? You've got always to recollect you must make as little disturbance as possible, use your loaf, don't let the patients get any idea there's something up. Go about it quietly. Don't rush in a ward shouting where's the fire? There may be people in there through no fault of their own. They're to be pitied." He would be careful not to look at Richard. "It might send them altogether crazy, a sudden shock just like that. Women that a sudden shock," and the whole class would laugh. "No, I'm serious." "No, that's right," from Piper. "Women," Pye would go on, "they might be our own folks, lads, being treated lying there in bed because of some kink, or misfortune, taken by force out of their own homes most likely, so use your loaf."

Knowing what he then knew, lying on the cushioned

seat, covered with material so rough it was like glasspaper, Roe gave a cough of embarrassment. Those lectures haunted him.

SEVEN WEEKS AFTER he had first been home, Roe worked four days and nights straight off to get another forty-eight hours' leave.

The life he now led was not hard. There were still no raids and they waited at the substation, in their periods of duty, day and night, night and day. At all times they had to be ready to ride out on a pump to civilian fires, fully dressed, in under sixty seconds. But they thought the strain of waiting for raids prodigious. So much so that when, at last, he got into a train, travelling seemed an unnecessary waste of leisure hours which had been dearly bought, and his fellow travellers did not seem to be fellow beings in the war with him, but an odd lot of unpleasant individuals who did not have to go through that which he endured, and which he was now, miraculously as ever, forgetting.

At Oxford, young men of military age, elegantly dressed in last year's Austrian outfits, skated on each pond. He wondered how they had the time. Then at Evesham, where the Avon was frozen over, townspeople were out along the stretches by the town.

Tired, his expectations lost, Roe found his sister-in-law, Dy, had again brought Christopher to meet the train. This time it was light and they could see each other as they gravely shook hands. The boy blushed. On the drive home he asked what his father was going to give him the next morning, his birthday, but Roe would not tell. Then, after some other talk, he said twice he wished they could have come home a different way. It was plain that he was bored. He became restless. He began to irritate Richard, whom he would not allow to finish a sentence when speaking to Dy. In fact, on this occasion, he was extravagantly self absorbed.

It was his bedtime when they arrived. Roe did not go up, once he had been put to bed, to say goodnight and, when he was asleep, did not bother to help fill his stocking.

The next day Richard gave a bike Dy had bought for him. Many months later, at the height of the first blitz, Roe could not remember how the child was given this present. It was certain, clear in his memory, that Christopher had come into the bedroom quite late in the morning, because he could still see the boy's face stiff with excitement. He knew Christopher had called him because he was so thankful that he had not been called earlier. In times of peace, when staying a week-end in that house, the boy had often woken him with a stammered good-morning at what had then seemed unearthly hours. So he knew he had seen his son first thing on the birthday morning because he remembered how glad he had been to have a long lie in bed, but he did not recollect how much pleasure the bicycle had given. He could see only that face, solemn at the opening of the day, at the present to be received. Further, he realised he could not, at that length of time, distinguish between the bike or the tricycle they had given the year before. He could remember some trouble over tearing wrapping paper away by how afraid he had been that Christopher might burst into tears at being helped or, alternatively, that he might cry on not seeing the thing soon enough revealed in all its glory. But he could not tell which, before the war or after, bicycle or tricycle.

So the father, trying, during the blitz, while he was being bombed on twenty-four hours' leave, to make himself believe that the war was an interlude, found his memory at fault. But the rest he thought he remembered very well.

The boy had been good all that day. When he got over his first excitement at the presents he said several times how much he was looking forward to having Rosemary, who was staying nearby, to tea.

In the morning he constructed battleships with his bricks, using the strong light which made all the rooms sharp, and which was reflected, beaten in by the still wings of snow on window ledges. He used shadows cast by these bricks to build up substance; thus he set three bricks a little apart and the shadows between gave two guns.

In the afternoon they went to a bonfire in the pied garden, all hard mud and dead soiled swans of snow. Last year's leaves lay frozen under a grove of beeches, next to the green yews. Two gardeners were raking in these leaves. He insisted on taking along his scarlet handcart, two clappers, and a toy rake he said would be handy. The gardeners had a better way. They were getting the leaves over two old turkey carpets. When they had made a heap they would gather the corners, stagger with this load on their backs right up to the fire, and then let go. Flames would take minutes to come through but, when they did, all called to Christopher to watch them lick out, making a hole and not even seeming warm, the colour taken away by the sun on snow. There would be sparks, a roll of smoke, and, in the end, that same mound of ash growing imperceptibly, glancing rose in places with the wind.

Christopher had not used the rake once and found the clappers too difficult. He picked up a forked branch. He used this as a pitch-fork. He would let no one near, he prized the thing and hurled small quantities of brown leaves towards the fire, warning the others they must not even touch his stick. His father had shewn him how to use the clappers, and possibly this had been too much. He seemed to be absorbed. But the instant word was sent out from the house that Rosemary had arrived he was so excited that he turned round without another thought, shouted, "Here you are," as he threw the bit of wood, which had been precious, towards his father, and then ran so hard to get to Rosemary that he tripped and twice fell flat. They all laughed, pleased that he was glad.

The children were going to have their tea with the nannies. Roe had to leave for the station before they could begin. He was due for some annual leave in a fortnight's time, Christopher could hardly wait to say goodbye because of his birthday cake, but, on this occasion, Richard did not mind departing. He was to be back in a day or two, so that his night at home seemed to have been a week-end before the war, his life in the Fire Service, so easily forgotten once he was away, no more important than a routine.

When Roe first joined the Service, when the nations were still declaring peace, it seemed ludicrous to be trained by firemen in a real fire-station. He signed on because he had for years wanted to see inside one of these turretted buildings, and also because he had always been afraid of heights. He did not know there was such a thing as a public night each week, when anyone is allowed to wander round, and he had not had the energy to run up a ladder thirteen times to find out if he could lose the feeling that he must throw himself off.

When he finished training, lost his fear of heights, and was allowed to go to fires, he never had one in all the time he waited fully dressed there, and he had gone every Tuesday for three hours until war was declared, that is for nine months. He had never felt war was possible, although in his mind he could not see how it could be avoided. His feelings were usually uppermost. As a result he did not expect ever to go to a fire, and he did not consider that his life in the station, what little he had, could at any time be real.

He was called up three days before the outbreak and, certain of death in the immediate raid he expected to raze London to the ground, he was soon saying farewell to Christopher away out in the country whenever he was alone, losing him because he loved himself so well that he was afraid. In his self pity he might have been sighing goodbye to adored unreality. All that was real to him then was his death in a matter of days. He kept on saying, falsely, and over and over, that he was to rejoin his wife.

Then, when there were no raids, and he was happy at the substation because it was a complete change of scene, he forgot Christopher until, on his first leave, he found he was still terrified of dying, perhaps because his son was older, but almost entirely because, now that he had been parted by life as well as by death, he could not bear to leave for ever, never to share life with what was left just when he had discovered how it had been shared.

A year later, when raids began, and he faced death, he loved his son fiercely, not so much for himself as for something between the three of them which he felt made life worth living, as his son grew up, for father, the dead mother, and their living child.

But while being trained, that is before the war, when he was still working through a joke discipline with regard to heights, it had seemed too amusing to be true, being put through it down in the yard by a burly fireman who took them all in ladder drill, who could not see a girl of any kind but he was struck dumb, followed her with his eyes until she was gone, and only then was able to pick up the lecture he had learned by heart, where her legs had scissored it off his tongue.

All his period of training meant to Roe afterwards was flashes of a kind, scenes such as those when below the single arc lamp, an instructor's bulbous eyes followed the girl's criss-crossing legs, under silk stockings her skin a sheath of magnolia petals beneath the blue white light.

Magnolia and rose was what it meant to him, the country house in which he had been born, and in which he was to spend his next leave with Christopher.

He came at last, at night. He found the shutters closed, shutting out all he had left. He came upon Christopher playing in the library with his bricks. The light was soft, soft as in the day the cedar outside lay about the room. He sank back on to cushions covered with a willow pattern, forgetting the hard pews they had at the substation, lent by a church, and that had racks at the back in which to place hymn books, forgetting the train, the car beginning to recede, coming gradually out in the old comfort, and the remembered warmth of home.

When Christopher demanded that he should help build something, and he was about to ask if Christopher would mind his sitting quietly by to watch, he was annoyed to see Dy frown and nod her head. She had noticed he wanted to refuse. She meant to make the few days they were to have together as much a memory to the boy as they would be to the father. She was determined they must share what little time they had. He had the grace to give in. He sat by his son to put up a harbour.

When his father had finished the lightship it was Christopher's bedtime, but the next morning Dy added a custom's house. She gave it a Carolean front. Then he bombed the whole thing down, and the time had come to go out to find Actress.

Actress was a hound bitch. For some reason her name was to be changed to Acorn. She lived about the stables, not right in the head. Her eyes were brown, but she was mad by a never-shuttered grey light in them, even when smiling. She was shy, wild with everyone but Christopher.

To go out to the stables with him was to go back years, Richard felt, to be the age again when he was always drifting out to the saddleroom, when the last day of the holidays he had said goodbye to a terrier, which had been his uncle's before the Germans killed his uncle in the last war, and it howled as he said goodbye for another term. This morning he now went out with Christopher, so many years later, there was no snow, but the roadway was slippery with ice. The boy wore rubber boots. In shrieks he called "Actress," and "Acorn darling." She did not come to him. His father was shewn where she slept, and was asked if he did not think her bedding comfortable. They visited the red setter Bruno. Christopher called again, but still no Actress. They looked through the kitchen garden, at the other empty rabbit hutch, then went back to the lawn. By this time the boy had forgotten all about the bitch.

As they returned towards the stables, Sam joined them, a cross between bulldog and mastiff, huge and awkward. Every now and then this animal would go sideways into the boy, almost knocking him over. As they came near the stables Christopher began to call Acorn again. There was still no sign. The one response in a muffled day was the frantic barking set up by Bruno to attract attention, and, at any pause, the rattling of his chain as, unseen, Bruno spun about his kennel. Yet again he cried "Acorn." This time she did gallop up at last, as though from a great distance, blown, with heaving sides. At the sight of Christopher, while she covered the last few yards, she flattened herself from her ears down her head. She crouched with love even along her tail. She did not bark. Bruno began to howl. She did not make a sound. She circled Christopher, rising up when she was in front, and when she was behind, to put her paws on his shoulders, licking his face and neck no more than once, and quickly, at each turn she made. He got cross and bothered. Sam joined in. Suddenly it was over. She trotted away in front with Sam and began to worry the dog, hamstringing him in play. He was yellow in colour, she liver and white, and the road was like a dark glass bottle.

Actress coming back to the boy as though they had been separated for a year, and not, as was the case, for only a few hours, led Richard back to the abduction again. When Christopher was lost, and he himself had been driven out of his own house by the dry-eyed anxiety about, he met the parlour maid of that time in the hall when he returned. She was in tears. The place was dark. He turned on the light with the second great thrust of dread that he had felt, the better to face the news of what he was at once certain would be another death, and under a bus at that. He needed to see it in her face if she was not going to tell. She snivelled a smile and said, of all things, "I always knew," and thus, while he rushed the stairs, he had realised, with a strong sense of irritated guilt over his relief, that Christopher was all right.

Turning away, to his son by his side, and these five easy days ahead, he found Christopher wanted him to come sliding on the pond. When Actress ran across, the ice cracked, and that was that.

Then he begged Richard to help him break the ice. He had some idea he would store it against the summer and his father wondered, but could not remember, how it had been left after their walk in the park, whether it was admitted that where the fairies lived might be an ice house after all.

Then Richard persuaded Christopher to come with him to the moat, to break ice near where they had had the bonfire not so long ago. But it was no use. The day was too cold. Over and above this he found, with so much time on their hands, that nothing was special. This was no more than just another week-end, now that he had forgotten he was a fireman who had not even had a fire. When he made some excuse to get away the boy did not mind, happy to go back with Actress to the stables.

The stud groom, on his last visit, had let him kill with a spoon nine immature mice they had uncovered beneath a pile of horse blankets.

Each day they had down there, Dy arranged that Richard should be with Christopher in the mornings. He would come into her room first thing, and ask, "What shall we do?" "Why not go out with daddy after breakfast?" "Yes," he might say, or "All right," not letting it be seen whether he was bored or pleased, seeming to accept the arrangement because it had been settled.

When, at last, his father took him by the hand soon after eleven and asked where they were to go, it was Christopher, now that it had been agreed that they should be together, who suggested the visit they could make to this or that in the grounds. He did this as though he was the one to do the entertaining, cold, unquestioning, yet perfectly happy, and with no comment. He was still too young for chat. In whatever they got up to he was content to stand by while Richard did the heavy work, not helping while he turned over logs or pulled long sheets of ice from the moat. But Richard could not do anything on his own or Christopher would cry, "Wait till I come, oh wait."

Roe had been brought up in this house, among these gardens. The lawns, and most of the undergrowth in the wild garden, the trees, the beds of reed around the moat, all these had become a part of his youth. They had not altered in the twenty years he was growing up. It was he who had changed, who dreaded now, with a hemlock loss of will, to evoke how once he shared these scenes with no one, for he had played alone, who had then no inkling of the insecurity the war would put him in, and who found, when confronted by each turning of a path he knew by heart but which he could never call to mind when he closed his eyes, that the presence, the disclosure again of so much that had not changed and shewed no immediate signs of changing, bore him down back to the state he wished to forget, when he was his son's age and had no more than a son's responsibility to a father.

Also, the weather was so very cold. In the end Richard would drift back to the house, and Christopher to the stables. Neither was sorry to go his own way. The boy would be building up memories peculiar to himself. The father had his own of that kind. He could not add to them.

So it came about that he did not see as much as he might of Christopher, partly because he had dropped into the old way of doing nothing which made a background to every memory of the place he had, and partly because he found he could not, this time, leave his wife's memory alone.

When she was alive, days at the office were long, evenings brief by such time as he got back from work. At that period, when his life lay ready to hand, he had not bothered, had taken the companionship of wife and baby for granted. Now that he was back in this old life only for a few days, he could not keep his hands off her in memory, now that he did not see her every evening, rather mocking, aloof, as gentle as he had been curt always, the touch of her white rose petal skin an unchanging part of what his life had been before, her gladness when she had been with him a promise of how they still had each other, of the love they had had one for the other, and of the love they would yet hold one another in, the greater by everything that had gone before.

Because of this, and by the fact that she had not been with him for so long, he could not leave her alone when in an empty room, but stroked her wrists, pinched, kissed her eyes, nibbled her lips while, for her part, she smiled, joked, and took him up to bed at all hours of the day, and lay all night murmuring to him in empty memory.

It is unnecessary to say how Christopher spent the days. Actress was there all the time. He had his own jokes with the men about the place, who were of an age to have been a part of Richard's youth as well.

In this way the time for father and son passed quickly.

Neither was much with the other, the one picking up the thread where the war had unravelled it, the other beginning to spin his own, to create his first tangled memories, to bind himself to life for the first time.

So it came to the morning of Richard's return. His wife went with him for a stroll before the car came to the door.

There was a tall hedge of holly out at the back to hide the stables. Two gardeners were clipping this hedge. One of them came down off his ladder and gave a holloa. He might have seen a fox. Richard saw Christopher come out of the small iron gate. The other man got off the ladder and stood by his side. The two men holloaed together. A third time they did this and then Christopher joined in, his voice high above theirs. At last Actress came galloping, once more from a distance. The nurse came out of the iron gate to fetch him for his goodbye to his father. Then Actress was there. And as Richard turned back, and the car came out of the back drive to go to the front door, he did not know how he was going to get through his goodbye. What he had just seen was so like all he had known and might never find again, and, as he clutched at her arm, which was not there, above the elbow, he shook at leaving this, the place he got back to her nearest, his ever precious loss.

"When I was in Africa," Piper was telling Richard in the four-ale bar, "it didn't 'alf cause a rumpus, oh dear, quite usual too. You'd see a number of 'em, with their long sticks, kickin' up the dust on the compound where they lived, till you could make out only their 'eads and shoulders with all they'd raised. In the end they always got 'em back, yus, nearly always, but oh dear what a rumpus," and he laughed his high, cracked laugh. For Piper had got Richard's name from the copper Pye called to take Christopher home, this copper living along the same street as Piper these twenty years.

It was the evening of the second day in the substation. Richard was too worn out, too bewildered to deny that his son had been abducted. In peace time, to avoid getting involved with this old man, he would not have hesitated. Lying he would have denied all knowledge of Christopher. But now that it was to be war he thought he would say goodbye to evasions, or pretence. He foolishly admitted he had been the victim.

"When that copper give me the name," said Piper, "I said to meself I know someone, let's see, somewheres, why yes, you old bastard, it's that young feller training alongside of yer at the station. So then I looks you up and it is you. So there you are then."

"Yes it was me," Richard admitted for the third time.

"An' if it 'adn't been that your nipper would not tell 'im where you lived 'e never would 'ave called the copper but left 'im as if by accident along your street, I don't doubt. Fortunate to one way of lookin', but misfortune some ways, according to 'ow things turn out with him in charge of this substation with you in it."

Richard agreed. He saw there was no escape. It came to him that if Pye were to find out Piper knew, Pye would be sure to suppose that he, Richard, had been talking. In any case Pye must take it out of him. But he was tired, too lost to want more than companionship. And he did not mind what happened. He thought there had already been too much.

Three days before war broke out they had all been mobilised, mustered in a car park attached to one of the big stores, and sent off some hours later to the action stations they were to man. These were commanded by Regulars from the Brigade. Richard was posted to Pye's station.

It seemed weeks since he listened in to the wireless, did not wait for his red telegram, and went off to this asphalt park, fully dressed in tin hat, dark blue uniform, shiny black gas trousers, rubber boots, with axe and spanner in a blue belt, as soon as he heard the announcer call on the Civil Defence Services to report.

He took a taxi. He told the driver to put him down round a corner so that he should not appear as rich as he was. But when he turned in at the entrance, there, in wait, had been Piper.

"I seen you, Mr Roe," he said, addressing Richard thus for the first time, "an' if you don't mind, you're wrongly dressed. I wouldn't let them see yer like that. The order is uniform caps to be worn, tin hat to be slung on the belt. Boots carried, shoes must be black. An' where's yer blankets, with grub sufficient for two nights. I should go back, Mr Roe, they won't miss no one, I've 'ad experience, we shan't move out of this yard this night, not unless Jerry comes and bombs us out."

Feeling like any schoolboy who has created a wrong impression on his first day, Richard immediately took another taxi home. He kept it waiting while he dashed upstairs to strip his bed. He gave the between maid a fit of giggles over the muddle he made tying his blankets. A minute or so later the cook lost her temper as, in turn, the girl lost her head searching for more string to make a parcel of sandwiches. Thinking he would be too late he had himself driven back right inside the car park. Piper saw him, but there was hardly anyone else to notice. Richard need not have hurried. He was one of the first.

As evening lengthened under a rainy sky, and more and more turned up in their deep blue uniforms, the melancholy light, as it failed, seemed to stretch long as grey elastic.

A balm he had never experienced heretofore spread over

him, the blessedness of being without duties or appointments, in the midst of anxious muddlement.

He had nothing to do, and nothing he could do would make any difference. His companions had little to say. For the most part they stood in silence while the officers bawled at each other over their heads. He did not seem able to get away from Piper, that was the one snag, because Piper had seen the taxi. They hardly spoke again except the once, after it had come on to rain, when this man advised him to move his blankets under cover.

For several hours they had all to stand in different groups only to be regrouped, creatures of the utter confusion the London Fire Brigade creates.

They were mute in a vast asphalted space. The store towered above, pile after dark pile which, gradually, light after light went darker than the night that was falling and which he dreaded. For twenty minutes at dusk the scene was his wife's eyes, wet with tears he thought, her long lashes those black railings, everywhere wet, but, in the air, the menace of what was yet to be experienced, the beginning.

Earlier the balloons had been a colour of the blade of a knife.

He was so without anticipation he did not even fear that Piper might be stationed with him, as of course, once they were sorted out, the old man was. He did not suppose even for a wild moment that Pye could be his Station Officer. Indeed, when he did know, the rush and turmoil was too great. He did not care until the evening of the next day, until, as he was listening to Piper in the pub on abduction in Africa and to his own story so inimitably retold,. Pye came over. Piper at once got up to let them be alone.

They had all worked hard to get into temporary quarters. They had by now done some of the sandbagging. Pye had got through more than anyone. They were tired out. They expected a gigantic raid any minute. The conversation of hanging, civilian faces in bowler hats up at the counter seemed mostly of the pet they had had put away that very morning, in accordance with instructions issued against gas attack. Or, if they had drowned the dog themselves, then they would ask each other whether the dustmen would reject a bin in which there was a body. One hairless dewlap with mastiff's eyes spoke up. He said every dustcart was commandeered to remove human carcasses that same night. The black-out, new to all, was of a vault. All this, while he had not specifically observed it, moved Pye to get things over, to speak for the first time, and, as he thought, for the last, directly of his sister to Richard.

"Being a man," he said, "I 'ave my feelings, and I don't discuss family matters with no one. But a human being I was bred up with has wronged your wife," not knowing she was dead, "and, situated as we are now, I consider I ought to say to you that I was sorry. Mind you, I'm not saying that I'm sorry now."

"Don't misinterpret me," he went on, "there's nothing personal about it. But any system that can send an unfortunate woman into what is jail really, is vile, a filthy system. I know it hasn't anything to do with you, but they told me I must sign her away like a bit of furniture or they would prosecute. So I did sign, underneath two doctors I 'ad to give a dollar each to. That's why I'm not sorry now. Not because of the money, no, but the disgrace, the force majewer."

Roe forbore to reply.

"Of course," Pye went on again, "in the station, while you was in the class, there was no cause to speak. But I want you to know that it won't make any difference you're being in my substation. There's many in the Brigade would never allow a man beneath them, as you're beneath me now right enough, to forget a thing like that. Well, I'm not like that, I'm a man who has educated 'imself. Take education, what is education? I say it is a man's capability to see rightly for 'isself. I see my mother's daughter, in a manner of speaking, has wronged your wife, and has not been given leave, or I should say permitted, by the system we live under, to put it right."

An infinite sensation of tiredness, made fluid by the beer he had drunk flowed over Richard together with the certainty that he could never make this man realise what had passed, mixed with relief at the fact that Pye did not know everything. But he was anxious to keep on the right side so he said a few words to the effect that whatever happened before the war was best forgotten. He ended by calling him sir.

"Don't call me sir, Dick, but sub. Only Station Officers and above are entitled to a sir."

Roe took heart at this use of the christian name and was glad, when the round came up, to find Pye buying him a drink. In a way it was salt that had passed between them.

After Pye left him Richard noticed he was going from one Auxiliary to another, and realised that he was making himself pleasant to each man in turn.

Piper came back. Richard bought him another drink. The old soldier never paid a round. Knowing he was being sponged on, Richard had now to listen to a rambling account of the old man's fears.

"Yus, I went to find out me action station for meself the moment I seen we meant business. As soon as ever they told me it was here I asked them 'oo was to be the officer. An' when the sub officer that told me comes out with this 'ere Pye's name I says to myself, 'well, it's all up with you this trip, you silly old bastard, you've landed in it this time, that man don't like yer, 'e'll make it uneasy, you old fool, ah,'" and he slapped the back of his own head, too hard, Richard thought, "So 'e will. Soon as I gets back to my buildings I said to the Mrs, I says, 'Well, mother, your old man's in trouble again,'" and at this point he tried a laugh, "Well, 'ere's the very best," he said, raising his pint glass,

"Yus, 'e's found 'isself trouble again I says, posted to a station where the officer can't bear the sight of 'im, oh, you unlucky old sod you," he cried too loud, striking himself again with a board-hard hand.

It appeared that Piper could not understand why Pye disliked him. Richard investigated, found the old man was ignorant of the effect his interrogations and echoing had on the lecturer. Roe left him in ignorance. Then he heard Piper, at a time when everyone was expecting instant death, ask if he thought it the right moment to put forward a friend, a someone called Mary Howells, as cook.

"Depend upon it," Piper said, "we shan't always take our meals at this ARP canteen. I shall be sorry, mind, we've none of us 'ad grub like it at the price," this when Roe had been too nervous to eat, and had not yet touched the sandwiches he had brought, "but they'll give us cooks by what I understand, an' I've known 'er a number of years."

"It's a bit soon, isn't it?"

"Well, maybe it is a trifle previous, but if this sub officer was one you could talk to then I wouldn't mind puttin' in a word to nudge things along, like, and do meself a bit of good because I've known 'er years, she lives just along our street. Now you're a man I prize, what d'you think, Mr Roe?"

Richard advised delay. They were called out to do more sandbagging. Piper did twice his share, sometimes carrying as many as two full bags on his thin, wide, hollow shoulders.

Pye, when he took his rest, at the end of one more chaotic day, was no less calm than this old soldier; nevertheless, the imminence of war action physically excited him.

Pye also had been out in France last time and had known the earth he fought over cold, wet, frozen, thawed or warm, whichever it might be by the sky above, in mud, or cracked and dry, but, on occasion barely moist, cool so that it crumbled leaving hardly a stain on the fingers.

Yes, he had been close to the earth then, and it led him back to the first girl he had known, not long before his father took them away from the village in which their childhood was passed, for that too was of the earth. In the grass lane, and Pye groaned as he lay on the floor, his head by a telephone, that winding lane between high banks, in moonlight, in colour blue, leaning back against the pale wild flowers whose names he had forgotten, her face, wildly cool to his touch, turned away from him and the underside of her jaw which went soft into her throat that was a colour of junket, oh my God he said to himself as he remembered how she panted through her nose and the feel of her true, roughened hands as they came to repel him and then, at the warmth of his skin, had stayed irresolute at the surface while, all lost, she murmured, "Will it hurt?" Oh God she had been so white and this bloody black-out brought you in mind of it with the moon, this blue colour, and with the creeping home. He had been out hunting that first night right enough as he came home, her tears still on the back of his hand, with the cries of an owl at his temples, like it might be the shrieks of that cat on the wall over there, bloody well yelling for her greens.

He was too tired to sleep. His mind switched from one thing to the next. The bank against which he had pressed her led him to worry about his wall of sandbags, which he had hoped they would have finished that same night. He had wanted a clear run the next day, sandbagging windows but, close on half past eleven, when they had all had just about enough, the wall collapsed. Well, he said to himself, my lads are all in, and Trant, the District Officer who was his immediate superior, can go drown 'isself, they can none of them do more tonight.

Then he turned to the asylum and the letter he had received, asking how much he could afford to pay towards his sister's upkeep. Surely, as a ratepayer, he was entitled to that free? They could force him to send her in, but no power in the country could make him pay out money for her.

That night, so long ago, as he crept back, who would then have thought that he was in for two wars? And as he came along in shadow, up the sides of hedges, to get back home unheard, unseen, because his old man must not know he was out, as he came slinking like any other creature out at night, and there was that dog whimpering near, chained up on account of a bitch, he had seen another shadow moving in front towards their bit of garden at the back, creeping as he was but lower, more like a wild animal, heavier in shame because a woman, and, as he saw with a deep tremor, his own sister, out whoring maybe as he had been, up now from off her back no doubt, out of a low shadow cast by the moon.

Well, he never married, and she came to keep house for him when the old people were gone. From that far evening to this he never mentioned that he had seen her. She did not marry, for all he knew she had never had to do with a man. Was her trouble over children the effect of ignorance, or the other way about? He did not even pause at the thought that she might afterwards, for the rest of her life, have suffered from a violent distaste, as had Mrs Lane's little girl at the time. If he had not been so sleepy he would have smacked his lips as once again he remembered his own wench crying, pretty crying.

He called to mind how disgusted it had made him, the sight of his sister, like a white wood shaving, when she darted, huddled, across the last still stretch of moonlight, intent on her next difficulty, the creep upstairs. (What he did not know was the year after year after year of entanglement before her, the senseless nightingale, the whining dog, repeating the same phrase over and over in the twining briars of her senses.) At that, not interested, he fell asleep.

★

Richard, laid out on the bare floor of a gas-proofed basement, watched Piper settle down. The old man would tell his absent wife, whom he called mother, the next thing he was going to do, and in a loud voice. "Well, mother," he cried, "I think I'll take me boots off now." This he did, and added to the already heavy stench, for the room was unventilated. "I think I'll try a bit of sleep now, mother, yus, I think I'll try a bit of sleep now." How utterly harmless you are, thought Richard, sleepless, and how wrong he was.

Later, when it was his turn to guard the fire engines, or appliances as these are called, drawn up outside in the open, and, lifting wet blankets draped over the door, he came out into a gin-clear air pasted with blue moonlight, at no length his thoughts, for the first time except for that once when Pye had made out that Pye was the only sufferer by his sister's tricks, turned to those he had left. In a sort of holy falseness he bade them farewell.

There is, he thought, in any manifestation of the firmament by a dead calm at night, a grandeur, the remoteness of anything large that is highly polished. He was looking at what, on this occasion, came so bright that he might have been under a silly, bright plan of the whole geography of the skies.

The fumes of what he had drunk had not lifted from him yet. A Rescue Squad, condemned by their leader to wear full gas clothing night and day, wandered up and down. The complete outfit, because it excludes air, is stifling, and they were too hot to sleep. They had had a bonus paid them. Each carried a bottle of whisky. Richard got his share from one after another as they went by.

Every man jack was full of his little woman and the Edies, the Joans, and the little Marys, in their pinnies, he had left behind, sleeping in their little cots (most likely watching mum in bed with a stranger), in what each man was proud to call home.

The Auxiliary on guard with him had been in the Navy. Some time ago this man had seen "King Kong," the film of an outsize in apes that was twenty foot tall. Roe's explanation was that the experience had had a lasting effect on his adjectives. One in particular, "conga," he used to cover almost everything.

"A conga night," he said. He called each Rescue man "cock." He remarked that their whisky was dodgy. He went by the name of "Shiner," because his surname was Wright.

The Rescue men spoke huskily of their families. Richard half heard what they said. The black-out was new to all, this was their second night. It stilled the loudest voice, by that moonlight such as no town-dweller had seen except on honeymoon, if then, yet it encouraged men and women to keep quiet, not for repeated love, but by the menace in that highly polished sky which they felt might, at any moment, fall flat, and across which the stars began to skate or slither as he crouched drinking, nostrils dilated, the air he took in that fed, as will a forced draught, the fire which ran with the charged blood in his veins.

He was not sorry when their relief came. Shiner, of course, said he felt "conga," and that he could have stayed out all night, but Richard, who was not used to keeping awake, was longing, by the great weight on his eyes, for as much sleep as he could get in the stench of Piper's feet. He was to be disappointed. A great muffled din hit them as they came towards their gas-proofed shelter. When they raised the wet blanket across the opening they saw, in a deep violet light from three coloured bulbs invisibly wreathed with footrot, two Regular firemen, one with a twenty-eight-pound hammer, the other with a crowbar, racing cockroaches along a course they had prepared between Auxiliaries rolled in blankets on the floor out of which, as though about to rise from the dead, came heads and shoulders as they propped themselves up to watch.

A man's face, in that profound, dim blood of the flower, was dead white. As these two drunk firemen bellowed oaths while they pounded the boards to make those cockroaches go faster, as they hopped, crouching in sapphire shirt sleeves, someone shouting odds, then Richard knew this was the end. He saw it more than double, and could remember no more of that night although, so they told him next day, he had made as much noise as any. He had been asleep standing up but, even so, he had been eager, in common with most of the others, to curry favour by sharing these men's phantasmal antics.

When the bells went down next morning at five, and all were warned they were required at once to fight the whole Rescue Squad, now turned mutinous, the two Regulars dressed in about thirty seconds. In the grey water light of dawn, his wife's eyes in tears forgotten, they showed no sign, even about their mouths, of the night they had spent. Richard was so stiff he could scarcely move. He was also extremely nervous. The only trace of those Rescue men was some shouting in the distance. He was still doing up his belt as Chopper, back already, for in the time it had taken Richard to get his gear on this man had dressed and been along to see, called out to Wal, "Why wait, let's go," and pulled out his axe. Richard's one thought now was, would he have time to relieve himself. Then Pye came along, walking with exaggerated calm, but too worked up to speak educated. He said, "Now, Chopper, what's the bloody rush? What are they goin' to say at the station? Do you know they 'ad to wake the great Dodge 'isself to give me orders to call you lads out. I would never do it else. We're not 'ere to control riots. Now we don't want to get into nothing. An' I've 'ad no orders direct, the Old Man was too wide for that, 'e can easy forget what 'e told Nobby I was to do. There's the 'ole fighting squad from Bow Street up this lane. Let them take care of it. I said to Nobby on the other end, I says, 'The Old Man can easy forget, can't he? 'Ow do I stand? Oh, no thanks, no for yours truly.' The Brigade broke a man, demoted 'im for something like it in nineteen eleven. I said to Nobby . . ." and Pye carried on talking to the Regulars, Wal and Chopper. Piper said "That's right" to something Richard had not heard, for Richard could wait no longer. He had to. So he went up to Wal. He asked permission, as he might have done in class at school. This man looked at him expressionless, said no word, unbuttoned his own trousers and, for answer, sprang a leak on to the pavement. More modest, Richard moved to the wall.

In the end they did nothing. The Auxiliaries were sent into the twenty-four hour canteen next door to have breakfast, where they discussed Pye's motives. It was explained to Richard that Pye was thinking of his pension, small blame to him, and consequently of how much he could cover up. The opinion was that if one of his men had been injured Pye would not have been covered by his superiors. This was born out next day when Pye boasted of how he had got out of the difficulty. Although his instructions had come from the very top, from the Superintendent, to cover the Super Pye had invented a fire. Such a thing as this is known as "the Fire Brigade mind." The older men deplored its absence in Auxiliaries. Pye officially reported that the Rescue Squad had lit a small fire to warm themselves and of all things, that it had spread to a dustbin. He said buckets had been in use to put this blaze out. For several hours he had it in mind to set fire to a dustbin himself. He kept his men out of a fight, because it was their job to fight fires or, only if a Superintendent ordered such a thing in writing, to turn hose on riots. Dodge had given a verbal order to cover himself should something go wrong and the Chiefs hear of it. So Pye had played safe, or, as Shiner remarked, boxed clever.

That morning war was declared. They had their first syren. Richard was too tired to take notice.

In the local, after several hours sandbagging, when every civilian seemed cowed and many of the women had obviously been crying, Pye came out with his imaginary fire at dawn. He was highly delighted with the invention. "How was I to know," he asked, speaking freely, unrestrained, "if 'e meant it? You know what they're like at the station. As I said to Nobby, I put it to 'im, if the Super wants me to call the lads out to fight, if 'e wants us to have our eyes gouged and 'atpins stuck through us where it would do most bloody damage, I says, why, what Mr Dodge thinks best is good enough for me only why don't 'e tell me 'isself or pick up 'is pen. There's typewriters enough for copyin'. 'Mind you,' I said, 'I don't say 'e didn't tell you Nobby. But will 'e remember in the morning, Nobby,' I says. I got to keep my nose clean, that's what I told him."

"I get yer," Piper said.

"As for you," Pye went on, "I 'ad to consider what chance a man like you stood with those boys in the Rescue. They'd castrate you, Piper, like a starved bullock. Or they'd wrap those long legs of yours round your neck and stuff the 'eels in your gob. And then where would your new denture be?"

A number of the lads laughed. Piper flushed, said "Well, I don't know." But the older men were shocked.

"I got false teeth meself, look," Pye said, half ashamed. He near took them out. "There you are." He laughed.

Shiner said to Richard, "'e's a mad bastard, cock, no skylark."

While Pye did not often come into the local, for he was kept busy in the office, or watchroom as it is called, the two Regulars, Wal and Chopper, were always in the bar. They would talk a bit with Shiner because he had been in the Navy, all three of them had been gunners, but they would not say much to the rest. They accepted drinks, never paid for a round themselves, and let it be known they disapproved of Pye. On this, the third day they had all been together, some of the Auxiliaries spent a great deal of time and money trying to get in with them.

But Pye was a warm-hearted man. Richard was surprised to learn that Piper had gone to him about his friend Mary Howells, the charwoman he wanted taken on the staff as cook, and that Pye had promised to arrange this soon as ever they moved into permanent billets.

Later on he carried out his promise. He was to regret it.

After the first excitement of war died down, as it soon did when there were no raids, the fun and games started.

The moment they opened, work was dropped. Everyone who could afford it went over to the local.

"What's it going to be Wal?"

"Naw, this one's on me," from another Auxiliary, "come on Wal."

"If it ain't me old china, Chopper," said a third, "come on now, what are you 'aving?"

They drank wallop, that is draught ale. Richard bought the Regulars more beer than anyone. He was as bad as the rest, and more successfully, because he had more money. With him it was a sign that he was returning to normal when he began to keep on asking questions.

"D'you reckon they'll be over this night?" he asked, getting minimum replies, until his queries were as futile as, "And when you get to a job are you allowed to use a torch outside?" Most of the questions he put these two men the other Auxiliaries answered, but they were too inexperienced to have a reply to this one. Chopper surpassed himself. He said:

"Well Dick, there's no smoke without there's flame."

Months afterwards, when the blitz began, flame came to be called "a light," they talked of "putting the light out" instead of "getting the flames down." But on those first evenings there was not one Auxiliary, fresh to the blackout, who could foresee the white flicker, then the red glow which spread and, close to, the greedy extravagance of fire which would be bombed and bombed and bombed again to increase the moth's suicide it was for firemen.

Those who would have a part to play, who were to have fires to put out, could strike attitudes in this saloon bar into which no outside air penetrated, so that ferns, hanging stiff in wire baskets from false beams, seemed carved out of painted iron plate. And the stray women, who looked older, with hats tilted this way and that, black and brown, their lips sealing wax, the skin of their faces the stop press, were unnaturally quiet, murmuring oh dear to the brown beer.

"It brings everyone together, there's that much to a war," Richard said to Chopper.

"It does, Dick," he said.

One of these women spoke.

"When it doesn't put blue water between," she said, but Richard did not notice. He had begun to eat again. Even now that he was able to fill his stomach he still did not think except when he had a letter, or when, once each week, he wrote to Christopher.

Those Auxiliaries so inclined, who could not afford to buy the Regulars beer, sought favour in doing more work than the rest.

This was a time when girls, taken out to night clubs by men in uniform, if he was a pilot she died in his arms that would soon, so she thought, be dead. In the hard idiom of the drum these women seemed already given up to the male in uniform so soon to go away, these girls, as they felt, soon to be killed themselves, so little time left, moth deathly gay, in a daze of giving.

That same afternoon the train to Portsmouth had wives dragged along the platform hanging limp to door handles and snatched off by porters in the way a man, standing aside, will pick bulrushes out of a harvest waggon load of oats.

Limp, dancing as never before entirely to his movements, long-haired sheaved heads too heavy for their bodies collapsed on pilots' blue shoulders, these clubs were like hotels, from double bedrooms of which the guests came, gorged with love, sleep lovewalking.

On the way to becoming adjusted, Richard began to look about him in daytime.

At that period the Fire Service came next after pilots with the public. Auxiliaries were often given money by old ladies, they were stood drinks by aged gentlemen, and, when an appeal was made over the wireless for blankets, there was an abundance of these brought in next morning. Street cleaners called Richard "mate." Girls looked him straight, long in the eye as never before, complicity in theirs, blue, and blue, and blue. They seemed to him to drag as they passed.

Pye, greatly excited, spoke jubilantly of his success at night. There had been one that he described as "a real cow, a countess."

On his way back from posting Dy's letter an expensive girl, discreetly enamelled about her hollow face, eyes moist, amused, sang out "Fireman." She was foreign, disagreed with the way the landlord was building a wall of sandbags outside a window to her flat nearby, and asked if he could come up to give advice.

As she shut the doors and pushed buttons she smiled, almost openly amused but also as though she was laughing at the fool she might quite likely make of herself now, so she seemed to imply, as he promoted his feelings, she had really noticed him for the first time.

She did not say, "I don't know what you will think of me," but "I hope this will not be a bore for you, no?"

He muttered, overwhelmed by the luck he thought he ought to have, caught up in what he understood to be the way other people acted at this time.

He had to wedge himself into a corner to let her get out

of the lift. Her skin, where neck joined shoulder, covered by small colourless hairs, was cool to his eyes, like an unwet cake of soap. It was hot. She had run out in a frock. He was suddenly aware of his tunic, proofed against flame and water, heavy.

She went inside a white room. An acetylene lamp triangle of sunlight cut into the floor. At the apex stood another girl, dark. This light, reflected up the bell of her skirt, made her translucent to the waist. She said, "Oh a fireman." He turned his eyes away, burned. He chanced on a rectangular table set back against the wall. It had a black glass top on which, in a scarlet bowl, was a cactus, painted white.

At once he noted that he had passed a glass tank in the lobby, filled with cut daffodils. This made him uneasy.

While his girl explained in broken English, laughing, calling the other Prudence, telling him, "My name to you will be Ilse," he felt his hands, which were gorged with blood, swollen with work. He made out to himself they had grown enormous, that the fingers hung at the thighs like strings of raw pork faggots, filthy as he was who had not been able to change his heavy sweat-charged clothes. For the first time he was conscious that he must smell bad while these girls were like bird's feathers, cool and settled. He raised a vinegar-coloured palm to his chin, which was covered by that four-day growth of bristle.

They asked him if he was very tired. They said he could have a bath in the flat any time. Ilse brought him cointreau with water in a long glass and a cube of ice. He found it difficult to answer their questions. Prudence said they would rather be killed by blast than die of no fresh air. "It is like it is in Norway, just to-day," said Ilse.

By his faltering replies he now knew, as far as he was concerned, that there was more to this war and his part in it than the latest change in his way of life. In his dirt, his tiredness, the way the light hurt his eyes and he could not look, in all these he thought he recognised that he was now a labourer, he thought he had grasped the fact that, from now on, dressed like this, and that was why roadmen called him mate, he was one of the thousand million that toiled and spun.

He told them he was too far gone in dirt to dirty their bathroom and added, by instinct, that he would send up his officer in charge. He said it with malice towards them, because he thought they would despise Pye, and with the idea that, by putting them Pye's way he might do himself a bit of good with the Skipper.

He could not help remarking on the flowers as he went out, "Daffodils in September?" he asked, malicious, taking them to be perhaps from Greece. Prudence explained that Ilse made artificial flowers out of sardine tins.

Back at the station he sought Pye out. "There's a couple of cows up in number ten Smith Street," he said and winked. "They want advice about sandbags."

"Is there?" said Pye, and went straight up.

PIPER LEFT THE STATION one evening before the war. As he came out with the others, and they were calling to each other, "Will you have one before you go?" he left, crying his goodnights, which were seldom answered. He could not afford a round. The others, so much younger, were not sorry to see his back. Those Firemen Instructors, more of his age, and who went with the rest because they were going to be treated without having to buy a drink themselves, ignored him as a broken old man. He called, "Goodnight Mr Jones, goodnight Mr Pye, goodnight all." He was forgotten before they turned in to that light, sweet smell of mild and bitter which spread out over the lighted street.

Long, bony, knees bent, he tramped home in boots back to one of those two-roomed flats there used to be behind the houses of the rich about the West End, blocks of which the staircases, set outside the walls, zig-zag up to two doors on each landing. He had rented one at the top but, when mother's leg got bad, his landlord, to save her, let him move down to ground level. It was one of the few true stories he told. This evening, as on every other, he repeated to himself, soft but out loud, "Yus, we'll see what mother 'as for us this night, maybe a bit of that pie, we'll see what mother's got this evenin'."

He had three steps to get down, shutting the front door behind him as he came, with one hand in the letter flap. There was not much light. The sour washing was out between him and the one white bulb. Because she could not shut the door behind her when she came back Mrs Piper never went outside alone these days. Bitter by nature, she was more so now by a handrail she had been promised by which she hoped to come unaided down this little flight. Or she kidded herself that this was how it was. A son by a previous marriage of the old man's had bought her one. It lay aside complete. She did not trust him or it. She thought he wanted her somewhere else, the rotten sod. The rail looked too light to her. Another thing she knew, she dare not leave Piper to fix it.

He said, still the other side of that washing, "Well, mother, it's your old man." She called from her corner in behind, "If you're 'ungry you'll needs must go out to get some."

He stood, dismayed. Then, with no anger, he said, "All right, old woman," climbed two steps, and, his weight on the handle, sawing the back of his free hand across his mouth, he went up and out.

As he shut the door the washing swayed slightly. She said, quiet, to the youngest by her youngest sister, "That's right Alf, you 'ave that last bit of pie, seein' 'e did not insist."

Outside, street lighting, shop displays, electric signs made Piper's heavens dull pink, the houses brown, only their upper floors and gables were shrouded in that half dark which is night over a town in times of peace.

As he went under a street lamp with its yellow pride of light there stood a guardsman, by the coffee stall painted the same colour as his scarlet coat. Many smells were about Piper at this cross roads, from the fishmonger's, closed now, but with a stack of boxes piled outside drenched in kipper, from the local each time someone came in or out and the swing doors fanned a sickly waft outside, from the fish and chip round a corner that, when frying, as now, spread high over this street, and, last of all, boiling water in the urns extruded steam on to the laden air, creating a comfort in which these various smells were marshalled, and so damped down that they could not be lifted on the warmth a little way toward the high, chill, faint stars. Fat George, motionless, as much part of his stall as three chromium urns, one of which was crowned by two fat earthenware teapots, and with shelves of coloured tins at his back, looked as though he and his stall might be a musical box put up stage in an opera, the smells the violins brought all together into a main movement above which this instrument, this dwarfed plaything for eating, stridently, it was so coloured, dominated the strings in a major key, the well-fed eunuch.

Standing up against the counter, and she was so frail in dark clothes she seemed part of the shadow, he saw Mary Howells, the old friend, a char.

"Well, if it ain't me old sparrer," she said in a low, sibilant voice, in dramatic amusement despite she was played out.

"What then," she went on, "wouldn't she even make you a fresh pot of you and me," referring to what was generally known, that Mrs Piper would hardly lift a finger, not even to put on a kettle.

"'Er leg's been troublesome on account of the weather."

"Yus," she said, "yus, an' I wish I 'ad that leg but then I 'ain't, so there you are. You bin to your fire practice?"

"That's right."

"An' at your age. Who's ever 'eard."

He also was tired. He let this pass. He said:

"What's George's tea this evenin'?"

"The usual," she said, "'ow 'e does it I don't know, an' if you was to ask me why I allers come back I wouldn't be able to tell yer. More like water 'e's done the kippers in of the mornin'," she said, but, in a manner even older than his years, Piper was watching a short, fat, fair girl, whose hair fell in one long yellow curl down her bare head. After a violent effort he remembered he had seen her not above an hour ago.

"Excuse me miss," he said, and, afraid that he was going to ask for money, this girl stopped only because he was plumb in her light.

"I just seen you at the station, now isn't that right, this night's my day for goin'."

"Why yes," Hilly said, relieved, "Are you training too?"

"Yus," he said. "Yus," he went on, "if this 'ere war talk comes to anythink it will be my fifth campaign."

"Your fifth campaign?" She wondered at his use of words. "Yus," he said. Then he was at a loss, had no more to say. But once she saw it was not a question of money, of which she had none or she would have been glad to give, and because she was a person to bring out whatever she might have on her mind, she asked whether he had heard the latest, "That it's supposed to make us shy when we come into the watchroom to learn about the old fire alarm system and there are men in there, so, those that aren't on duty are to be turned out, isn't it too silly?"

"Yes, well there you are then," he replied, not having followed. "Yus, I thought I recognised yer when I seen yer comin'. One of the WAFS I knew you was after a minute."

"Well thanks," she said. "I say I'm in a rush, I must simply fly. Goodnight," she called, thinking you meet all sorts and kinds.

More than any younger recruit Piper should have been able to foresee their sleeping all together, the men and women in the Service, rolled each in his or her deep mystery within a blanket, on any cellar floor near the substation, asleep, yet groaning and calling out, fighting last night's fires before they were called out to those shortly to be started up above, below the already busy sky.

"Goodnight, goodnight, I must simply . . ." Mary echoed, then said, "Oh well, I never."

"I thought I knew 'er soon as I set eyes on 'er eyes. Knows one of the Chiefs or something."

"Take my word. You're too old for it."

"Well, they'll 'ave a use for me yet." He sawed a forefinger to and fro across his mouth. "It's buckshee, it don't cost nothing to volunteer. You would do wuss yerself."

"What," she cried, "me in trousers."

"It's right the girls do wear uniform trousies, but you got to consider there won't be no more floors to scrub, much."

"Ah, there'll always be them things. I 'aven't 'ad twenty years on 'em for nothink. I'm not worryin'. I can always get me a job of work with a bucket."

There was a long silence. Then she said,

"What would I 'ave to do, Arthur, on top of wearin' the things?"

"Keep the occurrience book."

"God 'elp us, what's that?"

"Where they write the telephone messages down."

"Oh no, not me, not much. Why, once at the Royal

College, you know where I've worked these fifteen years, they said, 'Mary, Miss Hofford, an' she was a nice girl you was glad to oblige, Miss O we called her's deaf to-day or I forget what, an' would you mind answering the telephone through the mornin',' I expect it was a cold she 'ad. Oh dear, never no more again. I don't seem ever to get used to that instrument. Oh no, I couldn't."

"Well then, there's the kitchen."

"What, me cook for a 'undred? Oh my Gawd."

Arthur Piper stood, enveloping the saucer from below in one huge fist, the thick cup in his other hand too white, too breakable for fingers like his own, as he sucked at the tea, and then sucked at his teeth.

Leaving Piper, Hilly went on past an Underground which was blaring out light, sending a hot breath stale from the bowels in steady wind. At every step, each time one of the high heels she wore touched ground, her hair shook from the crown of her head right down the long curl to where it turned, at a cost of twenty-five shillings each month, over her shoulders. While on her way thus, it so happened she ran into Richard. He was confused with office tiredness, sapped by pints.

"In such a rush," she said, and disliked, but accepted the smell of beer about him. "I've got to have a smoke test."

"Do they give you those? Whatever for?"

"Well Ginger, you know Ginger Garton, one of the Chiefs, rather a friend of mine as a matter of fact, he says when the fun starts, if it ever does, and we go underground in the watchroom, that it might be rather useful really."

"Yes I see," he said, and had no idea of it. He was not to know what real smoke was like for another eighteen months. He told her he had just come from the Rose and Crown, outside the station, and which was the place he had first met her. He said Pye was there this instant minute, declaiming against capitalists. He added, "It's sheer provocation."

"I know," she said, "and thanks for telling me. I'll steer clear. Anyway I haven't time. Have you heard the latest?" She told him about the watchroom having to be cleared when girls came in.

He replied he knew everyone in the Brigade was mad.

They said goodnight. As he walked away he thought the women would cause endless trouble. He was right. But then he would not admit there could be a war, that all this fuss would ever come to anything. It was play acting. He felt he had been a fool to join. But if a war did begin then these girls would be a sort of harem for the officer in charge, and, if they were not all wiped out in raids at the start, then the women would get their teeth into the organisation. Which might make Hilly useful, if she knew one of the Chiefs like she said. He wondered if she went to bed. Perhaps he had better take her out one evening. These inconclusive gin and its were coming so expensive.

IT WAS ON A MORNING twelve months later. Just three weeks after mobilisation Piper was having a cup of tea in the poky kitchen of that Mayfair mansion into which they had moved the day before from the gas-proofed basement. Their cook, in full WAFS uniform including trousers, was Mary Howells, who had never cooked for anyone except her late husband and her two daughters.

"It's Brid," she was saying, "my youngest." She twisted a corner of the apron in her fingers. "I don't seem able to keep 'er out of me mind. I don't know what to think. The 'usband's a rotter, a real rotter, but ever since she 'ad the baby you'd think it'd got worse, not better. She 'ad a terrible time 'aving it, really, but as I said to 'er in the 'ospital, I says, 'you take a pull on yerself. Come through this all right and you'll find it'll make a world of difference,' I says. 'I know things ain't been easy,' I says, and she said to me, 'Not a word against Ted, mum,' and I said 'I'm not speaking of 'im, God forbid, me girl, I'm not one to come between 'usband and wife, no,' I says, 'I was meaning the dreadful pangs of labour what every woman is 'eir to, and what can follow it,' I says, 'Illness,' I says, 'weakness,' I says, 'loss of blood,' I says, 'blood to the 'ead,' I says to 'er, Arthur, and that there is what I'm a'scared of for 'er. She writes ever such funny letters to me, really."

Pye had been glad to have Piper's offer and Mary had been signed on as third cook without, so great was the hurry and shortage, one enquiry as to whether she could even do boiled eggs. She would keep saying, "fancy me in this lot," but she was happy. The college was evacuated. The cracks in each floor she had come to know as friend or foe were filling with dust until such time as the place should be taken over by soldiers. But she had insisted on seven days in which to go up north to see Brid, and now she was sorry.

"Pore little mite," she said of the baby, "it did make my 'eart bleed, Arthur, and 'er so awkward with it, 'ardly a glance would she give. An' as for the 'usband, I won't call 'im me son-in-law, why, as I said to 'im, I says, 'I'll report you, me lad, yus, for cruelty, that's what Ted,' I said. It makes me 'eart drop when I remember the way 'e be'aves, 'is own flesh and blood too. There's 'usbands knock their wives about but there, a girl makes 'er own bed an' she must needs lie on it, but to treat a baby so, that can't fend for itself, then that's what I call cowardly. With Brid in the state she is after 'avin' the child, it's neglect, that's what it is, proper wicked. You understand, it's what 'e doesn't do."

"They was ever so kind at the 'ospital," she went on, in

full flood, while Piper, not listening, entirely empty headed, sucked at his teeth. He found his way down to the kitchen whenever the other duty cook was out. Mary saw to him. When she could she gave him a little extra. But she had to be careful of her job. As she said "It's not as though I'd 'ad much training, ever, leastways not at this game." She also said of her cooking that, "You'll never 'ear the lads complain, they're satisfied with what I give, they're good lads." Nevertheless she would not touch the range. All she could do was to prepare the simpler foods and vegetables. Added to this she was very nervous, almost prophetically so, as it turned out, of an automatic domestic boiler that worked on a thermostat. The moment the water inside went below a certain temperature the gas burners turned on by themselves. Mary used to drive the orderlies for the day crazy, she was so continually asking them to have a look. But before ever she began to voice fears about Bridget her limitations had depressed the cooks. Hilly, for lack of anyone else, had taken on the job of mess manager, so she had to listen.

"I'll never understand Mr Pye, reelly I shan't ever," the fair cook, Eileen, was telling Hilly later that day. Of the same age they sat side by side on the dresser, smoking, "I know I'll never like that man. Why, he came into my kitchen only the other afternoon and 'e 'ad the impudence to tell me his potatoes wasn't cooked. Now you know as well as I do, that Mary can't get through the work with the trouble she's got. I was late putting those potatoes in I know, but then I was late getting them. As sure as I'm sitting here they were reel nice. Of course they're not the quality potatoes I have been used to cook with," ("No, of course," from Hilly), "but they were reel nice when they were done. None of the men complained."

"He'll be all right," Hilly said. "He talks so much he lets his plate get cold and then imagines things. The men say he's not supposed to have had a hot meal since he's been a fireman." She went on, "What it would be to be his wife." "You're telling me," from Eileen, and then Hilly again. "But it's rather awful about Mrs Howell's grand-daughter, I wonder what it is?" "By what I can make out it's the daughter. Funny that what comes out of quite another bit of you should go up there. She's a loony I rather fancy. Oh dear, who'd be a woman. Talk of the devil," said Eileen, and both jumped to the floor as Pye came in.

"Now is there anything you want," he asked, saying nothing about cigarettes in the morning, "I can get you anything from the Stores, like pots and pans, good morning I should 'ave begun by saying, because I know, and as some won't bother to realise, that no woman can cook without the wherewithal, the utensils of 'er trade . . ." and so on. Eileen said to herself she would scream if he did not go in another moment. But he was still talking after fifteen minutes. Neither girl realised he was trying to make out that perhaps his spuds had been raw yesterday because the cooks had not been issued with a steamer.

"And Mrs 'Owells," he said at last without having directly mentioned those potatoes, "is she all right? Of course I couldn't leave one cook and you, Hilly, to do the work and besides we're supposed to have three cooks with the number of men at this substation, so I was lucky to find one, in fact old Dodger, the Super, he came to hear of it and when 'e was on the telephone not long ago he said, 'I hear you are engaging cooks now, Pye,' 'e said, 'make sure they are good ones,' and make good little pies I thought he was going to tack on," both girls laughed, "but 'e didn't. Queer his getting to know, when you come to weigh it up, but then you never can be sure what these men will 'ear next, they can't be so occupied if they've got time to pick up things of that kind, can they? Still 'e sounded sort of pleased. So I can't complain. How's she shaping?" he asked, just as Hilly became sure he must have forgotten his own question.

"Why she's very good, Mr Pye."

Pye knew everything. "Isn't she in some trouble with her daughter?" Hilly denied all knowledge, wondering if old Piper told him things.

"All you women are the same," Pye went on, "you're each in league with one another." Now that he had forty-five under him, men and women, he meant to keep everything in control, in his hands. "There's nothing that breathes to beat you things for standing together."

"Thanks for calling us things," Hilly said, and smiled.

"You don't get my point." She seemed to have education and this intimidated him, so that whenever he thought of it he said to himself "kid gloves." "No, when I ask a thing, I mean a question of that nature, what I'm getting at is, is there any way I, the individual responsible for the efficiency, and that means the happiness, of this station, is there any reasonable means by which I can alluviate the little things that count such a lot to everyone, not only men, at times such as the present." "Blast you, you lying blackguard," said Eileen under her breath. Hilly spoke out loud. "I don't think I quite understand."

"It's like this," he said. "If you think she came away from that daughter of 'ers before she ought, then, if it would make it any easier, I could what we call cover 'er, that is I could let her go away for a week-end without them up at the Station knowing she was away. Of course, by doing that I'm liable to run my head into a noose." "I can't stomach it, shut up, oh run off," Eileen cried out herself and he went on, "But I want you girls to know I'll do anything in reason, anything I can, I will."

"Well, Mr Pye," said Hilly, "she hasn't said anything to me. Perhaps she hasn't seemed quite the thing just lately, but then she hasn't been here more than three days, it's strange to her."

When at last he was gone, they burst into excited whispers.

"What d'you make of 'im, I could scream sometimes, reelly I could, he's the limit."

"I'll tell you what I wondered, if he meant to trap one of us into telling."

"You mean – she's a friend of 'is – of course he engaged 'er."

"No, not that, but to judge of us, to see what we're like."

"Oh my God – if it's like that – I'll go back to private service or get into a canteen – 'e thinks we're out to work against 'er – I see – and the first to say a word, reelly, is the one that man thinks 'e'll get rid of."

"No, I don't think so, at all."

But Eileen was not to be diverted.

"Oh, if it's like that," she went on, "why, while she gives that old Piper extra already whenever my back is turned, if that's how it is, then this is no place for yours truly. There's only so much to go round, and if I'm to see my kitchen invaded by a madding crowd of men asking for more because one's been favoured behind my back, then it's more than the job's worth, even if there is a war on."

"When she talked to you about her daughter did she seem upset?"

"Oh yes, I wouldn't like to say she was putting anything on, oh no, I mean, it did sound reel to me. It's dreadful when you come to think." She gave Hilly some pitiable details. "But she is slow," she wound up, "as you can see, not that you've 'ad much to do with kitchens before," she put in, "but there, I can't go tell that Mr Pye, it wouldn't be right."

"And you'd rather have her here than not, lass," Hilly said. She was nettled.

"I'd rather be without that officer, what do they call it, in charge," said Eileen, and her mood changed. "Oh dear, see what a pother he's got us in and the dinner hardly started. Don't notice what I said, I get like that." She began to hum, "She's been and gone and lost it at the Astor. She wouldn't take her mother's good advice."

Every nine days Richard's turn to do orderly came round. He was aware of the kitchen undercurrents, but paid no attention, not at first. He also began by ignoring Hilly.

He had sent Christopher down to the country. Unless he went sick there was no way he could manage to see him before he was given annual leave, or until they were allowed to work ninety-six hours to get forty-eight hours off, a practice that was not begun until well into November. He began to come awake, to get restless.

These first weeks of war firemen were still heroes to the public, and to women especially.

There was, that autumn, a great promise of spring, the same unease as can be felt on a day, in March, that the morrow may bring summer weather, and that women's breasts, it was a phrase of Richard's, would again, as at each turn of the year, make themselves evident under light clothes.

In night clubs, it has been described, or wherever the young danced, couples passed the last goodbye hours abandoned to each other and, so Richard felt, when these girls were left behind alone as train after train went out loaded with men to fight, the pretty creatures must be hunting for more farewells. As they were driven to create memories to compare, and thus to compensate for the loss each had suffered, he saw them hungrily seeking another man, oh they were sorry for men and they pitied themselves, for yet another man with whom they could spend last hours, to whom they could murmur darling, darling, darling it will be you always; the phrase till death do us part being, for them, the short ride next morning to a railway station; the active death, for them, to be left alone on a platform; the I-have-given-all-before-we-die, their dying breath.

Pye we have seen preoccupied by his past, revitalised in

a way that took him by surprise. Richard, after his fresh tide of longing for his wife had ebbed, found he was increasingly absorbed by what was left to him of the sights and sounds, and by the feeling, as he had it now, of that early summer they had first met, the year he got to know her.

Each spring seems new, the first. It seemed to him it had been in April, but the afternoon she asked to be shewn round his parents' country place was in July. The roses, when they came to the rose garden, were full out, climbing along brick walls, some, overpowered by their heavy flowers, in obeisance before brick paths, petals loose here and there on the earth but, on each bush and tree of roses, rose after rose after rose of every shade stared like oxen, and came forward to meet them with a sweet, heavy, luxuriant breath.

Sitting as he was on the back step of a heavy unit pump, with a mangy kitten swiping at flies attracted by a cod's head in the gutter at his feet, the nine years that had passed, the position he was now in, all this lifted him as though in a balloon made lighter than air by the scent of roses.

The afternoon, it had been before tea, was hot, swallows darted low at the level of her thighs, a blackbird, against three blooms bent to the height of its yellow beak, seemed enchanted by terror into immobility as the two of them halted, brought to a full stop at the corner round which this impermanence caught them fast. He turned to her and she seemed his in her white clothes, with a cry the blackbird had flown and in her eyes as, speechless, she turned, still a stranger, to look into him, he thought he saw the hot, lazy, luxuriance of a rose, the heavy, weightless, luxuriance of a rose, the curling disclosure of the heart of a rose that, as for a hornet, was his for its honey, for the asking, open for him to pierce inside, this heavy, creamy, girl turned woman.

He had been sticky, then, in flannels, but not so hot as he was now, dressed in thick labourer's uniform, proofed against fire and water.

Roses had come above her bare knees under the fluted skirt she wore, and the swallows flying so low made her, in his recollection, much taller than she had ever been.

Back in his present, he heard a tap of high heels. Looking up, he saw Prudence, dressed in green as of dark olives like to the colour of that cod's head. She smiled, but did not stop. Still under the influence of his memories, he thought how sharp she appeared against the black wall with AMBULANCE painted in grey letters three foot high, knife sharp compared to the opulence his darling had carried about in her skin, sheathed for display to his senses, in the exuberance of his mother's garden.

Her bare legs had been the colour of the white roses about them, the red toenails, through her sandals, stood out against fallen rose leaves of a red that clashed with the enamel she used, the brick paths had been fresh, not stained, as the walls here, by soot-saturated rain.

Here, as Prudence drifted quickly off, infinitely young, so much the opposite of his heavy serge in the lightness of her dress that he broke violently out swearing, here, where he had seen Prudence lit up from under her frock by a blaze of the midday sun directed through her window, and he broke out sweating, he poured with sweat, here again he thought he broke the spell of what had been and, accepting his new life for the first time, he momentarily determined to join in the delights he imagined men and girls were sharing out to each other in the desperation of the times.

"Conger eel chasing, cock?" Looking up he saw Shiner laughing, nodding his head towards Prudence, who was almost out of sight. "Go on, say it, that's right," Shiner encouraged, "get it out of the old system. And ain't you perspirin'. Conga, eh?"

Richard laughed back. As loud as he dared he swore all he knew. Shiner went on:

"It's muckin' awful, ain't it, the first few days, the conga little place you've left, the little woman there, eh, it's like the first days out at sea. Sitting on the old rail where they can't see you, the old ship trembling under your arse, and that mucking awful sea for miles. Then you kind of fall in with it and everything's conga. But stone me up a bloody gum tree, thank God I got a job on land."

"I know," Richard said, and then went too far, "and to think I put Pye on to that girl with the one she lives with."

"'Ow d'you mean, put 'im on to them?" Shiner said. He had not heard.

Talking too fast, Richard explained. At the end he said, "and the frightful thing was, I meant Pye to get off with them so I could do myself a bit of good," borrowing Piper's phrase, "with him," he wound up rather lamely.

It drifted into Shiner's bullet head that this what's his name, Roe, was pansy.

"Naw," was his comment, "no skylark?"

At this Richard saw that he had made an impression it might take weeks to live down as, when an individual is observed drunk, as Roe was accustomed to say, from that moment, to those who witnessed it, that man is a habitual drunkard.

But Shiner was not worrying. He had once been out in a foreign port with two girls and a pansy, the pansy paying, and it ended in smashing stroke, he'd had both girls in the same bed. So, with a look of childish cunning, he asked if Richard would introduce him some time, "as between shipmates." Richard could not credit being addressed as shipmate. His confidence returning, and to put himself absolutely right, he told Shiner that he did not ponce for them.

"Naw," said Shiner, equally at a loss in Richard's company as Richard was in his, "straight up, is that what you do for a living?" They had neither of them come across anyone in the least resembling the other.

"What d'you think I am, for Christ's sake?"

"Naw, your getting me wrong, mate," Shiner said. "I

only meant we're all in the same ship an' if you was goin' up you might need a pal for the other one."

Taking stock of Wright, Richard thought to himself that neither Shiner nor Pye would have much chance while he was in the room, even if those two girls were good for anything of the kind, which he doubted. But in this he was wrong twice, both times.

"I could manage more than those two in the same bed," he replied.

THE REGULAR FIREMAN, Wal, had notice he was to be transferred to another station. Pye decided that there must be a farewell do. He asked Richard to invite Ilse and Prudence. Richard telephoned. They accepted. At once Richard assumed that Pye could not have been up to their flat again or he would have asked them on his own.

Beer was laid in. Gin was bought for the ladies. Pye shewed ignorance when he supposed that one half bottle of this last would be enough. Richard pointed out there must be at least two halves, particularly if Hilly was to come. Pye could not hide what he felt about this expense. "If I'd thought that," he said, "I'd've got in the distillery, by Jimmy Jesus." Richard again considered the man had no chance with girls such as these, when he had no idea what they were like.

Then there was a question as to whether the watchroom women should be asked. If Hilly came, and they were not invited, it might lead to trouble. "Well, send them in a glass of beer," said Pye, "though, mind you, I'm running my head into a noose to hang myself with, the Chief Officer's very hot on liquid refreshment, it's not long since the wet canteen at Number Fifteen was closed, in fact no more than a matter of twelve months back, and as to gin, spirits is forbidden anywhere on the premises, let alone the 'oly of 'olies. But I'll chance my arm on this occasion."

Everyone subscribed what he could afford, and, on the night, as Richard stood lonely by the door to bring both girls in when they arrived, they were so very late, under the high brilliant stars, he wondered if they would ever come. When they did, and said something about hoping there would not be a fire to break the party up, it was symptomatic of this change which by then had come over people's fears, that they did not think a raid was likely. He was surprised to find they knew the station rode to ordinary fires. He was too dense to recognise this as evidence of Pye.

"Yes, we call those civilian jobs," he said.

Taking them through the appliance room, where the pumps were kept, and there they exclaimed at how dark it was, he wondered if they were nervous. But he saw, once they had come round a corner of sandbags into blinding light, that they were just amused and that it was Pye, Wal, and the other men at the station, on the silence their entrance made, who were confused.

"So there you are then," Pye said, and got a laugh, for this was one of Piper's expressions. As he introduced the two girls to Hilly, "My driver," he told them to take no notice, "the men's amusement is on account of its being a manner of speech one of us uses, you'll pardon me, ladies." He set Prudence down to the trestle table on one of the pews which had been lent from a neighbouring church. He took the seat by her. There was no room for Richard, who had to draw up a beer crate to get next Ilse. Hilly, rather coldly, said conventional things. They accepted stiff gins without comment. Piper unexpectedly called out, "All the best, ducks," as they were about to drink and suddenly they were in, conversation became general, only now and then each of the men looked at their sleekness and this, with the twenty or thirty present, meant that a dim glance, a dull enquiry, a muffled undressing look, shut on and off continuously at them from one after the other of these one hundred watt shadow-carved faces, as bulbs go on and off on an illuminated sign while it is still daylight.

The large room, part of a disused West-end motor saleroom, had plate-glass windows which, so polished once, had been coated with black paint. As with all showrooms, it was overheated, and because there were no civilian fires to fight the men were discouraged, in daytime, from opening what few doors had been left by the sandbagging for fear the public might be led to protest at their idleness. During black-out hours it was impossible to have any ventilation. They were not allowed to turn down the radiators because a General Order had been circulated which drew attention to the danger of burst pipes. All day long they spent under powerful electric lamps, however brilliantly the sun might shine on snow laid over gardens across the way.

The room was painted yellow orange. The floor was done out with flags of artificial stone which, whatever the scrubbing, gave off a thick grey dust. All, as they sat in this bare room, had purple shadows hacked out beneath their eyebrows, chins and noses by the naked, hot spotlights in the orange ceiling.

The library at Richard's home was old, long and low. Its daylight came from beneath a vast cedar on the lawn. The walls were covered by books as dark as their oak shelves. Where it could not be seen without getting up to look, a grandfather clock tick-tocked.

At night shutters, and in front of these, curtains covered by a Morris design, closed all sound of the cedar out as it groaned under the weight of snow or, in other weather, absolutely black in moonlight as the wind outside swept through and through.

He tried to explain to Ilse. He felt awkward. She was distant. He wished he had been next Prudence, who was deep in with Pye, laughing and sparkling. His old friends had left London. This meeting with a new girl made it necessary to share past experience, to exchange he did not know what. And with any female, it seemed, but this, whose cold country could have given her, so he thought, no such memories as his own.

In white paint over the black, life-sized skeletons had been drawn on the showroom windows.

"Ach," she said, breaking into his laboured description of the library that she had not understood, "So you remember. You are like my country. Yes, with your skeletons that you have painted." She meant they did not mind remembering they were to die. He fell for this.

Before war broke out, with girls, in the first few minutes, Auxiliaries, unless drunk, had been too diffident to say they thought themselves a suicide squad. The women considered perhaps they might be, but, for the most part, were too interested in chances for new society that the various preparations for war, the regrouping of men, gave them, to bother to assess danger as between war-callings. Now the Fire Brigade had no drill halls, and had never, so far as Richard's district was concerned, given a dance for the Auxiliaries. Accordingly, in those days, when he went out with a girl, a magnet, he relied on a lecture they were given at the time, or rather was driven to refer to it immediately so as to talk about himself at once. This lecture told how a gigantic death roll must follow the first raid, together with a great number of what were called conflagrations. This word meant the calling out of every available appliance within reach. So Richard was divided, when he talked, between a wish to quote from this official view of what was likely, which included the opinion that the AFS must suffer heavy losses, and a reluctance, falsely gallant, to alarm the sex. In the end he would give them this lecture in full always and at the earliest, as he proceeded to do on this occasion. He invariably found these girls had no fear but that the Auxiliaries would come out all right. At first he supposed they took this line to still his fears. But whenever he bothered to be honest he had to admit they were a long way from paying attention to what might be his final bit of trouble. As he told Ilse, while enjoying a return to this oft-told horror story, he was watchful, expecting the usual "Oh, you will be all right, we shall all be." So that he was daunted when she said, "Yes, and it is my thought that your people in this country have not done enough, not nearly, no, you are such a long way far to go even yet, you will not realise," she said. "I was so surprised," she said, "to see those death bodies, skeletons, up there, such a lot think bombs do not explode because they come from Czechoslovakia. I, I like you here, but oh how you are hated abroad, yes, even your own allies. I'm sorry," she said, "but you have chosen, ach, so dangerous a thing, this fire, and I wished I could tell you. Because," and she turned on his her serious, ice-blue eyes, intensely, most boringly friendly, "Prudence, she is English like you, she does not agree with me, she thinks all this is good fun and I . . ."

What she went on to say was cut off from him by a roar of laughter. Looking along to Prudence he saw her mouth agape, her broad tender shoulders loose with laughter, her dark eyes lapped with melted ice. Pye was laughing gargantuanly into her face. His sly pig's eyes assessed his chances, while, once he saw the Chief amused, across that table Piper slapped his own forehead, roaring.

"What makes you split yourself, darling?" Ilse called to Prudence, at which the yell of laughter abruptly stopped. Richard leant forward to listen, saw thirty pairs of eyes turned speculatively and dim on the Swede. He did not notice Hilly get up to slip into a vacant pew on his other side.

"Hullo," she said.

After he had shewn surprise and had partly explained how it came about that he had not noticed her, intending this as an apology for having seen so little of Hilly ever since war began, she whispered that he did not look to be getting on so very well with his foreign friend. He countered in a low voice, promising he was no friend of hers, and thus became a conspirator. "But," she said, "you asked her here, you know." He corrected this. He pointed out it was Mr Pye had asked him to invite the girls.

"I heard all about that," she said, "you went to the flat, and then sent Peewee up."

"So is that what you girls call him?"

"We think he's sweet. But why did you send him?"

He wondered if she had been drinking.

"Look," he said, laughing, "I know I sent your sweet Peewee up, but what about it? I didn't stay, did I?"

"You can't fool me," she said. "Anyway I think they're both very attractive. Which do you like the best?"

"You can't catch me," he answered, "they're just two girls."

"No, really Richard, honestly it's not good enough." She grinned at him, blue eyed as well as that other but fatter, the bloom, as he said to himself, of a thousand moist evenings in August on her soft skin and, on the inner side of her lips, where the rouge had worn off, opened figs wet on a wall.

"You're teasing," he said. She giggled.

"I'm not," she whispered. "Oh you are stupid. I'd have thought someone like you who has thousands of girls would keep them to himself. Such a chance you see, next door to the station."

"No, they're no use."

"But you thought they might be to our precious Peewee, and when we've been taking so much trouble."

"Of course, if you girls can't hold Pye, I can't do much for you."

"The dark one's away with him now, I'm afraid."

"Don't be silly," he said, smiling particularly. "Why with you about he wouldn't want to look at anybody else, except at a party."

"Thanks."

"No, I meant, of course, that as he's in charge he's more or less host, he has to take trouble."

She laughed outright. "You're only making it worse," she said and suddenly, as perhaps he had been meant to, he intensely considered her. The thought came – had she gone to bed with Pye? The horror of this idea made him stammer slightly as he said:

"Where have you been all this time?"

"Here, same as you."

"When's your leave day? Are you on the blue watch?"

"Yes." She was no longer laughing.

"Shall we go out and have an evening? You know, meet as we used after the station, have something to eat and go to a film."

She burst out laughing again. "No, Richard."

"Why, what do you mean?"

She made herself serious to say, "You know what," she said.

"You beast," he said.

"Oh well," she corrected herself, "I might, you never know," and looked elsewhere. He felt he regarded her now as a real person, not just the girl for a drink when the evening's training was done. By this time both of them had had a few drinks. Then another crash of laughter dragged his eyes away.

Prudence was being a success. She liked firemen. When she first came to London five years ago, she put up at a hostel. In those days she did not know the number of men she knew now. One morning she was woken by the thud of leather top boots on stone stairs, by scrambling, by oaths. Soon after, she heard something rattle the brickwork up her chimney, smelled burning. Before she knew it was no more than a chimney fire, she was frightened but, when the other girls told her she stood at the door, an overcoat over her. A fireman, blackened by soot and water, smiled brilliantly at her as he came downstairs. At that she decided she would give them all tea, went back into the room to fold her bed away into the wall, and abandoned this only when she came to realise that she had not enough tea, or a large enough kettle, for what she imagined must be at least twenty men. Still, she began to do her face at once. Then when she was ready to outstare them going downstairs, she found it was all over and that they had been gone some eighteen minutes. Ever since she'd had a soft spot for firemen. She felt it was hard on Richard that he was not next her now at this party. She felt firemen must be very brave, but particularly the professionals, which was where Pye had the advantage. They had those funny hats.

But the jokes were getting rather free. Prudence had only meant to look in anyway. She got up to go. Piper protested above all the other voices, at their going. She was aware that the lights were impossible really for a girl. As Richard took them back through the dark appliance room, she said almost severely to him:

"And don't forget our flat, the windows look out over the door here and, if anything happened, you could see it and come back, what I'm trying to say is I know they're awfully difficult about letting you get out but you could come along if you wanted to be quiet, we're out most of the day aren't we darling, I mean if your wife comes up to see you."

As he gave thanks Richard said to himself so that's that, Pye has been with them after all, because Pye doesn't know she's dead, though he would never have told about Christopher, surely. This irritated him, and he was so bored with Ilse he was almost rude to her. She did not notice.

As he came back to the party, hating Pye for not knowing, he wondered if Pye would be arch. But he found a violent argument fully developed. It appeared that someone had referred to the newspaper report of a Regular's sister who had been convicted of shop lifting. The Auxiliary who started this claimed they had brought the man up before his officers to be questioned. Pye asked, did the fireman's sister live with him. The answer being yes, Pye gave as short an exposition as he was able of the view officers took when stolen goods were found in the house of a servant of the public, "that 'ad the right of entry into any place, anywhere, at any time, just as you lads has that same right given you now under the Defence Acts 1939."

"It's a thing one can't fathom," someone then said about that kind of theft, "but even those what don't lack for nothing do it."

"You're not telling me a fireman's wage was an abundance even before the war. I 'ad to live on it for years."

"No, sub, nor ours now," for the Auxiliaries were getting fifteen shillings a week less than the Regulars. Another said, "Per'aps 'e kept 'er short, you know, stinted." "And when the rich get taken up they bring the doctor to say they're sick." "Maybe she was driven to take what she took." "What, by greed?" "If you're starving . . ." "There's no one needs go 'ungry in this country."

"I known a corporal in the army once," said Piper, "in me own regiment 'e was, out in India." As the main argument developed on every side, it grew so that several were speaking at one and the same time, but Richard could not help himself, he had to listen, as always, to Piper. The old man inevitably forgot the end of his own stories. "Yus, it was out in India, oh a long time back, I seem to remember it was in Oodi, no, come to think, now, it must 'ave been Parge. You're sayin' as 'ow it was a funny thing put me in mind . . ."

What Piper went on to say was obliterated by thick, angry voices shouting in the general discussion. "'E didn't oughter . . ." "I wouldn't put nothin' past 'em . . ." "You're telling me she didn't . . ." "Not on your life 'e 'ad no right . . ." "She never did . . ."

Once more the old man's patient voice came through. "It's strange, I can't quite seem to recollect, that's funny, it was something to do down in the bazaar."

Yet again the voices rose. Richard, as he could no longer hear Piper, watched his lips move and, almost at once, gently close, while a look of great sadness came over his drooping face. Then, as the noise died down, Richard saw Pye's face stiffen as a sly Welshman said,

"Why would they 'ave 'ad 'im on the mat up at the station?"

"Did they do that then?"

"They did so, up at Number Fifteen."

"Well," said Pye, a flush spreading over his forehead that the rest could put down to ale if they liked, but which Richard knew came from another cause, "as I tried to acquaint you before, if she lived with 'im and they got to 'ear what she had done, they would send for 'im. Most likely someone put the squeak in, told them, they're too ignorant to read up there."

A roar of craven laughter greeted this, his smack at authority. "Oh listen to 'im," Piper cried. "You may laugh," Pye went on, "but 'e'll tell you the same, 'e's an old soldier. You'd 'ardly credit the ignorance of those that 'ave got promotion and will get no farther." "That's right," said Piper. "They won't tolerate even the smallest thing," Pye continued, "for fear they get asked about it. I could surprise you with things I know. That I know, mind you, as true as I'm sitting here. Is that the truth, Wal?"

This man spoke for the first and last time. "It's the God's truth, mate," said he.

"But they're like that," Pye went on, "soon as ever you're in the newspapers, or your family is, they want to know. 'Now, fireman,' he mimicked, 'what could have led you to suppose . . .' and all that tripe from a man you was with in the drill class fifteen year ago, who cussed and blinded with you then. Once they get the peaked cap," he said, forgetting his own promotion, "they turn, every one of them, bar one of course," he added, remembering, and getting a shout of laughter, "but then perhaps I haven't had it long enough," taking exaggerated care with his aitches.

Richard considered the awkwardness averted. Unfortunately no one else at that time, besides Piper, had heard of Christopher's abduction. In consequence the Welshman did not know the swamp he was on when he asked,

"Did they account his sister's sin his own, then?"

"What else would they do, mate, being as they are," Pye said, and choked.

"It is the same where I come from. If my own sister stole his good cow from my neighbour in the next field, in Llannethry where I come from, I should get the bloody blame."

"And indeed to goodness they wouldn't be far wrong mate," someone yelled, grinning at him, "a bob to a dollar you'd've put 'er up to it."

"God stone me blind in both my eyes, why should I do that when I can take my enamelled pail and milk her before he's up, for he does not rise till late."

This brought the house down. The trestle was banged and purple faces, with gaping throats fringed by green gaps for teeth, turned to each other, bellowing. Piper gave himself up for lost, exaggerating his pleasure, for he had not properly heard. He gasped, "Oh mother." As the noise died a man, mirth strangled, said, "Would you bloody well credit it." Richard laughed with all his heart, thinking the danger past.

"And if my sister had a bastard," this Welshman went on, but he was drunk, besides it was long ago that he had left Wales, "would these head officers put me bloody inside for it, the druids."

"They would that you ugly sod, you," one remarked and laughed, though not so freely. The man had gone too far. All listened to Pye when he spoke. He pronounced,

"A man's sister is sacred to 'im," and looked at Richard, then looked away, "who has been nursed at the same pap, and is 'is own flesh and blood." These were fine words, and, in the general assent, the moment was wild and free. "When I was a lad, me and my sister used to go out in the kingcups, soft of an evening after supper, and make gold chains we put about the other's neck. They were better than pearls fine ladies wear that they most likely got by whoring. If his dad and mother's own daughter takes a wrong turn, and it may be not by her own fault, but something in her circumstances, per'aps they could not buy the right grub to feed her, if she slips up and commits what the law of this land says is a felony, or a crime even, if they were men, lads, they would have him in, give 'im a hand, maybe assist him to send 'er to a place where she could be put right, not ask him what he had to do with it, same as it was he was the criminal."

At this Pye left dramatically, white faced. After three minutes all except Richard had forgotten him in baiting the Welshman.

THE DOOR OPENED as Mary Howells was putting tea leaves into the warmed pot for a last cup before going to work. It was Brid. The baby was in her arms, carelessly held.

Mrs Howells said, "Oh my Gawd." The expression

about her mouth, lips pursed for the rite it was when she prepared a cup of you and me, altered to horror, lips opened wider at the shock yet still pouted weak like the discharge end of a large size in spouts. The daughter came right in. She put this sleeping babe down plumb centre of the one table, by its grandmother's WAFS cap. Then, still saying nothing, she went back for her case, brought this through the door, and just stood, holding it with both hands in front of her knees.

Mrs Howells, with shaking fingers, put down the china teapot covered with pink roses her sister, Aggie, had given as a wedding present; which had reflected Brid's conception by that liquid rose flower light of a dying coal fire twenty-one years back; which now witnessed Brid's return, deflowered, but married, and with the fruit, a child.

"If I didn't nearly drop the pot. Oh me girl . . ." Mary began, then stopped. "But let you 'ave a fresh cup," she went on, and poured boiling water, "there now, it's making. Why that won't do," she cried and took three long black hatpins she still used on her uniform cap out of it, where the little innocent could not reach, "There my little sparrer, out of 'arm's way even if you is asleep. Now, me girl, whatever would you be standin' there for? Put the old case down, you're at 'ome now," she said, "at last," she added with a theatrical grim meaning.

The small room was breathless with curtains, knick-knacks, dark wallpaper and carpet. Every particle was clean but had gone dark from the years. Brid looked askew at her mother's trousers. "Thanks mum," was all she said. She sat down to table. Mrs Howells had her mouth lemon open once more, this time to ask her fill of questions, when Brid was spared because baby woke up, began grizzling. Mary bustled. She let out on the child a flood of appeals and pleased threats which was all her urge, given in a thick, loving voice, to ask Brid why.

There was snow outside. Two pools formed about Brid's

feet on the carpet, her that used to be so careful. The month was November. It was cold out. And meanwhile the sub-station was having its first fire.

The bells went down without warning, the long ring for a real call. As Richard fumbled his boots on, half suffocating, elated, he noticed someone motionless, flat on his face. He learned afterwards this man had fainted in excitement.

It seemed a long time before they drove out through the slush, but they were quite fast. In those early days taxis drew the pumps. Richard was upset that Chopper, who was in charge of the appliance, should ride standing on the step and not use the seat made for him next the driver. They careered along. They stopped. Pye's appliance had drawn up in front. Pye and Chopper plunged through a peacefully open door. "It can't be," Richard thought. But it was. He looked up. From a window came a blind of smoke, as though rolls of black-out material, caught in the wind, had been unwound and been kept blowing about. Just like the smoke from one of their bonfires at home. He said to himself, "So it is, at last."

Regardless of what they had been taught, both crews dashed in.

The staircarpet was white, and the walls. The banisters pink. He saw yellow curtains. He was out of breath. He found he had been shouting, "Where is it?" Then, in the way two dolphins will breast a wave and curve, Chopper and Pye hurled themselves downstairs past these lads coming up. He had a flash of their two set, dead-white faces. The crews turned round. They followed them out, three stairs, black now, at a time, right to the next front door, also ready open.

They had been in the wrong house.

There was a yell. "Still." The Auxiliaries stopped dead. This gave them time to see two red appliances, manned by Regulars, drawn up behind. These Regulars were standing idly by, bored. The man who had shouted said next with vicious scorn, "Why don't you git out of it?" Another enquired, "Do yer mas know yer out?" At that Pye shoved his head out of a window. There was no more smoke. His face was green. "A preventer," he hissed to the Auxiliaries, "and may God in his mercy strike every man of you cissies dead, you cloud of butterflies."

A preventer was taken up. It appeared that he had caught a can, in other words that he had been held to ridicule and worse inside, by the high officer Trant, for entering the wrong house. The fire was out. It had been extinguished by one old lady on her ownsome. She came down. She complained at the number of pumps in attendance. She may have had it in mind she would be made to pay. When she disappeared, the Regular who had yelled said to them in anguish, "For Christ's sake piddle off out of it." And, in their upset, the Auxiliaries did an unforgivable thing, they obeyed. They drove away. As a result, Pye and Chopper had to walk all the way back to the station, a full sub officer and a fireman, shamefully, Chopper carrying the pole with a hook on the end which is a preventer, right along three streets, every foot of the way on foot.

Pye was never the same.

Three hours later, when he came into the kitchen to fetch his dinner, he was still talking just on the fringe of this subject. He had not yet had time to begin to go properly into it. "And what about the occurrence book?" he was whining. "Would you propose to book me pump back, because you must surely know by now that everything must be booked out and in, book me pump back without me? But what do they know? Nothing," he said to the cook Eileen, then noticed Mary was crying. He paid no attention, but did not forget.

Later in the day he gave the station five turn-outs in three hours, that is to say, he gave them five false alarms. He put the bells down five separate times and on each occasion they had to drive out, turn round outside in the traffic, and bring the pumps back in again. After this it was not surprising that, while they did not claim they had done brilliantly at their first fire, the men considered their two officers had also lost their heads.

All day Mary Howells had done hardly any work. For hours she sat at the cain and abel in the kitchen, at that vast yellow kitchen table which the previous tenants had found too large to take away. Round her the cook grouped and regrouped various heaped dishes of veg. Meals had to be prepared for hungry men whatever the weather outside, or the weather in that meteorological disturbance which constitutes women's feelings. Cups of tea innumerable were poured poor Mary as she dripped and cried. And one by one the plates, brown enamelled trays, colanders piled high with the brown earth's fruits were taken from her, untouched, to be prepared by Hilly and Eileen.

For she mourned the fruit of her own body, what had, so to say, been grafted on her by Howells, but which in the fullness of time, when ripe, had dropped away alive, with a live life of its own she did not comprehend, to be grafted by a stranger with this helpless bundle that in spite of the process was part of Mary's flesh and blood, this baby that bore a strange name; this it was she mourned, not for the marriage, the flowering, the development or for that its mother had borne, all these being in the course of nature, but she mourned the mother, her own daughter, that she had come back.

Just as she got up to get ready to go home, for, in spite of anything that Eileen or Hilly could say, she would not make her way back before the usual time, just as she had taken the last cup, had dried her eyes for the last time, and said yet again she would never forget, ever, and never disremember the sight of Brid standing at the door, then, exactly, Pye came in. He had not forgotten. He came to suggest she might want to stay away a few days. With remarkable tenderness he described how he could cover her absence up so that, if she took no more than a few days off, she would lose no pay because he would see to it that the authorities did not get to know she had been absent from the station. Unfortunately for him she was too upset to understand. If he had said straight out he would let her have a paid holiday she would have understood. For what she confusedly had in mind was to visit the military camp in Doncaster where her daughter's husband was serving. But she did not hold with discussion at any time, with a male, of a plan she meditated which might have serious results. She held it to be unlucky. Besides she did not mean to discuss her private affairs with Mr Pye, whom she already disliked. But in any case she had not properly heard. She imagined he must suppose she was ill. Years of working for a harsh employer, a large corporation, had bred great wariness in any situation requiring her to admit her health at sixty was not that of a woman forty years younger. So she said, "No thank you," and that she was perfectly well in herself.

Pye felt slighted. He was that sort of a man. And the day's events had not helped.

Pye was discouraged. He knew now, for the first time, the sense of impotence which goes with authority, the feeling that those he commanded did not care. He had never before had to give orders, beyond the few shouted words at drill. In his ignorance he could not say what he felt. So it was unlucky for him, as he came back from the kitchen, that he found Piper on guard at the door of the appliance room.

This old man did not look his best. As usual his knees were bent, the trousers he wore were ingrained with sand, his tunic sagged from work hollowed shoulders, the medal ribbons were awry and that leathern jaw was covered by forty-eight hours of grey bristle.

"See here, Piper," Pye said, "there's 'igh officers go floatin' around in great 'igh powered cars. They come looking for what, why for trouble. When I enter the station I don't 'ave to look, I know it's there. Smarten up. We're in a service, not dustmen working for the council. You're an old soldier, give us a break. Sweet Jesus, what 'ave I done to deserve it?"

Piper said afterwards, "'e didn't 'alf give me a canin', oh dear," and thought no more. He was past that stage when he was able to remember any small incident which had gone against himself. But Pye could not put the substation out of mind. Unused to having men under him he assumed at any little bit of trouble that they were trying to get him down. And he had had big trouble. Trant had said, the words still rang out about his head, "Well Pye, while you was visitin' every other bedroom along this street, the fire was still behind that winder all the smoke was coming from. And it went on so until the old cow what was in the 'ouse put it out with a saucer full of water. Also, another thing, guard that tongue of yours before the public." For all he knew Trant might write out a report, in which case there would be an inquest at Headquarters on the fire. And it had been said to him before another sub officer. He could not shut his mind. He had the bells put down for work. He set all hands to clean out the appliance room a second time.

In their ignorance the men thought it was Piper had upset him.

Mary, highly dramatic in the black-out at having decided on action, stumbled home to Brid. She pictured at the back of her eye the descent she was going to make on this camp the rotten, good-for-nothing, lying 'ound her son-in-law hung out in. She saw a long straight road as dark as this she walked and herself making her way, collected, down along it. It was blue cold. She wore her coat and the warm gloves. Up in the sky giant silent trumpet searchlights swung like they were to herald angels. At the end lights twinkled from a thousand buildings. Soldiers always keep a rotten black-out. For sure, being as he was, they must crime him for showing a light out of that window behind which he would even now be waiting for the visit that was coming, the runt, the bastard. Great whited monuments, like the tomb in Whitehall, began to line the roadway. From under the first a sentry challenged her. It could very likely be his air-raid shelter. She caught the bayonet's flash. "Who goes there?" he would say. And then she could tell him. "A mother," was all she would reply. Yes, he must know, that had a mother of his own. "Pass mother." And the next. "Who goes there?" "A mother, like you have of your own." "Pass." "Who goes there?" "A mother," right until she was at the gates where that miserable twister would be waiting, froze with his conscience, wiping his white hands, the ponce.

The next day, she was going north. And, it so happened, Pye had a summons he could not ignore, to visit his sister that same day at the asylum.

As he lay in bed on duty, his head by another telephone, a myriad anguished conversations held, unheard by him, within the black, shining, idle handle, he felt he could not sleep and managed to forget the station only to fall to worry over the visit waiting to-morrow. He had not seen her from the time he put her there. He had never called at one of these places. He thought of it as by night, for the black-out, at that period, was at the back of all their minds.

As usual he pictured himself involved in argument. He imagined he was asking the bus conductor, "What's the nearest you go to the Hospital, mate?" "Cows Pasture." "And where would that be, chum?" "Where we turn off to the right." "Is that the only turn you take right-'anded?" "No, that it's not." "Then do I 'ave to wait till I see them eatin' grass on me left before I know this is where I gets off?" "Ah, it's all built over now, you would never recollect it for the place you 'ad known." "But see 'ere, chum," he would object, "I ain't never been this way before, and I can't say I'm sorry, be logical, 'ow am I goin' to tell?"

"Why, I'm going to call out to yer when we gets there, ain't I?" "You never said you was." "I allus were." "Then that's different."

After he had passed through a high wall, he saw himself groping to a vast pile that was raised black against him, for by now it was night and no gleam could escape into the darkness from this tiered tomb which shut those inside from the sky. He found he was under a large hall of bars that cast over him a zebra light. Dry, striped men with yellow surgeon's dress asked his business. For some time they would not admit they kept a Pye. After he had shown his fireman's pass, the letters he had, and the summons they had sent, one of them was away a long time. Then, from above, he heard her cry low, "Bert." Looking up, he could see Amy on the third floor of the cage, hanging to bars like they do in pictures, dressed all in yellow. Lying along his bed he groaned as Richard would, full length on the railway carriage seat coming back from his first leave, in six weeks' time.

As he pictured her she was pale, hair unbrushed, streaked with dirt, who had always been so fresh. "Amy," he called, "but we can't speak like this." "Excuse me," he said to the one expressionless man who now remained, "we can't speak like this, in public, shouting top and bottom to each other. This lady's my sister." "Them's the regulations, Mr Pye." "But man, it's not human." "Sorry, there it is." "But, by God, this ain't right." "You know what they are, you're in a service, Mr Pye, an' they won't have it." "But she's as sane as you and me, they put 'er inside, it wasn't nothing to do with myself, I signed, but they made me do it." "Now don't get excited," this man said in a meaning tone. He pulled a stethoscope out of his breast pocket. "Bert," Amy called to him in the same low, warning voice. "Is there any history in your family, Mr Pye?" "'Istory, what d'you mean, 'istory? I've twenty years service an' what I am and what I'm not is on my record card up at Headquarters."

The dry yellow-coated man at that instant turned into a Fire Brigade Superintendent, wet through, in full rig, dripping water. He said to Pye, "I'll take your number," at which Pye woke up, turned over, and fell this time into dreamless sleep.

The next day he said to Chopper, "I got to go on private business, mate. Cover me till roll call, till I'm on leave." It was his leave day, he would be off at ten, but he had been told he must see her doctor at the asylum. To be there on time he had to get away a bit early. He did not dare ask the main station, Number Fifteen, for permission. He did not want it known that he was going to see his sister.

Up at Number Fifteen, Trant's wife, as he left his quarters, promised him pork pie for dinner. This put Trant in mind of his sub officer who had made them a laughing stock the previous day, running about like a chicken that had its head cut off, with his Auxiliaries like a herd of sodding geese. "I wonder," he said to himself. He rang Pye up.

"Sub officer Pye is not here, sir, he has just gone out inspecting hydrants."

"Tell him to ring me when he gets back."

Pye was travelling. He could not be reached. A second time Trant rang up, on this occasion not five minutes before the roll was called at ten. He was informed Pye was busy on a private trunk call in the telephone box outside.

When Trant rang a third time, fifteen minutes after ten, it was to be told Pye had just that moment gone on leave, and that he must have forgotten, because Mr Trant's message had been given him.

Chopper rang up Pye's neighbours. "Soon as ever 'e gets back tell 'im to ring me quick," he said, "or 'e'll find trouble for 'isself."

Pye, unaware, arrived at the hospital with no difficulty. There were signposts pointing the way at every turn after he left his bus. He found matters simpler, but more horrible than he had dreamed.

The porter kept an occurrence book, same as they have in the Brigade. Then there was the paper he was made to sign, in which he undertook not to give anything to the patient. He read this carefully. To make doubly sure there was a list. Even toothbrushes were put down as dangerous, forbidden. What hurt could the sad, deluded females do with a toothbrush? But he signed. Being new to promotion, he put "Sub Officer, London Fire Brigade" beneath his signature. And, because he was a careful, law-abiding man, he gave up the present he had brought his sister, a comb with rose briars painted on the top.

The interview was so painful he could remember hardly any of it after. The room upset him. All in green, ceiling and all, the walls upholstered like an eiderdown, nothing but two armchairs on the floor. Amy had spoken rather quiet. When he tried to move his chair, padded outside and in to match the walls, so as to hear her better, also for old sake's sake to hold her hand, he found to his horror that it was bolted to the boards. She had talked sensible at first, said the food was good and all that, and then, towards the end, she went a bit wandering, asking when he was going to bring her child. But it had all been so strange that he was ready next day to reject any version left him of what she may have said. In a week's time, if he had had anyone to talk over his trouble, and there was no one, he would have insisted that she spoke no different from another.

Pye was a simple man. He had been wrought up by the outbreak of war. In the bus on the road back he cried part of the way, called himself wet. Then he forgot.

The moment Pye reached home from the asylum his neighbours gave him the message. He rang Chopper at once. As soon as he had been told he felt certain it was Richard had given him away. "It might be that soft savoury Roe's put the squeak in," he said.

"Why surely no one would do that, skipper, surely not?"

"Don't know so much, Chop. Got to keep our eyes skinned, mate."

Chopper was delighted with the expression. From that day Richard was known as Savoury, after the Row of this name, along which, in Chopper's home town, expensive tailors used to measure the well-breeched for their suits.

"I know what I'd call 'im, but then I can't, I'm a gentleman," Chopper greeted Pye next morning, on his return from leave.

"Who are you referrin' to?"

"Why Savoury, of course."

"'Oo?"

"You called 'im that yourself. Roe."

"Oh 'im. I'm not so sure now. It might be that simple old answering sod Piper. What's 'is name, that spy Trant has up at Number Fifteen, Osborn, uses the King's Arms, doesn't 'e, which is in the same street the miserable old 'ermit lives, ain't it? But what's Trant done? Posted me adrift? Yet you booked me out on leave in the occurrence book? Did you? At ten, same as the rest on my watch? Well, that's all right then," I don't think, he muttered under his breath. "I'll get Hilly to say she was taking me round the 'ydrants. An' you might slip out right away before you go on leave. Try and find one that's defective so as I can report it. I'll spin some yarn or other about that phone."

Roll was called and, as the cooks did not usually attend, it was only when Eileen sent over to say Mrs Howells had not turned up that Pye knew she was what is known as adrift, that is to say absent without leave, a major crime. He sent for Hilly. He was shorter with her than she had ever known. But she would not discuss Mary's affairs. She would not say where Mary was.

Because Pye was new to authority, he resented the fact that the whole station did not come to him with its troubles. Before the war, when promotion had been out of reach and he had had his dreams of the figure he would cut if he had his deserts and somehow, impossibly, attained the rank he felt was his due, that is, his present rank, he had imagined himself a father to the men, knowing about their children, even settling differences between husband and wife. And here was a case in which he had chanced his arm. He had offered to cover her, as much as to put his head into a noose, without even asking Mary to take him into her confidence. He blurted it out, saying:

"She's stabbed me in the back."

Hilly wondered if she would lose her temper.

"Honestly, I don't understand you."

"You don't understand me, eh? You know General Orders? Or you should. Where any member of the Service is sick they must acquaint the officer in charge. Else they're adrift."

Well, thought Hilly, I'm pretty certain I know where she is, it's obvious she's in the train on her way to that precious son-in-law of hers. It's a fairly sure thing she's making a big mistake. But if the old lady would not tell sweet nasty Peewee, no more will I, in fact I can't. So she said,

"Perhaps she has been knocked down or something."

If she had had more experience of the Brigade Hilly would have known better. The answer was obvious.

"Then I can't do any other than send 'er up as adrift in my return to Number Fifteen. The moment they get the report from hospital to say she's been admitted then I'm caught. You understand what covering is? It's pretending someone is at the station when they ain't. When I was in the kitchen dinner time yesterday I didn't think you girls did comprehend. I offered to cover her then. You heard me. She didn't answer. She may be waitin' to see the Chief Officer now with her troubles, whatever they may be. Or she may be inside, the police may 'ave took her in. I don't know, I can't tell."

So he still classes us all in the kitchen as "girls," Hilly thought, grandmothers and all.

"Well, I'm sure I don't know what to advise."

"And I'm not asking anyone for advice. Does the staff car want petrol?" With this he dismissed her. He prided himself that, at lectures and on official occasions, he could speak as educated as the next man. But he had forgotten. He realised it almost at once. He called Hilly back.

"And 'Illy," he said, smiling, "you took me out inspectin' 'ydrants yesterday morning when I went 'ome early, you drove me in the staff car, don't forget, and you omitted to make the entry in your log book. All right?"

"OK skipper."

"I'll tell you what I'll do. I'll cover 'Owells for to-day, though it may cost me my pension. You get in touch with 'er. Tell 'er to ring through to the watchroom and say she's gone sick. She don't need a doctor's certificate for forty-eight hours. You do that. Else to-morrow I shan't be able to 'elp myself, I'll be forced to send 'er up adrift. Get it?"

In any event he could do no other. He was simple enough to believe Hilly would not realise that the return for the twenty-four hours had gone in already, with Mary Howells included as present. And that return could not be scrubbed out, or altered in any way. Pye was caught if he was detected. He did not like it. He had already got the wrong side of Trant. He was jumpy the rest of the day.

He had reason. That afternoon Trant came down to turn them out, that is, to give them a false fire call and time it, to see how long they took to get cracking. As Pye said to Chopper afterwards:

"I couldn't bloody well believe the evidence of my own eyes, mate, couldn't credit it. I 'appened to be standin' at the door of the office, you know, just lookin' through the near window watching the ladies, the birds, the lovely bits of grub go by, when I sees two figures of men I takes to be cat burglars for a minute, they're actin' so bloody suspicious, mate. They're creeping along the port bow in front of this building, backs turned to the windows, and in their blue macs and caps being so you couldn't see the peak or the badge, they looked most like a couple of drivers that had done a 'old up. But I said to myself, I says, 'I've seen the back of that man's 'ead, I know that man's thick neck,' and it's so red I naturally think among all those that use the same pub as I do. Honest, it was just a drayman's neck, you know, one that 'as 'is beer all day long and most of the night, a proper drunkard's. Proper Guy Fawkes johnny. An' then, when 'e gets to the door he whips round an' dashes into the watchroom to put the bells down. Trant 'isself. Not so much as a 'ow-de-do to me of course. But the Job used to 'ave dignity. We was smart and we knew it. The officers didn't go creepin' around."

"You've said it skipper."

Fortunately, Trant took no notice of how many cooks were in the kitchen. He was too busy finding dirt. Upstairs he pushed a particular bed aside with his foot. "Not been swept for a week, this ain't," he said. Standing there, viewing the accumulation, he kicked the bed yet farther away. "Not seen a soft brush for a month." Getting angry, he kicked once more, so hard this time that the bed upset. "Never been scrubbed under since you got here, can't have been," he remarked. Of course it was Richard's bed.

Back in the appliance room Pye expatiated on the huge area of sandbagging that had already been completed, and on the immense amount that remained still to be done. In this way he managed to placate Trant, for the moment.

After Trant had gone, Pye had the bells put down again for work. He addressed the men. He did not specifically refer to Richard. "I'm speakin' to them whom the cap fits," he began. "'Oo the cap fits," Piper echoed, looking fierce. Pye went on to mention his pension at some length, "I have scrubbed floors white for twenty years, an' I'm not lettin' my pension be put in peril by one or two of you lads not doing your end of it." "An' I'm not blamin' yer," Piper added. Pye ended a long harangue by exhorting them "to keep on top line," the phrase Trant had used at parting.

Richard did not feel the backwash for several days. When he did he was surprised to find it came from his mates who began, as he thought in best public school tradition, to take it out of him for letting the guvnor, in other words, the housemaster, down.

One or two even refused to drink with him, although Chopper was not among them, nor Arthur Piper. Roe was bewildered. "Not so savoury," he heard said of himself a few times. Some ridiculed his habit of asking questions. He became homesick. He wondered if his wife had put up with a lot in him these others found out soon enough. It was the heyday of Regular Firemen, the Auxiliaries had not yet found them out. They were idolised. But Richard bought his way back into favour with free beer, plus extra housework. Before he managed, however, he crystallised in his imagination a false picture of what his home life had been, and sought advice from Hilly.

"Well, I'm up the pole now, as they say," he said to her.

"I know."

"What does one do about it?"

"Nothing I should think. But it's so stupid of the men. There's lots do much less than you. Shall I speak to Peewee?"

"No, no, for God's sake promise me you won't."

"All right, if you don't want."

"That would be disastrous."

Not many days later he came to realise he could have done worse than to get her to put in a word for him. But at this moment he had another use for Hilly. He began to describe to her, as he had tried with Ilse, the architecture of his life in old days, married, and with a son. The physical change that had befallen him he could still not escape. He had forgotten that he used to take office worries home at night. He remembered only the beatitude of those evenings and began by asking if they should, either of them, ever see those days again, "nights," he corrected himself. "I mean after work was done, when the office was over."

"Why on earth not?"

"Oh I don't know."

She wanted to ask whether it was Ilse or Prudence had given him that feeling, but he looked so miserable she thought she had better not.

"What do you mean, quite?"

"The obvious thing," he said, shying at the thought of his wife, "having worked pretty hard, really, and got a home together, and a child, and now I shan't be able to afford to keep it up. If the war ended to-morrow I suppose everything would be different to what we have known."

"I don't see still. Whatever happened to your money you would be able to keep things going."

"I suppose we shall all be killed, which makes all the fuss about cleaning and dusting pretty silly."

"But it's discipline, Dickie."

"No never. It's mad this public school business from the proletariat, about you've let the old man down. If he wants the work done why doesn't he see that it's done? And anyway," which was consciously untrue, "I've got cleaner habits than any of 'em. And when my wife wanted the house spotless she didn't trust the servants to keep the place clean, she saw that they did their work. We do enough for Pye, I'd like to see him do something for us."

"Oh he does quite lot. Really."

"Well what?" he asked.

"I can't tell you yet," she said, "I'm sorry, but it's still going on, you see."

"All right, I don't want to know. But I thought you wouldn't be able to give me an example."

"I'm sorry. I will tell you some time."

There was a silence between them. Then he began again.

"We've had to turn in everything over this war, all our private hopes, all our plans. We come here ready for at least death, and then we get into trouble for not doing under our beds."

"But, Richard, of course. It's quite right."

"I know," he said, "it probably is, but not the way it's done. Be punished, get crimed, but not this schoolboy stuff about you're endangering the skipper's pension. That's crazy. Would a corporal in the army lose his stripes if one of his privates was dirty? And anyway they pushed all that stuff under my bed to save picking it up themselves."

"I'm sorry. I really am."

"Nothing to be sorry about," he said. "But it does make me long to be back where I could make my own way, without having to make someone else's for them."

"It must be miserable for you with Christopher out of London."

"It is."

"But come on, you see lots and lots of people in the evenings."

"Believe me I don't."

"No girls?"

"No, none."

"Truly?"

"I swear to you everyone I know has gone. Torquay's the place now they tell me."

"Well, that's all wrong," she said, thinking what a fool some girl she did not know of was to have left him, so to speak, unattended. Like a fire. She smiled to herself.

He went on, "And I don't know that the Regulars are so very wonderful at fires. They actually are supposed to know all about those things."

"You're going too far," she said. "You know the reputation of the London Fire Brigade is right up ahead of any other."

"Yes, well look at the other morning. Your Peewee and the magnificent Chopper were beside themselves, they truly had no idea what they were doing."

"I'm not so sure. But I promise you they'll be all right when raids start, when the time comes, if it ever does."

She was wrong about Chopper. Almost twelve months to a day after this conversation Richard was number one, that is in charge of a pump, called during the night blitz to an incident at which two heavy bombs had fallen within a hundred yards of each other.

He found the driver had brought them to a statue, which still looked blindly on, in the centre of a London square.

Two great streets converged ahead at a sharp angle, and he could see up both because the gas mains had been set alight. Two thirty-foot high sprays or fans of flame lit the face of ornate hotel buildings, or what may have been the east and west sides of a vast block of flats fronting these two streets, and illuminated them so well that, at the distance, he was able to pick out details of brickwork and stone facings more easily, and in colours more natural, than would have been possible on a spring morning, in early sunlight.

Against this livid incandescence stood the old war horse, pitch black, his bronze rider up, pitch black, both, as always, facing south.

Richard was told by the officer in charge, whom it had not been easy to find, to take his men and help another crew lay out hose up one of these streets that might have been twin approaches to a palace in a story, the story of ruin. As they stumbled along, and the sickly sweet smell of coal gas got thicker, over small debris which lay like a vast slumped down load of slag, he looked up and found he could now see beyond this lighted gas main, up a side street decorated by black hacked-out house fronts flickering above large, flame tongue leaping mounds of broken wood and stone.

He laid out the last length of hose. He was told to go back to his pump and keep the crew in reserve. As he went he thought he saw a shimmer out of a roof in the agitated semi-light which half lit, half shrouded those buildings nearest the bronze rider that he could no longer see, now his back was to the gas glare. Accordingly he stopped and shone his torch up at the sky. At once he heard a cry that was lost, "Put it out, put that light out." It was Chopper's voice. At that moment, with what seemed a final crash, every gun opened up on a chandelier flare which, with infinite ease, with the greatest menace, had begun to float swaying down like pearls on fire, dropped by magic.

Then for a space the din stopped. Richard heard Chopper moan, "They've seen us, the bastards've seen us." He looked down. The Regular was lying flat at his feet.

Richard had had similar nights already. And it was not until he was back among dams that had been erected on each side of the bronze horse, black on one flank, rose coloured on the other towards the now spreading fire beyond the gas mains, it was not until then that he was frightened. More dangerous than the fire those lighted mains must attract bombers. Through shattering silence he heard two aircraft. Then machine gunning. He looked up. He expected a dog fight he would not see. That flare, nearer, was still coldly, majestically descending with his fate. Rising in a long arc from the ground red tracer bullets now lobbed up at speed, and kept on missing. At last every pump started up at once. The roar of their engines enveloped everything. The ground shook. And then the guns opened again, firing this time at the bombers.

There was a surface shelter close by. Richard went inside, making the excuse that he wanted to find out how many Regulars were hiding. The structure seemed to shake, the one light to flicker with that percussion, concussion of gun fire up above. And in the near corner a girl stood between a soldier's legs. He had been kissing her mouth, so that it was now a blotch of red. He held on to her hips, had leant his head back against the white painted brick. Hair came down and trembled over his closed eyes with the trembling in the wall. Man and girl were motionless, forgotten, as though they had been drugged in order to forget, as though he had turned over a stone and climbed down stairs revealed in the echoing desert, these two were so alone.

Richard went out, abashed. Also he resented the way they were passing time. Leaning against the outside wall he found Chopper, second in command at this incident, jawing with the crew. He had packed it in. Even at such a moment Richard could not resist the temptation to be friendly to a Regular. He went up. The noise was now so terrific that, to make himself heard, he knew he must cup his hands to Chopper's ear and shout. He yelled, "Have you looked in there?"

A reluctance came over Chopper's spade-shaped face. He thought Richard was telling on some Auxiliary who was too flare struck to come outside. But there were witnesses, so he went in. He stayed a longer time. When he came out he had a soft, serious look on him. He cupped his hands. He shouted in Richard's ear, almost with reverence, "More power to his elbow mate, more power to it."

He might have come from seeing a Prince and a Princess.

Richard shouted back, "Pity old Pye never saw," and wondered if one of these bombs they rained down each night on London would turn him out of the cover he had taken, willy nilly, in his coffin, eaten by worms six foot underground.

At that moment two ambulance men carried a stretcher up. They laid it down. The twisted creature under a blanket coughed a last gushing, gout of blood.

Two police brought past a looter, most of his clothes torn off, heels dragging, drooling blood at the mouth, out on his feet from the bashing he had been given.

Then, alone, carrying a music case, handkerchief to her mouth, her thin body made angular in the glare, sharp as a saw, an old lady came slowly by, on her own, looking to the ground, ignoring it all.

And then that soldier tottered out. He was drunk. He shouted in Richard's ear. "Would you boys like to 'ave a whip round, see, to raise me a shilling so I can 'ave another go?" Chopper leaned over. "What's 'e say?" Richard yelled it. Chopper turned round and was sick. The crew nudged one another, and wryly smiled.

Twelve months almost to a day before such things happened every night, Richard wound up the talk with Hilly by saying:

"Well you never know. Raids may not be anywhere near as bad as we imagine, when we shan't know who's right about the Regulars."

"Don't you worry," she replied, having the last word, "they'll be much worse, and these men you think so hopeless now will be wonderful, honestly wonderful, you'll see."

THREE WEEKS LATER Richard asked Hilly out for a night. He took her to a small place in Soho, and was glad to see no one he recognised also having dinner. Halfway through a bottle of claret she began to tease him that he did not hear a fraction of what went on at the substation. He was thinking of Pye's sister when he replied that he was willing to bet he knew more than she did.

"All right," she said, "what?"

But he did not mean to tell the story of Christopher's abduction. He did not want to bring Hilly into family secrets. He must not, he repeated to himself, realising that he would when he had had enough to drink. It would be too intimate. He knew she would only plague him asking after Christopher, as his relations had. It was over now, there was no sign that the boy had suffered in any way. He could do without her enquiries in the substation at odd times just when his aunts and cousins, after so many months, had begun to forget.

"Isn't there something up between old man Piper and Mary?" he asked, to head her off.

"Don't be so silly,"

"There could be, you know."

"Anything's possible, and all the more so now, but not between those two, please."

"Then you do feel, as well, that anything is possible between people now?" said he, with a purpose.

"But, Richard, of course. This war's been a tremendous release for most."

"Not for me."

"Really and truly?"

"No, it hasn't. What were you before the war?"

"Didn't I ever tell you? I was a sort of superior filing clerk, that's all, in my uncle's business. I hated it. They sold umbrellas and walking sticks."

"Well you understand Dy, that is we, decided Christopher, that's my son," and as always, he felt pompous when he brought out that he was a parent, "we made up our minds he ought not to stay in London in case there were air raids, so we hoicked the old chap down to the country, for Dy to be with him. He doesn't cost any more, in fact it's an economy. But I can't get rid of our house. So there you are," he ended lamely. He had shied away again. It was too intimate. He knew well enough the only change must be in himself, that the alteration in his circumstances, by which he was more alone every evening on leave, had made him restless. He imagined, as has been described, a great deal going on all round between girls and men. What he might be missing haunted him. "And I enjoyed my job," he went on, getting back to firm ground, "I still look in there on the days I'm off, to keep them sweet. They make up my salary. I'm going sick for a few days to help get out the dividend warrants."

"When?"

The moment she asked Hilly told herself she was a fool. She could not think what had made her. He would realise she was interested, and really she never even considered him. As she formulated these words to herself she knew she was lying. It gave her the old, the remembered, small thrill. But he had not noticed. He went on to tell the date their year ended, and how they prided themselves on holding their Annual Meeting within three days of the books being closed.

"Well, you're quite right to keep in with them."

"I've got to. But I say," he said, "I wonder how many of these people here are going to bed together later?"

"I don't know, Dickie," she replied brightly, thinking I'm sure most of them are. But you aren't, not with him my dear, she told herself, oh dear no, because it makes you quite sick to think of it with him, though you know what you are, after a few drinks, but not even then, she concluded, knowing she probably lied again.

They had not been out eating together at night before. So that they had never until this moment shared the spectacle, dreary, commonplace and sad, of dim lit faces leaning two by two towards each other beside pink-shaded table lamps, solid, rosy, not so young couples endlessly talking, talking within their little coral pools, in half whispers, waited on by those hopeless, splay-footed, black-coated waiters.

"It's a bit disgusting when you look at most of them," she said.

"It sure is," he agreed, "but there you are. Piper for instance."

"No, I know you're hopelessly out about him and Howells. Honestly, they're past it. Besides he's married."

"Well a few weeks ago you said that made no difference,

d'you remember, when you were twitting me with going up to that Swedish girl's flat."

"Was I?" she said, remembering perfectly, "I forget."

"I believe you see a lot in very little, Hilly. I expect you made a great deal out of my trying to help Ilse and Prudence when it was entirely innocent."

"I didn't, I wouldn't bother," she said, looking huffy.

"I'm sorry, I didn't mean you would."

"That's quite all right. I might have, you know," she said and smiled, because she felt she had been a bit rude really. "No, but if you want me to tell you Richard, quite a lot happened about them, and is still happening, but not with you. Does that make sense?"

"No, it doesn't, and I can't believe it."

"It is true, cross my heart."

"Well then, what?" he asked.

"I can't tell you."

"You must. You can't not tell me, it's unfair not to."

"I really am sorry, I know it's too tiresome, but honestly I can't, I promised. Look," she said, and drained her glass, holding it out to be filled again as though she had decided, "we haven't finished what we were on with about the war. I don't believe there is anyone who hasn't enjoyed the change." She put this to him because she was curious to know more about his dead wife.

"Of course," he replied, content to talk of himself, "it was a great relief to have done with being polite to Hitler, and let go at last. The summer was an awful strain. But what I miss is family life. One of the troops said to me about his small daughter in the last war, 'I was away at sea most of the time, so missed all her pretty years.' I never really used to give Christopher a thought, but I do now. D'you see?"

"Yes, and it must be horrible for you," she said, wondering is it? At the back of her mind she added, and his wife is dead.

"It is," he said truthfully but, as he spoke, a sensation that he was being false attacked him. He thought he had made himself sound pathetic.

"I'm sorry," she said.

"No, no, I'm all right. It's mean of you not to share Arthur Piper and Mary."

"I never said I wouldn't," she replied.

"Then do tell me."

Because of the fuss she had made she decided she would. She said, severely:

"It's simply this. Her only daughter ran away with a soldier. They were married, and she's had a baby. But he treats her badly, and now she has come home. The sad part is that she has gone a bit silly in the head. Something to do with having the child. And Mary has gone up to Doncaster to see the husband. Old Piper doesn't come into things at all."

"Probably the worst thing she could have done," he said.

"I know, but I couldn't make her change. You know what old people are."

"You're telling me. Well, I must say that's very dull."

"What made you think the old Pied Piper had anything to do with her?" she asked.

"Is that what you call him? Oh, Hilly, I don't know, he got her the job, didn't he, and someone was saying they'd overheard Pye make some remark about Arthur being the cause of her not turning up."

Why doesn't he take me some place where we can dance, she thought, but explained what had occurred over the daily return of personnel at the substation, how Pye covered Mary for a day, and posted her sick after that, which seemed a shame, and how Pye feared Piper would tell on him if he did otherwise. "As a matter of fact I heard Peewee thought you might have let them know up at Number Fifteen about his being adrift himself. You see, he imagined, once, you had something to do with Trant turning the station out."

She was, of course, hopelessly wrong in this. She was confusing the episode of Richard's bed with the fact that Trant had caught Peewee absent when on duty. Roe, however, because his relations with Pye were awkward, had no alternative but to take her assertion at face value.

"What me," he asked, horrified, "how could I?"

"I can't imagine, but you know what they are."

"But what would I have to do with Trant?"

"I shouldn't think of it again. I was only telling you as I heard it. In any case, you know who really must have told the DO, why, the old Pied Piper. Now that he's got this job redecorating Trant's quarters up at Number Fifteen, I'm sure he repeats everything. Still, how he can have got to find out that Peewee was going off early is a bit of a dark mystery, isn't it?" she asked, though she had some days ago discovered the way she thought he had found out.

Richard said:

"He mentioned nothing about Christopher?"

"How could he? Pye d'you mean? No, of course not."

"Well, it isn't exactly of course not," he said.

"What d'you mean?"

At that he came out with the story of Christopher's abduction. She was so interested she forgot to slide her glass forward to be filled. At the end of his tale he leant over to pour more of the dark, tale-telling liquid in.

"Honestly," she said, "how perfectly terrible for your poor wife."

He ordered another bottle. He went on:

"And now that man is trying to set the station against me, because his sister walked off with my child. As if that was my fault. Saying that I tipped Trant off about him."

"No, Richard, he didn't," and she reached to put a hand on his arm, "it was only talk."

He drank up his glass of wine. He said angrily, "where's that damned waiter?" In his own way he became dramatic in the Howells manner. "I'd like to kill him. As if I'd lower myself by putting the squeak in, to sneak. I knew it would be hopeless the moment they put me in his station. I hate the lot of them. Damn."

"They don't hate you," she said, telling a white lie, "you're very popular with the men."

"I wish now I'd gone into the Army. I could have got a commission any day. Only the other morning, as I came along in the bus, an old lady said in front of everyone when she saw the ridiculous uniform, 'Army dodgers, that's what you are.'"

"Richard, you know that's silly. Who cares what they think? I told you about Ginger Garton, my friend who is one of the Chiefs. Well, he is all for Auxiliaries against the Regulars, and they wouldn't let him go back to the Navy, they told him he had more important work to do in this Service. So there."

"Well, well, I suppose I'm being ridiculous."

"I don't think so at all, and it's most frightfully important that there should be men like you in this, I mean who are different. Look, has the skipper ever mentioned Christopher again?"

"Only once, the first night in the pub. I say, I never knew old Piper was working on Trant's quarters. It's quite an idea his passing bits on. Very awkward too. As far as I can tell they've never heard up there about the skipper's sister. Suppose the hermit, as they call him, tells Trant, what d'you think?"

"Honestly, I don't see they can do anything to the skipper now, it's all over and done with."

"I'd like to see them try. I'd have something to say about that. Christopher has got nothing to do with the Brigade. And Pye's a decent enough old stick when all's said and done." She breathed again.

"But you must promise you won't tell anyone," she said, "about Peewee being caught adrift, I mean, it's not supposed to be known."

"Why is everything so secret in our place, I can't see why?"

"Don't ask me," she said, "but the more you get to know them, the Fire Brigade I mean, the more terrified they are of letting things out. They seem to be every minute spying on each other, and telling."

"As if there was any Auxiliary would bother to take tales back. Why," he said, voicing a common grievance, "they won't even give us the same training as they get when they join, in case we become more efficient than they are, and so rob them of their jobs. It's a farce." But he was wrong. There were already men who, for no apparent advantage, were more than willing to talk.

Only that morning old Piper, who had volunteered to whitewash the ceiling in what was to be the Trants' bedroom, by which he hoped to touch Trant for half a dollar, took that opportunity.

"I been wondering if I might make so bold, sir," he said, "as to put a question? Now in a certain substation there's a woman that works there, I could give the name, but no names, no pack drill, no nothing, now this 'ere woman's a married woman if you get my meanin', an' she's in trouble with 'er married daughter, same as can 'appen any place. 'Er son-in-law's no manner of good. Now a certain sub officer 'as been told by 'er all the roundabouts of it, as the sayin' is, but 'e's taken no notice, though the trouble's in 'er 'ead like the toothache. Till she goes, just like that, off to see 'im, the son-in-law I've mentioned, an' what does the sub officer do, why 'e straightaway seeks to send 'er up adrift. What's 'er position, sir, what I'm gettin' at is, 'ow does she stand in circumstances like I'm referrin' to?"

"What's the officer in charge at the substation done about 'er?"

"Nothin', like I told you, sir."

"But there's a return made to us up 'ere every morning of 'ow many's on duty."

"Ah, now I'm getting you. This 'ere return you speak about, I 'appened to catch sight of it on the two mornin's." In this way he betrayed that he was speaking of his own substation. "The first said she was on duty and the second one, that would be the next that was sent on the morrer, gives her as absent without leaf."

"Well, there's rules and regulations in every job. You're an old army man, is that right? Well, you've seen the King's Regulations?" "To be sure the King's Regulations," said Piper. "We've got nothing so complicated in the Brigade," said Mr Trant, "but, by God, you men ought to make yourselves acquainted with what there is, and these sub officers should 'ave them off by 'eart. It's their living, it's not as if they was playin' at it like so many of your posh Auxiliaries." Oh, oh, Piper cried out beneath his breath, posh is what you are now, then, you old bastard, doing 'is dirty ceiling what'll take four hours for 'alf a bloody dollar if you're lucky. "That is their livin'," he echoed aloud, servile. Trant walked off.

In substations the men had no work given them after fourteen hundred hours. One of the reasons which led Piper to volunteer to carry out decorating for the District Officer was that, accustomed in peacetime to an eight-hour day when he was not unemployed, in wartime he could not stand the idleness with which Englishmen begin hostilities. Now they were settled in their new quarters they had nothing to do. The idea was that they were to be kept fresh for the night raid which never came. At the same time they were forbidden to get their heads down, to go to sleep, before twenty-two hundred hours. Not everyone could afford to play cards. There were many who would not read. Thus each afternoon was ripe for gossip and crawling to the fireman and sub officer, ripe because these two men had almost unlimited power to make an individual's life comfortable or otherwise in these small substations.

That very afternoon there was a man closeted with Pye.

"Yes, I reckon it's quite a romance," he was saying of Hilly and Richard. "They're meeting to-night on their leave day."

"Champagne, jazz and all the rest of it, eh," said Pye, the hypocrite. "Champagne pressed out of the skin of the grape by the feet of starving peasant women, boy. Drunk to the accompaniment of music made by tubercular niggers tempted away from the climate their bodies is acclimatised to by luxury wages. It's a knockout."

"It certainly is."

"And yet if we 'ad the money," he said, "we'd do just the very same. It's 'uman nature, but saying as much is not to make out that it should be allowed, it shouldn't, it ought to be stopped. Yet I don't blame 'er, I don't blame any woman. If she can get 'im to spend some of the dough 'e won't 'ave much longer, when we get this new world they say we're fighting for," he sneered, "then I say let 'er."

"Roe's a dopey bastard, though."

"You've said it, mate. A dopey bastard's correct. Why, d'you know what 'e did the other morning? You wouldn't 'ardly credit the thing unless you knew 'im. It can't be three days since I read out that order about not smoking before thirteen hundred hours. You was there. Well, I go to put the bells down for a drill the following morning, and there's Savoury, one of the ruling class, so called, riding the front of the taxi as number one with a fag on. I shouts to 'im, 'put that fag out.' What does 'e do? The miserable so an' so stubs it on the coachwork, it was the tool box actually which 'ad been simonized up the day previous. Now what can you make of men like that?"

Later, Roe squashed his cigarette out on a large china fig leaf. It was warm in the half dark of the club he had taken Hilly on to, lights were low from table lamps with violet shades, dark palm leaves canopied each girl's bare, sapphire gleaming head; naked, fat round shoulders were chalk white; the blues negroes played were to foreigners in a foreign land of the still farther south which, with simplicity, became everyone's longing in this soft evening aching room; bottles on tables held stifling, moonlight from that south; cares melted; still they sang, played in the band, or one played alone, or it was all piano and drum while couples danced no longer in farewell but, on the part of young beautiful ladies, with the assurance that there were weeks and even months of more nights still to live, and chew, and love not very much, before it might be they would have to be dug out of the heaped ruins.

He told her the light reminded him of that first guard he had done, when, coming back with Shiner, they found cockroaches being raced before an audience drenched in deep light from a gentian bulb. Now, with excitement, so that his throat was constricted because of her nearness, fat, soft, and soft eyed, with sea flower fingered hands, and to bring the talk round to the two of them, he asked what gossip she had in return for Christopher's story. He expected she would refuse. At first he was surprised, then, for a little, disappointed, when she began at once on a tale of Pye.

She had been wafted off, was enchanted not entirely by all she had had to drink and which was released inside her in a glow of earth chilled above a river at the noisy night harvest of vines, not altogether by this music, which, literally, was her honey, her feeling's tongue, but as much by sweet comfort, and the compulsion she felt here to gentleness that was put on her by these couples, by the blues, by wine, and now by this murmuring, night haunted, softness shared. Thus, not caring, neither did she notice if she spoke the truth, she began to tell. She told so as to bring in, most particularly, everything ever so closely back to their two selves.

"Well, darling, it's like this. Oh isn't what they are playing a wonderful number? You were very naughty when you introduced Peewee to those two harpies. The thing is, he's not ready yet for things like that. I suppose if I really tell you you'll think the oddest things about me." At this point she gulped some more champagne. "Oh, I think this is a divine place," she broke off.

"Yes, it's about the best band in London. Now go on, darling, do go on."

She put her hand in his. "You mustn't hurry me," she said, "just when I'm getting a little bit tipsy, it's not fair, I won't be rushed, d'you hear? Well, to get back to our precious officer in charge. Have you ever thought about them, the Regular Firemen, I mean? The older ones are getting about twice as much money as they've ever had. Peewee had no chance of promotion before the war. He's told me so. Now this has come along, and there he is." She stopped.

"There you are then," Richard echoed Piper.

She took her hand away. "Oh look at that couple, darling," she giggled, "dancing over by that darkie waiter. D'you think she's pretty? No you can't, you mustn't. Where was I? Yes, d'you think Prudence, or whatever her name is, really lovely, honestly? Because our Peewee does. It makes me a bit worried for him. No, he's not ready for girls like her yet."

Here again she stopped. To help her, he said, the dolt, "I don't know that it's for anyone, man or woman, to judge for anyone else."

"But don't you see this war is Peewee's great chance. There's all you amateurs have joined. What's going to happen? The Regulars will promote themselves, none of you will get a look in, a man of his age with his experience may end anywhere, quite high up, honestly, if the war lasts long enough."

"If there are no raids," he said, "as there have been none, they may quite likely turn away every Auxiliary who can't stand on his head on top of a ladder without having been trained how. And then Mr Pye will revert back to what he really is, an ordinary fireman. In that case," he went on, "not to mention myself, men like old Piper, who are utterly past it, will be altogether out, and a good thing too, if what you say about him is right."

Drink had made Roe rather more intelligent.

"Darling," she said, "you should pay greater attention to what your pretty Ilse tells you." He made a face. "No, I was only teasing," she said. "You are so sweet. We shall have plenty to do when the time comes. But, even if Peewee does go back to what he was, just think of what he is now and what he used to be, pedalling back home on a byke to that sister, after his spell of duty. And now I know she's nuts I see it's ever so much more dangerous. Even if she raved and stormed every night she must have been a habit."

Richard thought the evening was not going right, or fast enough.

"A bad habit," he said, "or, anyway, one that didn't pay." If they had any more of Pye their going out together to-night would be ruined.

"I say," he went on for obvious reasons, "tell me, is there any man dancing here you would like to go to bed with? I mean on the floor at the moment," he added, so as not to seem too direct.

"Yes, there is, not counting you," she added with a look at him, and went on, "that one over there, with the girl that's dressed as if she was in diamonds fathoms under the sea, oh dear she's much too lovely. But think of my Peewee in this place, just think."

He could not make up his mind if she was only being polite. To gain time he said:

"Pye here, never."

"Why yes, he comes most evenings, and it's so bad for him, stirs up all his boring political views while actually he enjoys the place madly. But he's finding it terribly expensive."

"He's never paid for anything here, don't you worry," Richard said, still wondering if she meant what, deaf as he was, he thought he had heard her say about himself, "I know all about the only time he did come, which was the night we were mobilised. He got the proprietor to stand him three star brandy for two hours, then left, cursing the rich."

"That was the beginning, yes, but it's Prudence now, didn't you know? Every night that he's on duty. But thank God not when he's on leave yet."

Richard became speechless. She went on to give convincing details but he was wallowing behind.

"Pye comes here with her?" he asked, dumbfounded.

"Every single night. When you think he's in the watchroom."

Not that he minded, Richard told himself, not that anything made any difference. So Pye had told Prudence he was married, it confirmed the night they had had gin at the substation. So Pye saw her every night. He felt excited and jealous.

At this moment all the lights went out. A blue lime was turned, sizzling, on to the small stage. To have what little he that minute had he leaned over, in pitch dark, and kissed Hilly on the mouth. Her lips' answer, he felt, was of opened figs, wet at dead of night in a hothouse.

"Oh darling," he said, low and false, "the months I've waited to do that."

"Sweet," she said.

In the steep purple left behind by that beam of intense blue light casting on the famous coloured lady, who had begun to sing, a shiny film of dark blue, so that he might have been looking through Christmas cracker paper, he took Hilly's right arm and began to stroke the soft inside of it, which he could not see, nor tried to, watching as he was, as though in stained glass window light, the singer sing of what goes on at all times. He was rapt, lips still wet from hers, while the fingers of his right hand, toying with her arm, passed under his the softness of her skin.

As she stood there, gently telling them in music, reflecting aloud, wondering in her low, rich voice, the spot light spread a story over her body and dazzled her cheeks to bend and blend to a fabulous matching of the mood in which she told them, as she pretended to remember the south, the man who had gone, as she held all theirs with her magnificent eyes guardedly flashing, slowly turning from one couple to another, then again dropping her voice, almost sighing, motionless, while beads of sweat began to come like the base of a tiara on her forehead as she told the audience that he could see only as the less dark below her and whose clouded heads, each one, drew nearer to a companion's in this forced communion, this hyacinthine, grape dark fellowship of longing. The music floated her, the beat was even more of all she had to say, the colour became a part, alive and deep, making what they told each other, with her but in silence, simply repeatedly plain, the truth, over and over again.

She was beginning the last bars. Hilly opened herself, enfolded his fingers in her hand. "Let no one breathe a word, nobody say anything," she uttered in prayer, voiceless. Her eyes filled with tears. The stage grew impossibly brilliant. She shut her eyes and settled down, not, as she told herself, for long, to love Dickie.

During the applause he kissed her once more. She was empty, she was nothing. It was such ages since she had felt like it. She thought she made her mouth a sort of loving cup. She said to herself, "If you go on like this, my girl, in a minute you'll actually snore." She had snored once, with intensity, when kissed. Accordingly she pulled herself together, patted her back hair, began to get out lipstick. They might put the lights on. With several other men Richard called for an encore. She hoped they got it.

When she had done, and the lights went up, the singer stood revealed as what she was not, a negress with too wide a smile. The same with Hilly. As he looked at her he thought it wild that the touch of the unseen inside of her arm should have been so, and saw her not as she was.

Richard found it natural to put this next question immediately, and had no pang of jealousy when he asked:

"Then has Pye slept with Prudence?"

"Of course," she said, to be on the safe side, and looked at him. Actually she had no idea, but she was not going to risk saying that Prudence had done less.

For no reason except this looking answer, and with a rush of excitement that made him feel sick, he was suddenly sure this must mean that Hilly, who had not yet been asked, would go to bed with him that night.

WHEN MRS HOWELLS got to Doncaster she found the son-in-law Ted had come to meet her.

"'Ere I is, Ted," she said forced, very different from the way she had pictured it, "but where I'm to find me a bed for the old bones I don't know," she put in at once.

"Well, mother, we'll 'ave to ask." He had a careless way with him.

"Lucky for Brid she's got a roof over 'er 'ead," Mrs Howells answered.

"Ah," he said.

She thought he looked better back in the army, more of a man.

"You look stronger than you did, Ted. 'Ow's the chest? Would you be coughin' easier?"

She smiled. He smiled back. He gave her no reply.

"Well, I don't know," she said, "but I could do with a nice cup of Rosie Lee."

"Ah." He looked helpless about.

"This way then," she said, and at that started off for the buffet quick, "gawd love a duck, 'urry or it'll be all gone." She carried Brid's case she had borrowed. He pushed along behind, medium sized, clumping, blank in khaki.

As she fussed a way for them through the crowd, regardless, knocking knees right and left with the case she carried, she said to herself it was awkward as much as to be seen with him, the useless good for nothink.

Once inside, however, he did manage to get them two cups, hot, not the same as at home but still tea, and there was sugar.

"What would they charge for this?" she began.

"Thruppence."

"Oh – isn't it dreadful really. All that! Oh dear. 'Ere," she said and pushed over a tanner she had grappled with difficulty from her old purse. He pocketed it without comment. He had made tuppence out of her.

On the way up she had decided she would come straight out about Brid the first moment. But now he was across the table she did not have the heart.

"Ah, that's nice," she said, laying the cup back in its saucer as though it was porcelain, "most likely Brid's pourin' one for 'erself this minute. Though wasn't the train late! It's terrible really." She looked about.

She saw there were too many crowded in on either side to be confidential. This made her think here was a chance, which might not come again, to ask after lodgings. It was not as if Ted could look out for her. The party next them seemed just the thing.

"Excuse me," Mrs Howells said, "but could you put me right? Would you 'appen to be h'acquainted with any place I could lodge for the evenin'? I've come north to see me son-in-law 'ere, my girl's boy."

This made Ted squirm.

"You'll never, not in Doncaster you won't, not this night or any night in the year, packed tight as pilchards we are in this town I should know," the unknown lady said, "none better. It's a hole, that's what it is, you have me sympathy," she ended with hidden delight.

"You don't say, oh dear." Mary went on, "This dreadful war, really. It's all on account of the rich, they started it for their own ends. Now everything's topsy turvy."

"You up for long, Mrs?" Sitting a bit farther off at the round table the man who asked this looked respectable. He was white-haired, and lived with a sister, he explained. Work was taking him away that night for eleven days. The sister was next him, she hardly spoke, but in a few minutes everything was arranged, Mrs Howells could spend the night there for rather less than she had meant to pay. Relief led Mary to explanations, which made Ted squirm again.

"Yus," she said, "I'm in the WAFS in London, a real cockney I am, 'ardly ever been out of the old place, an' I 'ave to wear trousers, though I'm not that sort. What my 'usband would say if 'e was alive I can't imagine," she said, knowing full well. Within half an hour they were off in a bus to the address; within the hour Mary had taken Ted to a free house for a bite to eat and a drop of the other. She entered into a long, careful, surprised description of the living room they had just left. She could not bring herself to mention Brid.

"Busted up everythin'," she said over a glass of port, paying for his, and at last getting nearer it, "but it won't never come to nothink, mark my words, I wasn't born yesterday, I've seen two of the things, this is my third war, an' the last wasn't no picnic let me tell yer. Ted," she went on, leaving off because she was inquisitive by nature, and seldom got away, so that the fresh scenes, the small differences on either side, were too distracting, "Ted," she said, "I don't like this place, some'ow it's not 'omely, I couldn't live 'ere, never. Why look, that man's 'avin' gin in 'is pint. If anyone did that in the Running 'Orse, corner of Maypole Street, the customers would break the old place down for strugglin'."

They never got any nearer to Brid but the once, when he opened his mouth for almost the first time to tell her he must get back to camp. Then she did say "Ted, Brid's sick." Two tears took a dog's leg course down her lined cheeks. He said nothing at all. He left. She sat on, found another woman from London, and was well away by closing time.

The next day she went back to town without seeing Ted again.

When she landed home she found Brid had taken everything in the two rooms the girl could lay claim to, like the clock her auntie May said she would leave and never did, so that they had had to carry it out of the house when she died, and had put all in the old trunk which she had locked up, Brid, her own daughter had. This so upset Mary that she did not go to work at the substation for two days more. When she did report on, she was told Pye had posted her adrift.

"What I can't stomach, Arthur," she said to old Piper as she boiled him an egg on the side, extra for his supper, when no one could see, "what I can't rightly seem to get into me mind, is me own daughter, my gel, doin' a thing like that after I'd taken 'er in. 'Uman nature's 'ardly understandable, I should know, that 'as lived in the one street these twenty years, married and a widder, but to go an' do what she's done is downright unnatural, is that right or isn't it? I couldn't believe me own eyes. 'Why Brid,' I says, 'where's the mirrer,' thinking per'aps she'd broken the thing, 'whatever's 'appened,' I says, 'and the clock an' the bit of a jar I keep me pins in, you thief,' I said, forgettin' meself, 'you've pledged 'em.' 'They're mine, mum,' she says. I wasn't goin' to arguify with 'er. 'You tell me what you've done with 'em this minute,' I said, and, to cut a long story short, in the finish I found them all locked away in me trunk like I told you. I don't know. The trouble there is in this world. Sometimes I feel as if I should go crazy. And it come over me at the time, very queer it was, 'ow this trouble was on the way, like, not a day before she walked in. Children, they say, is the salt of life. Our parents looked on their children to 'elp at the end. But nowadays it's wars every generation, so it's not as if a woman, rich or poor, can call 'er child 'er own. An' with the marvels they speak about science, there's more deadly sickness now than ever we see in our young days, Arthur. On top o' that there's the worry. Sometimes I feel me head goin' round and round. For she can't go h'out to work, not in the state she's in. The expense! An' I've got to see about 'er allotment, or whatever they call it in the army these days. She can't do nothin' for 'erself. Some mornin's I'm afraid to leave 'er with the baby. If it wasn't for the neighbours I wouldn't honest."

She came to a stop.

"So there you are then," Piper said, gloomy.

At that instant, in great haste, on leave, and for only the second time, Richard tumbled into bed with Hilly. The relief he experienced when their bodies met was like the crack, on a snow silent day, of a branch that breaks to fall under a weight of snow, as his hands went like two owls in daylight over the hills, moors, and wooded valleys, over the fat white winter of her body.

"But I told 'im, Arthur, you should've been there to 'ear. I said to 'im, I says," she went on, imagining every word, "'You're no good to no one, and I got a daughter, I 'ave, 'oo you took, an' when you'd used what you wanted you sent 'er back,' I says, 'more shame to yer, call yerself a man,' I said. 'E went white, Arthur, even if 'e didn't say nothink. But I wouldn't spare 'im. 'Yus,' I said, 'yus, you 'as your pleasure of a gel, and then what,' I says, 'why, you want another dish. The best won't do for yer but you've got to ape them as can afford it, the rich with their filthy cases every day in the paper.'"

"Every day in the paper," Piper echoed.

"Oh I told 'im, Arthur, told 'im proper. I said all 'e'd done to get in the army was to be after those ATS girls, pretendin' 'e was doing what 'e did for king an' country, then when 'e 'ad a child it was too much trouble, 'you lazy bastard,' I says, 'that's got no right to call yourself a man.' Only since I been back I can't but wonder if I done right. Oh dear. To think of it. Locking up me things in me own box, an' then makin' out I was robbin' 'er. It's all 'is fault, though, I'll swear blind to that." Saying this, her face settled to a look of a grim, bleak horizon, and she fell silent.

There was a long pause while Arthur ate his egg and drank tea. When he finished he said, "That was very tasty, very sweet." He scrunched the eggshell up in his fist, dug in the garbage bin, and buried it so that no one should see that an egg had been eaten. Yet he put the egg-cup back on the dresser dirty with dried egg meat, exactly as it was. He wiped his hands. And he sawed at his mouth. He sucked his teeth. Then he said:

"First things first, what's Mr Pye goin' to do?"

"What do I care?" she broke out. "Arthur, I'm telling you as true as I'm standin' 'ere, I don't care so much I could laugh right in 'is face. If I don't give satisfaction I can get me a job of work with me bucket same as I 'ave done these many years I've brought Brid up alone. But there's times," she said, "you wish the old days was back. The money was less, but they did look after us."

As with the return of summer, a beginning warmth ran in their limbs where they lay together, on leave, in naked bed. Richard fetched a great sigh. What he had now, and had only held before when drunk, was so much to his contentment that he wanted nothing more. The small warm movements of her were promises she made, and which she was about to fulfil. He had no further questions. He had the certainty of her body in his arms. He grew hot.

Pye sat with Prudence in the half dark of that night club Richard had taken Hilly. He wondered impatiently how soon he could suggest that they should go back to her flat. His small, questioning eyes did not leave what he could see of her face and that darkness, with the deep stains the infrequent lamp shades cast, irritated him, gave him no feeling, as Richard had, of the shared, woman-hunting cause. But then he was only drinking beer. Even so it was an offence against his upbringing that he should have to pay six shillings for a jug of washy lager, less than two pints. The entrance fee, plus her "white ladies" at four and six of which, on average, she would drink three in one of these evenings, sobered him by the exorbitant expense. With his house still not paid for he could not possibly afford it. Yet he was too foxy to let her see. He spoke steadily of his troubles at the station, keeping to the last, as always, such excitements as had come his way on peacetime fires. It was these, he knew, that got her, the silky bitch.

Prudence was tolerably miserable about another man, a pilot, who had gone way in August, who was now said to be marrying someone else. Also she had had a row with Ilse over going to bed with Pye, whom she called Bert. What could it matter? He was different. It was something. He would not remind her of John. But the lighting in this room made her think of John on a leaflet night raid, his darling face with much of Bert's look who, anyway, had had to be brave in peace, who was staring at her now with just that glare John would have into the dangerous, dangerous night, which might be the colour that was here before her eyes. What little he could see of the land or ocean beneath might be like this deep light she drooped in, and the beat of his engine possibly a bit like this music.

Of course Bert was looking at her, and always did like that, for bed, sitting up, begging. It was different, but John would want his target so much it would really be the same. War, she thought, was sex.

"Yes," he went on, speaking as refined as he knew how and with an utter lack of interest that she shared, for bed was all they had, and were not to have much longer, in common, "Yes I sometimes wish I'd never taken promotion, turned it down same as many have in the Brigade. It's nothing but a worry. There's Howells. Her snivelling daughter's got into trouble with her husband, she's gone up north to see him, now we're short of a cook and I'm expected to say nothing. She thinks I'm going to pretend she's still cooking for us. I know that sort. It pays her not to see my position. I daren't do it. Besides I don't know where she is, she might be in Russia for all I know, it was too much trouble on her part to tell."

"Darling," said Richard, "I thought it would kill me," while she thought well anyway I never snored or did I, it was such heaven I shan't know unless he tells; or would he have noticed, but it certainly didn't seem as if he could. She said, "Oh it was worth the candle."

They lay now on a sofa, naked, a pleasant brutal picture by the light of his coal fire from which rose petals showered on them as the flames played, deepening the flush spread over contented bodies. She wriggled over on top, held his dark face and drank it with her eyes. She had never been to Venice. She murmured to herself, "This man's my gondola."

Brid at that instant was crying. She missed her Ted, so feckless in everything except when he loved her, "flyblow" his father called him, her spot she had to clean up after, feckless with money and all but he loved her, only sometimes he forgot, leaving trousers, boots, and socks all over, one boot here, the other beyond. But he was everything to her who had had to come back she wouldn't know why exactly, something to do with mum, and of course there was baby. Nothing had been right after it came, it was such a worry, a girl didn't know what, not for the best she didn't. It was so difficult, and she was no hand at it. She cried on.

"Did I never tell you about Bossy Small, at Number Seventeen?" Pye asked Prudence. She turned herself towards him, said no with her head. "Which is Number Seventeen?"

"I don't know, Bert."

"Come on now," he said gallantly, "how many times must I tell you?"

"I never can remember."

"They'll never make a WAFS of you if you join. It's Dryden Highway station off of Great Clarence Street. It was when I was standin' by there one afternoon, and we got two calls to the same address. That's what we call it, see, only it was two adjacent addresses, one backing on the other, and we sent attendance to both. You might think that foolish, but how are we to know there's not two separate jobs going, and on this occasion it was very fortunate there is that rule in the Brigade.

"Bossy is on the Pump and he dashes up through the first room over the fire to find a person that was reported to be inside. First thing 'e knows is that the floor gave way beneath him. As it went he jumps for what he'd caught out of the corner of his eye, the window, because there's nothing heroic in getting fried. He goes clean through, head first, landing in eighteen inches of drink, as we term water, two stories below in the basement area. That's where the other crew came in, that'd gone to the back, to the other address. They saw 'im go, got a line round him and had 'im up pronto. He was invalided out."

"Oh," she said, thinking this was not one of his best, "and who got him out?"

"Your humble servant," he said.

He knew that she knew he lied. But he did not worry, he felt she was straight about it, that she would admit this was the sort of story she wanted for afterwards, when, the third "white lady" finished, they were to go up to her flat.

In the silence which followed, what seemed to Pye outstanding, as always, was her hands. Yet he did not see these because he kept his eyes upon her eyes, on that remote fire in this half dark as of fireworks released at a distance in a night sky, the points of brilliance when she turned her eyes towards him the only evidence he had of what went on inside her; as of a dead king's birthday celebrated on a hill seven miles away, with rockets, in frosty weather. But her hands would be warm. Although they were not touching him, he knew the feel, the soft touch. He had achingly learned their milk whiteness in daytime, not chalky, as they would now be under the violet-hooded lamps. He coveted her fingers because they had not worked. With all her other warmth they set a glow about him just as, in childhood, when, watching the impossible brilliance climb slowly high then burst into fired dust so far away, so long ago, over that hill the time his sister put her hand inside his boy's coat because he was cold, to warm his heart.

It was danger Prudence sought in this lull of living, before the enemy went into Norway.

But the peril was drawing closer and heavier about Pye; Prudence, for the spring and summer months, would be as safe as houses.

"It's strange, it is," Piper had said to Trant that very afternoon, as he mixed colours yet again in an attempt to get the shade required by Mrs Trant, "I'm an older man an' yet I can't seem some'ow to get accustomed, a 'eart it's known by in the 'uman frame, but the bowels is the word they employ in the Book. We know very well, sir, that if it's not the one thing like marriage then there's the bloody other, that when they're not back at 'ome, men are poachers. I remember the last time I danced," he went on, naturally, "in South Africa it was. I was dancin' with the Colonel's daughter. I was colour sergeant at the time. An' the wind of the dance sent 'er skirt into my spurs. Tore 'er skirts right up they did, and there was I not knowin' what to do. A beautiful blue robe she 'ad on, with white stars set about it. It would've cost a quid in those days to buy another. But seein' she was the Colonel's daughter I didn't rightly know for the best." He dropped his voice. "So there you are then," he murmured.

Trant wondered whatever made this old man, at his age, want to be a fireman, and how on God's earth he had been accepted. It must be he had needed to wear uniform once more.

"There was many was stuck on 'is daughter," Piper went on, "many, with not one out of all of us but knew she was above our station. Yet in this 'ere campaign they seem to set themselves after it unleashed, spendin' maybe twice what they earn, the crazy lechers, on bits of stuff that would turn up their sniffin' noses at a man's own mother."

"She'll find that a shade too yellowy," Trant objected.

"It's your sleepin' room, not mine," said Piper. "Now, beggin' your pardon, sir, but take your own cloth. Look at the goin's on of young Fire Brigade officers. I know one sub not many miles from 'ere crazy after a tart, just like the lad 'e used to be more'n fifteen years back though I 'adn't the pleasure of knowin' 'im, I 'ad a war on me 'ands then. Lunattic. Why, of a night, 'e's never in, duty or not. An' layin' out money on 'er. If 'is sister could see 'im as 'e is to-day it would break 'er bloody 'eart."

"Is she under the sod, then?" Trant asked, disinterested, idly thinking that if she was dead, whoever she might be, he would and must get back to his desk.

"Not on your bloody oath she ain't," said Piper, "she's inside, in one o' them places, right out of 'er mind."

Trant did not say another word. He went away. He had not even forgotten that Pye had a sister. He did not know the first thing, yet.

"A shade too yellowy, the tight-fisted bastard," Piper muttered after him.

That very evening, as Richard was still enjoying Hilly while she revelled in him, with Pye still waiting for Prudence to drink up her third "white lady," the Chief Superintendent, Mr Dodge, was talking to his District Officer, Trant.

"There'll be trouble over that substation, you don't have to tell me, I know," he said, "the rates are too high by far, out of all proportion. I've got a feeling we've not heard the last of that place. If the telephone rings now something seems to tell me it will be the Chief Officer on about these Auxiliaries bein' in palaces, and put there by me, naturally. Who's the man in charge?"

"Sub officer Pye, sir."

"Albert Pye, the individual that was with me up at Number Seventeen when I was Station Officer? How's he makin' out?"

Trant could say nothing about Pye's absence when on duty because he had not reported it. But there are other ways.

"He's very much the same, sir."

"A bit of a red he used to be in the old days. But we're not in the Navy now, Trant, and the Council's Labour."

"He's behind with all the returns."

"That's wrong, that's all wrong. I won't have that, you understand?"

"Yes sir. And a cook there is adrift."

"Adrift?"

"Yes sir. I was going to ask you. Been gone without trace these four days. Though I do seem to remember seeing she reported back to-day, I think it was."

"Don't think, Trant, I don't want you to think what you remember. Well, I don't have to tell you what to do. Have her up before me at the end of the month and I'll have to fine her. We must have discipline. Why, in the Brigade, men have been thrown out for less."

Trant said, "Very good sir." But he reflected that as the

women were not on the run, did not ride to fires, it could hardly, in their case, be such a crime when they forgot to apply for compassionate leave.

At that instant the Auxiliaries in this substation were discussing Pye's excursions.

"Every bloody night he's on duty."

"No?"

"Yus."

"'Ow d'you know?"

"Because he's not about now. I went to see 'im on account of my bed, you know the one we scrounged off the place next door, well it's in a terrible condition an' I went to ask if 'e could get me a Brigade issue, them bloody trestles they use up at Number Fifteen look all right to me. But he's nowhere to be found, not in any place. An' when I asked the women in the watchroom they was 'ighly indignant, so much so I could tell there was something up, nosey Charley they call me. An' every night it's the same."

"The cows in there would make a mystery out of a bit of window glass."

"I don't pay no attention. But the doorman at that posh night place up the yard just beyond where the 'eavy unit is parked, he moved over one night when I'm on guard. ''Oo's your geezer,' 'e says. 'Sub officer Pye,' I said. 'Don't spend much time on fightin' fires, do 'e,' 'e says. 'How's that,' I said. Then he comes out with it. Makes out old Pye's in 'is place every evenin' till late, in 'is glory, then comes across with a tart and goes up to 'er apartment."

"What a lark, eh?"

"Is 'e a married man?"

"No, 'e lives with his sister by what I've 'eard, but she's evacuated or something."

"Dodgy, eh," said Shiner, speaking for the first time.

They were draped in a half circle about the trestle table that served as a bar, beneath the orange ceiling with harsh indirect lighting, behind them one of the fluted pillars and a barrel of beer on a rack, like a secret in the naked light, and which dripped into its enamelled pail. Their shoes were coated with white dust from the artificial marble floor. They had white faces. On and off they had been months indoors. The skeletons were there, painted over blacked-out windows.

"It's conga all right for the Regulars," he went on, "why they're like petty officers run amock." He then spoke a line of what he said was Maltese, and which sounded like abra kalay kalamooch, "Every night up in that bloody flat, with a lovely bit of 'omework, the old matelot. Does 'e run up 'is pennant, I wonder, like an admiral, on the bit of stick there is on the top of 'er building when 'e's up there."

"How do you know where she lives, Shiner?"

"It was Savoury showed me, mate."

"And you didn't go up?"

"That'd be tellin'," Shiner said, mysterious as you please. "But what a lovely bit of ong dong."

"That's as may be," another whined, "but it won't do us chaps any good."

"'Ow d'you mean, won't do us any good? 'Ow come it's the business of any man in this place the dodgy way the skipper passes 'is evenin's?"

"Because when they get to 'ear up at Number Fifteen they'll be coming down to turn us out so as to catch 'im."

"Gawd stone me up a bloody gum tree but they can't say nothing to us," Shiner said. "If old Pye's a man 'e'll take 'is punishment when 'e's caught, dong, like that. It's not hurting you if they do come round 'ere. Be fair to the bloody man."

"There's nothing fair in this game, mate."

"It's not like the Services, I'll agree with you so far. But what bloody rat come to tell them up at Number Fifteen?"

"Well, you asked. That stinking old 'ermit, Piper."

"Good God," Shiner said, "that old frayed end of old rope? 'E might. 'E'd be capable of anything, that bastard."

"Or Savoury."

Here they disagreed. It was admitted Richard did more crawling to Pye than any, but it was cynically held that if half the station had Richard's money, Pye would be drowned in beer. The majority believed Roe treated no one besides Pye, in other words, as was true, that he no longer bought drinks for the Regulars up at Number Fifteen.

Not one of those present knew about Christopher. Shiner asked:

"Is Roe a pansy?"

Shiner turned out to be alone in thinking he might be. "I've seen 'em in the Navy, the quiet, well-spoken sort. I got nothing against 'em, mind," he said.

"Nor I 'aven't," another went on. "What would you say to the diabolical stroke like pushing the dirt under a man's bed, and then, when it's brought to light, blame him whose bed it is for the room bein' dirty." They laughed.

"There's a canny lot of bastards in this station," said a third. At this their talk moved to football.

The following evening old Piper sought Richard out in the pub next door. Roe preferred this to the wet canteen in their recreation room, because it was an escape from shouting, gargantuan, mushroom pale firemen. Nothing was said, yet, to his staying out thus when on duty by reason of the fact that he started Pye off, buying him drinks before, as he now realised the skipper went to his Prudence. Nothing was said to Arthur if he went to get a wet or a wine off Richard because he was protected, he worked for Trant.

"Why, it's Mr Roe," Piper said, when he came upon him, pretending it was accidental, "what d'yer know about that?"

"What'll you have Arthur?"

"A double Scotch an' a large packet of Players," the old man answered, sawing his moustache. Richard laughed, as was intended. "Why, thankin' you, a wallop, Mr Roe, to your very good 'ealth, sir. This is a queer job, I don't remember another similar, an' this is my fifth campaign. It must come strange to you, that's lived a life with those that never lacked for nothin'. Yus. There's occasions it dunders me, grieves me, but then I've 'ad my time amongst all sorts and conditions, I've 'ad no choice."

Richard said that although he had knocked about the world a bit himself he had never come across anything quite like the London Fire Service.

"You never said a truer word, sir." Piper drank, sucked his moustache, sawed a forefinger across his chin, and shook his head. "Not 'uman, that's what they are, not men, more like women. T'ain't right. Course you light upon some like it in the army, officers that never was nor couldn't be officers 'owever 'igh they rose if you get my meanin', but on God's oath every one o' them is alike in this Service."

"What's troubling you then?"

"I never was a man to meddle in another's business," the old man replied, "I keep me own counsel, 'ear no evil speak no evil, that's me. But this mornin' up at Number Fifteen I get the buzz they're intendin' to crime Mrs 'Owells. Now I've known that party years. A respectable married woman, mind yer. She's a widder to-day. I knowed 'er old man same as I knows me own brother, 'e was one o' my mates oh years back."

"Why run her? What's she done?"

"Well she's got a daughter that went an' got 'erself married to a young feller in the army, Oxford and Bucks Light Infantry 'e's in. She comes to me for a bit of advice every so often, there's many do along our street I couldn't tell for why. She's in a spot of bother now an' takin' it rough. I'm acquaintin' you because I know it won't go no farther. It's like this. On account of one thing or the other, I'm not clear about that part, see, this daughter's back 'ome an' the mother, my friend that I was tellin' you about, went north to 'ave a word, or maybe more, you get me? with the 'usband."

Richard, of course, knew that part of the story, but he could not admit to knowing.

"So what does sub officer Pye do," the old man went on, "'e posts 'er adrift as they call it in the Brigade, 'e so much as calls 'er a deserter. And now they're making out a charge. She'll be fined most likely. It does seem not right, Mr Roe, though, of course, I couldn't say if you would be to my way of thinking."

"Right? I think it damnable," says Richard, up in arms at once. It was an outburst. One or two of the cowlike heads, under hanging ferns, turned towards him, ruminating. His eyes almost flashed, as though the lamps hanging before rows of bottles had been sent lurching, as they were to be, by a bomb. His righteous anger was flashy.

Meantime, back at home, across the table to Brid, Mrs Howells was opening a tin of sardines for their supper. Once they were emptied on a plate she began to powder the oil-soaked fish thickly with brown pepper. When she saw her mother do this Brid realised, it was proved to her, that she was being poisoned, no less. First she had come to know the things she had always counted hers were no longer hers, that mum was set on keeping them. And she had felt bad, somehow, about the way the room with Ted was so bare. That beautiful jar would have gone just right on the mantel. Then she had felt poorly, not up to anything, and it seemed worse after she got back to London. She could not think why at first. She knew now. She stared, fixed. Her eyes widened. She stuck a knuckle in her mouth.

"Don't, mum," she broke out, but in a tone so piteous that Mrs Howells stood, frozen.

"But you did always fancy pepper with 'em."

"Don't, you mustn't." Brid was moaning now. She had dropped her gaze to the cain and abel.

"Why, whatever," said Mrs Howells loudly, "you'll be the finish of me, my gel. Whatever's the matter, for Christ's sake."

"Poisonin' of me, I know, poisonin' she is. Where's my baby?"

"You leave that alone. In the condition you are if you so much as touch a 'air of 'er 'ead I'll bring a copper in to yer."

Brid was silent. She now held a hand flat across her mouth.

"Oh Brid," said Mrs Howells, "what's come over yer, love." While her daughter sat motionless, head bowed, Mrs Howells covered her face with her hands. She broke into a loud, ugly, persistent sobbing.

Richard went straight back to the substation. He sought Hilly out and, against all rules, sat alone with her in her room, a thing he had never dared before. She accepted his presence as another proof of love until he began talking, and this he could not manage at first because he was almost out of breath with his love for her.

"Surely, if it's true," he panted, "this about Mrs Howells, it's very bad, isn't it?"

"Is that why you've come?" Hilly said, giving him a chance to affirm.

"Of course," said he. "But it's monstrous, don't you think, that a woman can't go north without getting into their bad books, when her daughter's in such trouble?"

"I know," she answered sadly, "it does seem hard."

"Darling, you don't sound very certain."

"Well, you see, it's discipline, isn't it," she said rising above herself. "After all, if everyone went away, if every fireman did . . ."

He interrupted to demolish this proposition.

"I know you're right," she replied, "of course everyone wouldn't go off just like that, but still, in any other Service, darling, I'm sure you would find them making trouble for those who did." It seemed too much that he should be able to sit opposite, talking angrily like this so soon after. He went on:

"But it's exactly that the AFS isn't a Service, in the proper sense, that they simply can't run it on these lines. Besides, any proper officer worth his salt would never report someone for that, much less a mother. He'd cover them."

"But, you see, he tried."

"Did he? I shouldn't say he did."

"Yes, Richard, he did, honestly. But make an effort to look at it his way. He did not dare cover her after she'd gone. He offered, only she didn't undersand. She just went off without saying a word. He couldn't know where she was."

"I can't understand your taking this line. It's just when it is awkward that the real officer does do something for people under him."

"Richard, darling, you aren't angry with me, surely?"

"What d'you mean, angry?" Secretly, and he had not even put it to himself, he was irritated, mainly because she had gone to bed with him. He found it made her of no account. "Of course not," he went on, "but do try and see how monstrous it is that she should have to go up before old Dodge. She may get even worse treatment. It's Pye the super ought to run for not seeing that she went up north at once."

"But you agreed with me, on our night, that it was the silliest thing she could do, to go to Doncaster."

Then, probably because he knew this last was true, he was short with Hilly. They had their first row. And kissed and made up after.

If he could only have witnessed the appearance Mrs Howells made before the Superintendent he would not have excited himself.

The moment she set eyes on Mr Dodge at his desk Mrs Howells liked the look of him, recognised him as a man she could talk to. "It's me daughter, sir," she began at once, hurrying forward, looking absurd in uniform, and before the formal preliminaries, usual with a man of his rank, could be opened. Pye, who had to be present as her immediate superior, literally held his breath. But Mrs Howells had made no mistake. Behind a front of purple, whisky-drinking ferocity, under wide shoulders, beneath the show he made of great strength for a man of his age, she had smelled the gossip in Mr Dodge. She was right. At the first pause in the rattle of her narrative he said, "You can go, Pye, dismiss." Once Pye was out of the room he began, "You know I 'ad a niece get just like it." Before long they were deep in the topic of afterbirths. In the end he dismissed her, without even a reprimand, after what had been to him a very interesting discussion. As for Mrs Howells she would, for the rest of her life, at a word, have followed him through fire and water to the end. What is more, she never troubled the Superintendent again, either by appealing to him or by telling tales. For he knew what he was about.

So did Pye. It made the sub officer extremely uneasy that she had not been reprimanded. As he knew the Brigade, he expected to catch it because she had been let off. He tried to get out of Mrs Howells what had passed after he was sent out of the room. She would only repeat that Mr Dodge was a gentleman, a proper gentleman. This made Pye sure she had told the Super some lying tale. The incident weighed on his mind. He dared not ask Trant. He thought he was going to come on it any minute round the next corner, as he was. He became so nervous of making some mistake in the returns he had to send up, returns which, day by day, seemed to breed, that he got to be more and ever more behind, until his desk was littered.

It was the beginning of the end.

SOON AFTER MRS HOWELLS had been before Mr Dodge, and as a direct result of that visit, Trant came down to give Pye a shake up. The District Officer did not refer to Mary but it was as Pye feared, the fact that she had been let off put Pye in the wrong.

When Trant arrived he went straight to Pye's small office by the watchroom. He saw Pye alone. He began about some return that was overdue. He broke off to dress him down about the condition of his tunic. Even the office was dirty and untidy, he went on. Papers all over. Pye interrupted to point out he could not do much with the tunic, that it was second hand. He voiced a grievance by saying he hoped to get issued with new clothing shortly. Trant objected that the buttons were filthy, had not seen polish for a month. Glancing down his chest Pye had to admit they were in bad shape. The way they looked even came as a surprise to him. But he had no time to marvel. The DO was carrying on alarming. He swept all forms, returns, petrol dockets, doctor's certificates, etc., to the floor. He cleared the table. "Who's runnin' this station, you or the men," he shouted, then went so far as to state that Pye was only an Acting Sub, Temporary. By this time Pye had seen the light. He was standing to attention. At any interval he piped, "Yessir."

"Let's 'ave no more of it. Keep on top line," Trant said when at last he went.

Pye did not like the state of things. It was very awkward. There would be all hell let loose the next stroke his bad luck played. He got out of the tunic. He brushed it so hard he was half afraid he might brush right through, the cloth only held together by force of habit. New sub officers had second hand issues. It was misery. He fell on his buttons. He had to admit these were on the dull side. He asked himself how he had not come to notice earlier. But there was so much on his mind. It was different in the old days, before the war, when there was time for spit and polish, when that was all there was to the Job. Now you only had leisure to go "ha" at buttons. Yet he had known subs in those times, real officers mark you, who didn't look no different. You could never say Bossy Small's brother up at Number Ten, had been smart. But it was any stick to beat a man with these days, anything. And once in their bad books you were for it.

He was too disturbed to notice the invasion of Norway. In any case he had not read a newspaper for years. As a disillusioned trades unionist he had given the Press up as corrupt. To his mind, in politics, he had been betrayed even by his own people. Now his own class was putting his job in peril, his own cloth, or so it seemed to him.

He began to blame everything on the AFS. He would still admit the new Service was necessary but he came, in that first interview with Trant at which they had not been mentioned, to recognise cut-price firemen, the Auxiliaries, as an evil. He cracked hard down on his. He would shew who was running the substation.

He chose this moment to order that the guard outside was to be properly rigged at all times, spotless. This man was to see that no other Auxiliary within view of the public had so much as a button undone on his tunic. It seemed oppressive to the personnel, all the more so now that Piper had blobs of distemper all over his trousers, and nothing was said to him because he was on his racket redecorating the DO's quarters. Several supposed Pye must have a relation out in Norway.

He stopped Richard going off to the pub.

He stopped them getting between blankets in the afternoon, even in the case of an off-duty guard who had been up half the night.

But Piper still did not have to do general duties, could go out for a drink whenever he pleased. This led to comment. The comment grew pointed, niggly. When eventually a deputation went to see Pye in his room about the privileged time old Piper had, the hermit made out he was bewildered. He said no such thing had happened to him in all his four campaigns, that he was humiliated. But Pye refused to have it. The men even put in that Piper was receiving special rations. On this Pye emptied his office of them. He said they had the remedy, in other words, as was true, that the messing was for the station's food committee. "You get your grub allowance separate each week. The Chief Officer leaves matters to you lads yourselves to manage between you. There's Auxiliaries in this station claim they've held down big jobs before the war. Can't you organise your own grub, or do I have to do your pants up for you in addition." He ended with, "And I don't want to see you lads here again. The Brigade don't recognise round robins and the like. If I have any more I'll run you, every one, before Mr Dodge. It's more than my pension's worth to talk as I am doing. If I wasn't a man that tried to see reason, was amenable to it, I'd charge each one of you now. This place will be the death of me. A babies' button, a comforter, is what you want, some of you. What a ship!"

He did not stop his visits to Prudence in the evenings. "'E's like a tom that must get back up on the self-same wall," they said.

Coming back after his second spell of leave, Richard found he could not remember what his home life had been only a day or two before. All he had then done lay ready to hand, but as dried fruit is to fresh off the tree, tasteless, unlike. Now that he was kept all hours in the station he had no privacy with which to ferment those feelings, shrivelled after so short a journey.

Pye went along to the kitchen. On thinking things over he had decided it was part of his duty to investigate the complaint. He found Hilly and Eileen alone with a blank white readiness of the electric range.

"Where's 'Owells?" he began, very sharp. Hilly explained she had sent Mary out to the butcher's.

"I thought maybe she had gone on a trip to Sheerness," he said. He went on to ask what had happened to the orderlies. When it was explained that these men had done all they had to do for the next meal, which was dinner, and had been allowed upstairs, he was indignant. He pointed out to the cooks they had no right to vary the men's routine, which called for work throughout every morning, bar Sundays. He said if one of his superior officers came to find the state of affairs he had just found, he, Pye, would get a bottle for it, would be landed in trouble. He told Hilly she must think up something for the orderlies to occupy themselves with, no matter what. If necessary they could scrub the kitchen floor again.

Eileen took offence.

"My kitchen's clean, Mr Pye," she said.

He replied it was not for her to say what was clean or otherwise and that, in any case, he had not said it was dirty. "And there's another thing," he went on, "some of the men have had a moan to me that Piper's been favourised."

Eileen went white all over. She opened her mouth and was about to start when Pye interrupted. He said to let him finish. He pointed out he was not accusing any individual of being special to the old man, that he was not saying it had happened, much less who had done it, if it had been done. "All I have to tell you is, it's got to stop," he said.

"Then you are accusing me," Eileen shouted, whiter, breathless with rage.

"No, Eileen, let me," Hilly began.

"I'm not so green," said Pye, "I've not been twenty years in the Brigade for nothing. What's more it's natural, sometimes you can't help yourself."

"There's not a man at this station gets anything special

in my kitchen," Eileen said in a small voice, breathless.

"There's occasions you can't help yourself," Pye continued, "when certain food don't suit a individual and he asks if there's any left over from the day before. Anyone who's a bit out of trim that mornin' will claim that man's getting preference. I don't say it's right, I say it's 'uman nature."

"There's nothing of the sort goes on here, Mr Pye," Hilly said, bowing her head before the outburst she saw was on them. And break it did.

"Get out of my kitchen," Eileen yelled, dead white, surprised herself at where she got the breath.

"Now look," he said.

"Get out of 'ere," she shouted, "I don't mind, get out of 'ere, Mr Pye, can't you leave me alone, get out."

Upon which Pye left. Eileen burst out sobbing. And that same day she gave notice.

The news from Norway was worse.

With Eileen gone Hilly gave of her best in the Mess. But Mrs Howells was no cook, the third woman hardly any better. The men began seriously to complain about the food. "It's good grub spoiled," they said. No one came along to take Eileen's place. Pye could not be certain some lying acccount might not get back to Trant, through Piper, of the reasons which had led Eileen to resign. Besides he was afraid Mr Dodge would blame him for losing what had already become a rarity, a woman who was prepared, in return for good money, to cook hot meals for men.

About this time an elderly gent walked right into the station, cried in a loud voice, "You won't be getting my money much longer." Boys, riding bikes on errands, called out to them "Why don't you join the army?" And Pye was summoned to the asylum for the second time.

Before he could make arrangements to pay this visit, the first blow fell, with no commotion, and officially, yet with deceptive softness. He was summoned to appear before

Trant in his room up at Number Fifteen. As it was some days after he had been told off by the DO at the substation, he thought it could only be about Eileen's giving notice. But when he got there he found Trant was giving him the official caution in connection with his work, the traditional warning. Nothing was directly specified. He was led to understand in dangerous, gentle language that if he did not change his ways, he would find serious trouble for himself. He took the wisest course. He said "Yessir," to everything he did.

The next day he went down to the asylum. He was to remember afterwards how fine that afternoon had been; sun, a blue sky, the air mild; so that he had to remind himself afterwards it was a false spring, just one of those days come much too early, a break in the weather.

He considered they must want to see him about his sister's maintenance. He thought almost happily of what he would say, of his triumphant refusal to contribute towards what had been forced on him by a savage society.

They did not make him wait. He was shewn into a room, was asked to sit in a deep chair. In front was a big gothic window overlooking a big park which must have been the grounds. This window had violet-coloured glass in clover-leaf openings round the frame. Then he became entirely aware of a man at ease behind a large desk, who might have been, and wasn't, Mr Dodge, but who was properly imposing.

The man behind the desk introduced himself. Pye did not catch the name, only that it was a doctor. This physician began by thanking him for his trouble and then said they wanted his help. Pye reminded himself, "Anything bar money," he repeated behind clenched teeth. Aloud he said "Yessir."

"In all sicknesses of this kind," the physician remarked, soft yet firm, "when we deal with illnesses of the mind, or not even illnesses, breaks, such as the weather we have to-day, look how different it is from what we endured yesterday, and what will be our lot to-morrow." "It won't last, sir," Pye put in, intelligent. "Exactly," the doctor went on, "precisely as in high summer we can have quick storms, then fine weather again, so with the human being we get the sudden storm out of a blue sky." "And women especially," said Pye. "Men and women," the physician corrected, picking up a long ivory paper knife, carved at one end like the figure head beneath a bowsprit.

"What we have to do is to dispel it, to prevent the storm from persisting. If we can," he went on, and stopped.

If they can't, Pye remarked to himself, surely they won't expect me to pay towards keeping her on. But he said nothing.

There was a long pause. In the end Pye cleared his throat. He said "Yessir."

"Mr Pye," the man at the desk began again, and he might have been telling about a scientific game of draughts, "your sister's had a relapse. I'm sorry to say she's not so well." More expensive treatment, the sub officer thought at once. "Now why, that's what we've got to consider," Pye heard as, in self defence, he let his eyes wander out to the cream yellow sunlight on the ungrowing, still winter grass. "Why," the voice came at him again, "Why? There must be a reason. That is where we want your help."

"Me," Pye said, turning back to him.

"Yes, you, Mr Pye, you see we have no one else."

"Me? In what manner, sir?"

"Very simply, by telling us about your sister."

"Me tell about her? I'm sure I don't know. We don't discuss matters much in our family, we never did."

"I fancy we're rather at cross purposes, Mr Pye. What I'm getting at is this, I want you to let me have your time so that I can get some inkling as to why she is like this. You see, just now, we can't ask her."

"Now I understand," Pye said slowly, with dread. "But

I don't know that I'll be able to assist. It was like this. Somehow or other, we can't tell, this kid hitches 'imself on in the department store, just how 'e done it we'll never get at, and that was the start."

"Oh no, Mr Pye, that was not the beginning. What I want you to do is to take me right back, back to when you were both children."

"Can I see her, sir?"

"No, I'm afraid that is quite out of the question."

There was another pause. Then Pye said:

"I thought if I could 'ave a chat with her, settle 'er mind, then between the two of us we could get at what you was desirous of knowing."

"No, Mr Pye, you can't. It is impossible just now. Now, let's see if we can help each other over this. I had a sister. I was brought up with her in the country." Waited on hand and foot, Pye thought, now that he could concentrate on the story this man had begun to tell. "It was near Godalming, I don't know if you are familiar with the country round there." Pye said "No sir," readily. The doctor got up. He began pacing the turkey carpet behind his desk. He went on:

"There was a heavy fall of snow in the winter of nineteen eight, though I don't suppose you will remember that, I should say it was before your time, and one afternoon my mother let us take one of those large japanned black tray things there used to be, with a key design in gold round the edge, off to a hill at the back of our garden, for tobogganing. It was most imprudent as it turned out. For my sister had an accident, she crashed into a tree and broke her leg. Now my mother, my sainted mother, had one unreasoning prejudice which seemed stronger than herself, she was one of those who call themselves Christian Scientists. I'm confident that we, as children, could never have been in more loving hands. But, despite the pain her daughter was in, my mother would insist that a qualified doctor should not be called. For ten days Mary must have been in agony, without even a proper splint to support the fracture. Then at last my father prevailed. Well, that is why I chose this profession, why, to this day, my sister stutters which, in turn, is, to a great degree, the reason that she never married. Why did you join the Fire Brigade?"

"For the pension."

"And your sister," the doctor said rather impatiently, Pye thought, with that tone of authority back in his voice, "She never married? How was that?"

"I don't know I'm sure, I couldn't say."

"But there must have been boys round."

Without any warning, and with a shock that took all his breath, Pye saw the dry wood shaving creep, bent in the moonlight, the back way to their cottage. He saw it again as though it was before his eyes, which he now tried to draw away from the doctor's. He had never before thought of his sister's creeping separate from his own with Mrs Lane's little girl. In a surge of blood, it was made clear, false, that it might have been his own sister he was with that night. So it might have been her voice, thick with excitement and fright and disgust, that said "Will it hurt?" So in the blind moonlight, eyes warped by his need, he must have forced his own sister.

How could he have been mistaken, how not recognise that neck of junket, dew cool then. What a judgment! And he could not call to mind how they had come on one another that night. It must have been stifling, and her skin clammy hot, sticky. Why had she not said, the unnatural bitch. But if he had not been so quick, could he not have told who she was? Of course he could. And he had always known, and never realised.

He searched back, frantic. His pairing with the other girl had started a year before he thought he first had her. He was shy. They were gradual. She had begun to be on the look out when he went down to fish of an evening. The path went round the back of the Lanes', by that pear tree. Was that why, when in the end it occurred, she made out she was so surprised, his second time, her first with him, when he had thought it was her second occasion?

With a suffocation of loathing at himself, which quickly passed, he grew hot with the idea.

He remembered there had been nothing doing, his float had not moved, the river slipped by, the blazing day had begun to sink, flies and wasps, the manor clock chimed, the kind of swallows that live in holes along the river bank squeaked as they flew. He left his rod, came up out of the rushes to the grass. He ate his step of bread and jam. He had lain back, eyes shut and pink, shirt open, the breeze flapping, so you could hardly notice, all over his heat-wet body. And a smear of jam must have been across one corner of his mouth, for the first he knew was when she mouthed it off.

She had come up barefoot, shoes and stockings hung about her neck to stalk him, and there was dust, he could exactly see it now, over her scruffy, absolutely flat brown feet. As he sat up they almost trod him by that difference there is in a girl's foot, which he had never before had occasion to feel. But what a difference again to Prudence's enamelled toes, the silky white bitch. So that must have been the first time with him for old Lane's daughter.

"Well, Mr Pye?"

Brought back to himself, Pye decided he must box clever, else he might lose the old pension.

"I'll think it over, sir," he said. He got up, unsteady. He wondered if he should thank this man for reminding him about that late afternoon, the rotten-gutted bastard of a doctor. Or should he thank him for minding his sister? Then he thought no, sod it, they pay him well, trust him for that, the quack.

"Yes, precisely," the doctor said. "And let me know so that we can fix an appointment. I don't want to worry you but she is just at a stage when a clue will make all the difference." At which Pye recollected his sister. What with believing, then disbelieving, he could not remember afterwards how he got out.

But she did not last in his mind, not then at any rate. For, in the bus back to the substation, and their driver must have been late because he drove them swooping round the streets always, or so it seemed, downhill, Pye began to observe a girl. She was fair, that was all he could see for some time, and her tweed shoulders above the back of the seat. But, as this double-decker swayed and banked, and she, the lily, let her lovely head and neck incline with it, he caught sight of one protuberant, half-transparent eye, sideways, blue, hedged with long lashes that might have been scythes to mow his upstanding corn. And a straight, grave nose, curved like a goose neck at the nostril. Elated at his release from the asylum, he asked himself what he would not give to have this puss mouth jam off his cheek by a river bank on such an evening as the weather to-day seemed to promise after the first long winter of war, and to see her quietness overflow into laughter, into the pleased shrieks of Mrs Lane's little girl and, so much more to his taste, the protests later and ever fainter, oh the gorgeous, up now on her dignity, bit of fancy lump of grub.

It might have been the same day, but just before blackout, that Ilse lay naked on her bed. Declining light, in which there was no sun, reduced her body. She lay dim, like a worm with a thin skeleton, back from a window, pallid, rasher thin, her breasts, as she lay on her back, pointing different ways. She had been complaining. The war with Finland. The invasion of Norway. Poor Sweden. Poor England. It was this last that irritated Prudence, as she sat on a cushion before the hoarse gas fire.

For Prudence much resented Shiner Wright, with whom Ilse had coldly begun to go to bed, almost publicly, almost as though to clear the skin. So sweet, lovely she thought

Ilse was, so cold of course. After all, it was too continental with this Auxiliary. It put one off Bert Pye even. She wondered if her John would be flying this night. It was real bombs now. Not leaflets. She said, to change the conversation:

"Darling, you've started painting your toes."

Ilse said something really quite coarse and unlike her true self about the Wright creature, who sat in the best chair and stamped cigarettes out on the carpet. She, who had seriously left her toenails natural, now said she had changed because he liked it. She did not even pretend she felt anything except the one thing.

"Look," Prudence said, "it must be black-out." She judged this by the sudden unreal depth of blue outside. "I'll draw the curtains." She got up.

"Ach you are so English, darling. No, I will lie in the night light."

"You can't. You know the fire shews outside." Prudence drew the curtains, shut the room up. It glowed with the gas fire. Then she walked across and switched on lamps. At these, in their logic, Ilse's body jumped out where it lay, fattened and stared. With her yellow hair in short curls, her washed, washed skin, fluted ribs, a stomach caved like sand, with long-fingered arms drifted to her whole violin-cut length, long fragile legs polished and fine, with painted toenails that had the look of objects thrown up on a beach, her mouth also and with the shut, lashed eyes which might have been the marks a tide that has ebbed can leave on sand, Prudence caught her breath, it was so strong, so falsely Wright's, what was thus coldly, virginally outspread.

Taking up the eiderdown from where it had been kicked, with disgust she covered, and left, and muted, this now victorious paper white violin.

So it came about that Prudence went off Pye. She would still go out but she would not bring him back after. Pye thought it must be to do with his sister, that she must have heard. She might even have met the doctor. That man would never hesitate, he thought, to discuss a case for which the asylum had not been paid.

And Pye of course was no longer sure that he had forced his sister that night long ago. He told himself it had been so bright out he must have known who he was with. But in an attempt to make certain he began experiments. Once he went up to Shiner when this man was on guard, peered right in his eyes. And there were moments, always at night, that Pye could not get away from it that it might have been.

ABOUT THIS TIME Dy brought Christopher up to London for a week at the flat. On Richard's leave day they all went to the Zoo for tea. That night, she suggested she might bring him to see his father at the substation. Richard was not keen, but he could not refuse.

The next day, Sunday, Dy changed her mind twice, but in the end she brought Christopher along in the morning. They gravely shook hands with Richard. While he shewed her what they had by way of equipment, Christopher drifted off to the back.

Dy, in her dislike of anything to do with the Service, was extremely reserved.

"What's that?" she asked coldly.

He noticed she was dressed in her smartest. He still did not like her coming. "Oh that?" he said, "why that's what we use for lifting static water," and went on to describe the suctions at some length. She thought this was rather like before you were married, when you went to see a young man or other, and he shewed you round.

Meantime Christopher had wandered behind a corner of sandbags. He stood at the entrance to the recreation room. Shiner was lying on his shoulders, feet in the air, exercising leg muscles bicycling above his head. As soon as he saw Christopher he said good morning.

"I'm quite well thank you," Christopher replied.

"Then everything in the garden's conga," Shiner said. Christopher watched. Not a word more passed until Shiner completed his exercises. Then he began, " 'ow did you come to blow in, mate?"

He got no reply. He lay, immensely broad and long, staring at Christopher who stared back.

"You wouldn't be lookin' for much by any chance? Or anyone?"

Christopher did not say a word.

"Then wee wee off," Shiner said.

On Sundays the men were now allowed to use their beds. Christopher turned to another voice under electric light which said, "You wouldn't be Roe's kid by any chance, would yer?" He saw Piper, old and unshaven, laid out with bare feet sticking from his trousers. He stared fascinated at the twisted broken toes, armed with nails like doll's trowels. He did not realise that the smell came from those stained feet. He turned. He went off, looking over his shoulder. With a vast shout, Shiner called, "Guard."

Richard heard Shiner, saw Christopher come away.

"It's all right, cock," he cried, "it's only my nipper." Dy thought, what horrible expressions he does use nowadays.

Piper murmured to his toes, "The minute I seen 'im I known, the minute I seen." He was overjoyed at having, as he thought, guessed it. To have even more, he quickly put on his socks, then his boots.

Shiner also got up. He was upset that he had not welcomed someone's son. "Hi, Dick there," he shouted to Richard, "I'll be with yer, 'ang on there."

Another voice said from between blankets, "Why can't you bastards make less din."

At this moment Hilly came into the appliance room by a side entrance and saw Dy not more than ten feet away. She had so often imagined what she would do when in the end, as was inevitable, she came face to face with his sister-in-law. Contrary to all her plans she went straight up. She said, "Why, hullo." Then, because she remembered they had not been introduced, she added, "I knew you at once from your photograph." This last remark embarrassed her. She blushed. "And is this Christopher?" she asked, flooded with blush, to Richard's fury.

Fully dressed, Shiner hurried round that corner with a bellow. "There 'e is," he remarked to Piper behind him. "Look mate, we didn't know 'oo you was, see," he went on to Christopher. "Good morning Mrs," to Dy, thinking to himself, what a smashing lump of stuff. "Say Chris, see 'ere, there's a fire in this place, see. It's up to us to put it out." He picked up a roll of hose as though it was no more than lavatory paper, unrolled it, that is he ran it out, chased back, calling to Piper, "The branch, man, the branch," by which he meant the nozzle, got one of these out of a locker on the pump, tore back, snapped it into the coupling on the hose and yelled, "Down with the pump." Nothing happened.

"'I can't make this out," he pretended. "Look," to Christopher, "you be number four. OK? You run back along this length of 'ose and when you find Fireman Piper you sing out to 'im, down with the pump. Becos' it's dodgy, this fire's fryin' us alive, there's not a second to lose, man. Get me."

Expressionless, Christopher trotted along the hose. "Not a minute to lose, not a minute to lose," Piper remarked, sawing his chin. "Down with the pump," the boy cried, high and clear. "Bless me," said Piper and made motions with his hands. "What you must think," Hilly said to Dy, hating her, as Dy called out, "Be careful, darling." Then, when Piper yelled, "Water," and Wright began to shout, "Another 'and on the branch, it's taking charge," by which he meant that the imaginary pressure was threatening to pluck the nozzle out of his huge fists, at that instant Pye came in.

He saw, and seemed to pay no attention, turning aside at the door to speak with an electrician, who was there to fix a fire sign outside the entrance. He was dressed in civvies. Dy had no idea who he could be. Shiner was much embarrassed at being caught fooling. Piper let his mouth fall open. Richard was appalled. This was Pye's leave day. He had agreed to Christopher's visit only because he had been sure Pye would not be there.

Standing with his back to Pye, facing Piper, Christopher repeated in his treble:

"Down with the pump."

"Water," the old man echoed, in hushed tones.

There was a regulation which laid it down that all visitors must be reported to the officer in charge. Also it was in Richard's mind that they had brought Christopher round out of visiting hours. So in spite of the fact that Pye was on leave, but in deference to Pye's latest attitude by which he demanded elaborate respect for his rank, Richard thought it best to report Dy and Christopher. He went up. He said in confidential tones.

"The old sister-in-law and my nipper have come, sub. All right?"

"Your sister-in-law and your son? Why yes, go ahead. Now don't fix that sign where they can't see it for the other one," he went on to this electrician. "I thought the best place would be about three foot east of that soil pipe, but excuse me a minute, mate, I shan't be long."

He came across to Dy. As Richard introduced them, and

Pye held the brim of his hat before taking her hand, she gave not a flicker of a sign of what she really felt, for, once she knew who it was, she loathed him.

"So that's the son and heir, is it?" said Pye, not taken in, thinking to himself the crafty whore. "Going to be a fireman like his father," he went on, sly, "well, I must say, he's shapin' fine at it. Taking orders back correctly into the bargain."

The situation Richard hoped would always be spared them was present. Piper was alive to it and could now hardly mask his interest. Pye had instantly decided not to recognise the boy. But Christopher, at this first encounter with him after the abduction, behaved as if it was most natural.

He said "I say." He came across to shake hands. He said "I say" again, and then, before he could be asked, "I'm quite well, thank you."

Pye, giving no indication, said, "That's good. Now would you like to see the engines? You take 'im round Dick, let him ring the bell if he wants. Mrs," he went on, turning only to find that she was no longer there, "Mrs," he said again, moving over to where she stood, in conversation with Shiner, "Will you excuse me while I see to this fire sign? I've come back particular on my leave day." "Of course," she said, sweetly smiling. Then she spoilt it. Abruptly she turned her back, walked off to pretend to look at one of the pumps.

Christopher trotted after her. "What's that?" he asked, pointing to an adaptor. Richard joined them. Shiner and the hermit hastily cleared up, then followed Pye over to the electrician, to see if they were still all right with the skipper. Hilly, furious with herself, saying "Excuse me" in a low voice to no one, went out to look at her face in the big mirror, where the girls washed. And Dy said, for Richard's benefit:

"Mummy doesn't like that man."

"Why?" Christopher asked.

"Look at this funny thing," she said.
"Why don't you like him, Mummy?"
"Sh . . . Sh . . . or he'll hear."
"Why don't you Mummy?"
"No I can't talk about it, darling, not now."
"Why, Mummy?"
"You let Mummy be. Richard what is this for, oh what did I tell you, never mind," she said in the one breath. Roe began to explain the apparatus they carried. This was not the time to shew what he felt.
But Christopher would not listen at first.
"I say Mummy," he said brightly, "that man came to tea when I was lost."
"I know, darling. Now listen to Daddy."
At that Christopher gave all his attention to his father.
"What are they painted grey for?" he asked.
Richard said he thought it was because by keeping them Admiralty grey, like battleships, these appliances would be less easily seen from the air at night. He even pronounced this grey to be almost the colour of the night, and by that he meant moonlight. Who was he to know, before he had been in a raid, that it would have been best to paint them pink, a boudoir shade, to match that half light which was to settle, night after night, around the larger conflagrations.
"I want to be an airman," Christopher announced.
"Would you like to ring the bell?"
"Oh yes. I say, may I really, please?"
"Go ahead," his father said. He climbed up, barely reached the strap while Richard steadied him where he was perched on top of some rolls of hose, and violently rang that bell. The warning, flung out on the pitch peculiar to all bells on fire engines, made pedestrians outside turn round.
"Look, Christopher, the traffic policeman's watching behind him. He thinks we're coming out."
"Wear this and be a real fireman." It was Pye. He had gone to his office and brought out the Regular Fireman's

helmet shaped like a goose's head, black, made of a cork wood composition. It was much too big for the boy, sat down over his eyes. He began crowing with laughter.

Dy said, "Now that's enough darling." Christopher climbed off at once. In a few minutes she took him away, at long last, Richard felt. They shook hands all round. Pye again held the brim of his hat. Piper sought to play the fool by saluting. His attempt to exaggerate this was ludicrous. As Piper and Wright went back to the recreation room Shiner said:

"It was decent of the skipper to bring 'is 'elmet. Went to fetch it on 'is own as well."

Piper answered mysteriously. "Right glad I am they brought it off at last," he said, "brought it off at last."

"Brought what off?" But Piper would only mumble in answer. Shiner went on, "What beats me about you, you bloody old 'ermit, is the way you will talk in riddles. It's dodgy. I'll tell you another thing, you carry on like that in the night. You can't ever get your rest. Watch yerself, mate, you'll be goin' pickin' violets off of stones before you're finished, stone bonk, you will."

If the old man would not explain at once, he let fall so many hints that a story of Christopher's abduction eventually got out, for Piper considered the visit paid by this lady he thought was the mother, with her son, had been prearranged, that the old score, if you liked to put it that way, must now be settled. He was the kind of man who could never credit coincidence. And he was glad, for his own sake. He did not care in the least about Roe. Piper had got it into his head that Pye was down on Piper because he happened to know about the abduction. This was a fixed idea, although he kept it to himself. But even if he had let it get about that he thought it was the reason Pye was always chasing him, no one in the world could ever have dissuaded the old man. He was one of those who are beyond even the common or garden interchange of doubts and petty fears.

He said to the Welshman later, "That's the reason 'e's been sortin' you out, the skipper 'as, ever since you said what you did the night them two tarts drank three bottles of gin. I said to meself then, I says, 'You watch out, Taffy, you won't get away with that, you won't, oh dear.'"

"But skipper and me's close as a snail who's riding on another's back."

"The minute I 'eard you say them few words that time I says to meself, that's done it."

"Man, you're making me all nervous."

"When you said about the Regular what 'ad a sister that got took inside for bein' sticky fingered in one of the big shops."

"Stiffen my crows, what about it?"

"Gawd, you young fellers will never learn. 'Is own sister was put inside for walkin' off with Roe's nipper, that's why."

"What sister, sister to what man?"

But Piper would say no more to the Welshman. This was how the story got around in bits and pieces, and it was in this way that it grew, and grew in a short time, for there was not much time left.

When he had finished with the electrician Pye went into his office, and picked up the telephone as though taking hold of a black handle of the box which held all his hopes imprisoned; delicately, so that he should not break his luck which had broken; fearful, because before he could make the connection, he already knew.

"Yes, hullo," she answered, bright.

"It's Bert."

"Oh yes," Prudence said, in a very different tone, "how are you?"

"I'm terrible," he moaned, "sweetheart. It's the change in the weather, or this war, or something. What about me and you meetin' some place?" He knew better now than to propose going up to her apartment.

"I'm not sure," she answered, after a bit of a pause, "it's rather difficult this week." But she thought this is awful, I shall never manage to get rid of him.

"You've become a different girlie altogether," he said.

"Don't be like that," she answered, sharp.

"Oh yes you 'ave," he replied in a low voice of great unhappiness.

"Don't be silly."

Her educated accents cut him.

"Is it somethin' I've done, sweetheart?"

"Don't call me that," she said. But he was following his own thoughts, the will of the wisps. He could no longer take in what she told him. "Was it something I done the last time," he asked. "I rack my memory," he went on, "because you know I wouldn't do the least thing, not for worlds, to put you against me. When I 'ad all that trouble with my sister I think I'd've gone stark crazy if it hadn't been for you. When I think," he said, all at once speaking in his official tone but in a way that would have alarmed his men, it was so interrupted, so indistinct, "I realise I owe more than life to you, my dear, all the trouble I've been through these last few weeks, yes more than life, for what is it if it isn't happiness, and you gave me more of that, yes you did, than any human being, than I 'ad the right in my position, that is, the likelihood to expect."

"Well, but you're all right again now," she said, brisk, at the first opportunity.

"Am I," he said, "that's the big question."

As he went on and on she settled down, slumped, over the stool there was by the phone. It was of black glass, bitterly cold. Ilse had taken the cushion for her bed. The glass struck at her through her thin, flowing clothes. Her soft back got quite round.

Ilse came in about the middle. She chose to ignore the fact that Prudence seemed to be listening into the receiver which, as she held it close to her ear, made a butterfly sound for Ilse about that bent head to which, unseen, this voice from another world was speaking.

"Darling," she interrupted, "shall you be going out presently?" Prudence put her hand over the mouthpiece. She told herself it was the final limit. Here was Ilse trying to turn her out of her own flat so as to ask that horror Wright.

All she said was, "I don't know. I don't expect so."

"But darling I'm so very sorry, I did not see that you were busy," said Ilse.

"That's all right, darling," Prudence answered. She put the receiver back to her ear. It seemed Bert had had the threat of a writ, the asylum was insisting that he should pay some money for his sister. But she did not care. Nothing would make her see Bert again this week, no, not till she felt quite different about firemen.

"What about you an' me meetin' some place this afternoon," said Pye, falling back on his fatal banter.

"I'm afraid I can't."

"Now sweetheart," he objected, but she had had enough. She softly put that receiver back, as though shutting a linen cupboard, and said, quietly, "damn."

He did not immediately ring her again. He came out of his office into the watchroom looking for trouble. He picked up the first thing he saw, which happened to be Hilly's log book, an official record of her journeys that she had to keep. She was passing the outer door just then.

"Here a minute," he said.

She thought how terribly ill he had seemed these last weeks, honestly he looked deathly this morning. Not that she cared.

"How often do I have to tell you drivers?" Then he began, "What is the matter with this log book? It is yours, isn't it? It's got your name and your staff car number on the cover? What's wrong with it?"

"I'm very sorry, sub, let me see, well I suppose . . . but honestly I don't notice anything."

"What about the end of the month? How many times do I have to remind you that there is a double line must be drawn after the entry on the last day of each month."

Oh, she thought with satisfaction, what an awful doing your Prudence must have given you.

"So soon as you've made the appropriate entry for the thirty-first or the thirtieth," he went on, "whichever it may be, rule a double line under." He enlarged for some time. When at last she was able to get away she locked herself in the lavatory again. She had never felt so depressed in her life.

Once Piper opened his mouth about the abduction Richard found the substation rapidly altered their opinion of him. In fact he became almost popular, that is with as many as heard what grew to be the fable started by the old soldier. This was largely possible because he no longer gave Pye drinks. Richard's companions were interested, or were influenced, only by actions. That Richard would have gone on standing him ale, if Pye had allowed it, did not affect their view. This change of attitude was also due to his having kept his mouth or, as they called it, the trap, shut. Again it seemed wrong to them because word had gone round that what they thought was his wife looked to be a smashing dame. Thus the whole story made him someone in their eyes. For the first time he became real to the substation, and all this from a tale that had expanded remarkably within thirty-six hours. Because it was now the sub officer who had taken Christopher away from where the boy was left when Pye found him, in a cloakroom of one of those night clubs, while his parents drank champagne within.

Shiner remarked that Roe was playing the white man when Richard refused to discuss the matter, shoot his mouth. It was generally understood that he did not dare, in case Pye took reprisals. In this the men were wrong, but the effect was the same, as much as if they had given him credit for the feeling he had, which they ignored, that he must never let them share, even though it was only in the telling, in the agony, the death of his wife, not in the abduction, but in her death.

Conversely Piper came to be even better hated.

The invasion of the Low Countries had begun. Although they hardly ever discusssed the war these men listened to news broadcasts three times a day. With the first shock of retreat overseas there was hardly one of them who did not transfer some of his sense of frustration into active dislike of old Piper, and, with each defeat across the Channel, into a hope, now the fighting had started, that his kind, the crawlers, the creepers, the old enough not to fight and know better, would at last be sunk, would be put in a situation where they could not bother anyone again. This feeling was intensified by the fact that they, who were young enough to carry arms, had nothing whatever to do at such a time but scrub floors and polish brass. This made them ridiculous even in their own eyes, and they knew that the public, seeing a man of Piper's age in the Service, must think it gallant of the hermit to be in even their uniform. No one shouted out to him, as was done more and more to the others, "Why don't you go and fight?" Still the men dared do nothing again about Piper, not yet. He was protected, too well in.

But threats began to be made. "The first blitz we get I'll drop a flue pot on the old oyster," someone said.

Because he worked for Trant the hermit was excused more and more of the station fatigues, for instance, he was never orderly in the kitchen now, although he made his way back for meals. As a result the others, when their turn came, waited on the Pied one, washed his dirty dishes. They objected to it. Also he got out of doing guards at night. He said Trant had given orders that he should get his night's rest in return for the extra work he put in. At last, about the time of Weygand's stand, three men were deputed to see Pye once more. The sub officer was almost tearful with the spokesman. Pye sometimes knew when to drop his official manner, to forget his threats.

"I was expectin' this," he said, "all along I was, but what can I do? 'E doesn't get the grub up at Number Fifteen, 'e's got a sweet tooth, the old fool 'as, and in addition 'e spreads 'imself, 'e lives like a lord at present, waited on by all alike. And what does 'e do for it? Nothing, mate, sweet dam' all. The Germans will be in Calais before that bloody bathroom is done, 'e's been three months already." But the Germans were to be quicker than that.

The deputation was pleased. Pye had been acting so strange lately there was no knowing how he would take anything. Emboldened, one of them spoke up to enquire whether Trant could be asked if he had excused Piper doing night guards. But Pye did not intend to go near the District Officer if he could help, and he was not prepared to let his station know that he lacked the courage.

"Now," he said, "be careful, you'll be beyond everything permissible in a minute. We're in a Service lads," he told them, "we all have to obey orders whether we like or not. I'll tell you something else, it ain't healthy to question lawful orders. Get back to work, to what you was doing, we won't call that work. You all know what I said to the lads the first time. It might be worth my pension if the DO got to hear that I'd listened on a second occasion."

That night, when Pye asked Richard to slip out for a drink, as had been their custom some months back, Roe thought it must be to discuss Piper. But, once they were settled in the four-ale bar, the sub's first words were almost an echo of those he had used the day war was declared.

"As man to man, Dick," he said, "what sort of a government is it we live under, eh? Look over in France. This marvellous system of ours can put a sane woman within the asylum but it can't put inside the lunatics who've landed us in the pass we've come to, because we've lost the entire British army, mark my words, there's no mistaking it. This self-same system can't get rid of the very men themselves that's at the top now, and responsible. That's something no true man can comprehend."

Richard sighed. He realised he was in for a session. But Pye was not in the mood to stick to one subject.

"Now a woman I was born and bred up with has wronged your wife." For Pye did not know his wife was dead. "It's what it comes to," he went on. "But wait a minute. When I come in unexpected on my leave day the other morning I was glad to meet her, yes and to see the nipper again, because of the way it turned out. For the reason that 'e didn't take no notice. I couldn't 'elp remarking the manner your wife switched 'erself away but I made no account, don't misunderstand me, it was only natural on her part. I'd've done the same myself. But I'm like any man, I can control my instincts, yet there's no one can put a halter on his thoughts. I don't mean anything personal. Being as I am I couldn't stop myself asking what she'd done still to be locked away as she is. Tell me straight, is there any accounting for it the way things have come out? 'As she done any wrong that has lasted till to-day? Can you see it?"

Richard thought he tumbled to what was in the wind. He foolishly opened his mouth.

"I know, sub," he said, "but after all it was none of my doing. And if you were to ask me to write in to the authorities calling on them to release her, or something like that, well it's going to be difficult, I'm in an awkward predicament, I . . ."

"I wouldn't ask a thing like that of anyone," Pye broke in, remarking to himself the sod, the awkward bastard, why can't he listen, "because it wouldn't be the slightest use," he went on, "once doctors get a grip they never let go. And even if I did wangle her out, because I've only to go up before the 'Igh Courts of Justice, put down fifty quid, and the thing's done so long as I swear she'll get as good attention at 'ome, even if I did want her back which I'm not so sure now, it wouldn't alter that she'd been in. No, if she's in she'd better stay, but the 'eartbreak is that she was ever there at all." He fell silent.

Richard drank his beer. He tried to think of something. In the end this was the best he could do:

"I know," he said.

"What d'you make of this moonlight, I mean in the black-out?" Pye began again, not changing the subject. "D'you mistake objects in it, 'ave you taken one person for another?"

"I can't tell one from another, sub."

"But I mean close to, right up. It's confusing you know, some nights."

Richard thought he could risk a joke.

"What have you been up to, then?" he asked. "Going up to the wrong girl?"

"You mightn't be so far out at that," Pye said. "Speaking of the same subject, they sent for me down to the asylum again the other afternoon. You know they're after trying to get me to pay for her upkeep and I say, no, you doctors booked my sister in and now you can toe the line, foot the expense. But that's another story. Anyway, this doctor I saw asked if I could remember anything in her past 'istory to account for her being the way she is. Now you're a married man and, you know, he meant anything to do with the sex life."

"I see," said Richard. He was sorry their conversation was coming back to the sister. "As a matter of fact I'm very doubtful about these psychologists, and yours sounds like he was one of them."

"You are, eh? Well, Dick, I don't mind telling you that by the time he'd finished with me I didn't know what day of the week it was."

"I don't know myself any more," Richard said. "This life we lead, every third day off, bewilders me. I couldn't tell you if it's Saturday or Sunday to-day, honestly."

"Come on, drink up, it's my round," Pye said, but he was not to be diverted. "Yes," he went on, "this doctor got me properly guessing. Then he starts to tell me about 'is own sister, quite uncalled for, something about a toboggan ride they had when they were kids on a black tray they had, and a lot more besides. I couldn't follow it. But, oh boy, was there a lovely bit of stuff on top of the old bus coming back."

Richard would rather anything than one of Pye's descriptions of the latest girl.

"How typical of a psychologist," he said, "making a song about a black tray."

"You don't have such a high opinion of them, then?"

"No, sub, I've not. Here's all the best. I know a man who went to one, and he came out crackers."

"Did 'e, the poor bastard. And he came out? What was his trouble?"

"Girls."

"Skirt, eh? Well that's sent many a good man off his nut. I've remarked there's a lot to do with the first one a lad has, and that goes for the woman as well. But what sort of a cuss would I be to tell this doctor things my sister's always kept to herself? It's not a question of class. There's subjects that are private, and that's all. But these doctors certainly make you wonder."

"You're telling me." Then Richard, through over-confidence, was rash. "You know," he said, "after what happened my sister-in-law was most insistent that Christopher should not meet you again. I can say it, can't I, we're talking frankly and we both know there was nothing in that little business," then he corrected himself, "or it's all over, now, anyway." Pye asked himself, why in God's name do I sit here with him, the wet sod, and anyway what's this about a sister-in-law. Could any man make head or tail of it? Richard went on, "Well she cost me a guinea the other morning when she rang up the psychologist to enquire whether he thought it would matter if you did meet although I told her you were on leave that day, and he said it would be dangerous, or it might be, I believe he said."

Pye muttered, "I'm sorry," and thought, does he want to tap me for that bill as well?

Richard took another deep draught of ale, "Don't be sorry, sub, there's nothing to be sorry about. You saw what happened, he came up to you perfectly happy, delighted to see you again in fact."

"I'm glad," Pye said, not glad.

"So you're having a quiet time still, fireman." They both turned round to find a nondescript civilian who had come up to get another drink.

"Yes," Pye said, thankful for the break, "but Christ help us all when it does start over here, mate." He would stand no nonsense with civilians.

Richard had come to an end, aware that he had gone too far. This gave the sub officer his chance to get on with the main subject.

"Tell us, Dick," he said, "can you remember after you've been with 'em?"

"What d'you mean?"

"Why, kypher, skirt. Listen, years ago the first I 'ad, see, I thought might be someone else, only it was a dark night and I couldn't be certain." He was talking so low that it was all Richard could do to hear. "What d'you make of that?"

"I still don't get you, sub."

"Well, do you think a man could be mistaken?"

"But didn't you talk?"

"No, of course we didn't. What was there to yarn about?"

"Then unless she had a mastoid, or something similar, I don't suppose you could tell."

"That's just what I keep repeating to myself. I'll acquaint you with it some day, Dick."

"It could be very awkward."

"Awkward? It was worse than that. It's a thing that only come to me not above a week or two back. Keeps me awake, that does. I bloody well lie there sweatin' of a night time."

"You don't want to let it worry you."

"Yes, but there you are, what we want and what we get is two very different things. Oh I know it's unreasonable, yet I don't seem able to 'elp myself."

"I'll bet you've been terrific with the girls in your day," Richard said, making up to him.

"Get out, what's the matter with you," Pye replied, not displeased, and ready to drop the topic. He did not wish to discuss girls with Roe. His instinct had been to find some comfort against the doubts which were sure to crowd him when, some hours later, after lights out, he would close his eyes alongside the black telephone.

There was a silence. Pye let his mind free-wheel. He went on dreading the night. Suddenly he said:

"I know who that man is. He's a plain clothes man."

"What chap is that, sub?"

Richard, after a few beers, would let himself drop into what he imagined was their way of talking.

"Why," said Pye, "the one that said we were 'aving a quiet time. I'll wager he won't stir out of 'is shelter under Savile Row when the raids start, either."

"What makes you think he is?"

"I always know one by the cut of his jib, mate. I can tell 'em in the black-out at fifty yards distance, the rotten swine. I hate their guts. Since I've 'ad to do with 'em any criminal's got my sympathy. They make crime, that sort do."

Richard thought they had better get off this subject. "Well, sub," he said, "what are you going to have now?"

"Thanks, Dick, I tell you what, shall we wind up with a round of shorts?"

"Won't you be going across the way to-night?" Richard

meant was Pye to meet Prudence. He ordered the whisky. The sub officer did not answer, so Roe thought he would risk another try. While he was jealous no longer, he was most curious to know.

"Not any more if I can help it, I'm not," Pye lied. "Not since that mad sod of an old matelot got up there with the other one. I can't afford to do it."

"How's that? Does it come expensive?"

"No, never on your life. But once one of me own men gets drinking from the adjacent source, to use an expression, even if it is on Swedish territory, then it's time for me to leave well alone, get back on the old Scotch. 'Ere's good health. No, an officer can't afford to get mixed up with his men on that sort of lark. Else how can he expect to keep authority?"

"You mean Shiner's having a thing with Ilse?"

"Well you brought 'em together, didn't you? But I don't know, don't go asking me. All I know is I keep right out of it now, bet your life I do."

Richard was flabbergasted at first, then much tickled. Hilly had made him immune for the moment. He laughed.

"What are you laughing about?" Pye said.

"I can't help it when I think of those two together." Pye looked at him pityingly. Then he turned round to see if the plain clothes man was still around.

"There 'e is."

"What? Who? I don't see them. Shiner and Ilse you mean?"

"No, mate, the copper in flannel bags."

Finally Pye brought out the first remark of many that were to alarm Richard. He said:

"Of course, being the age I am, I could join as officer air gunner in the RAF."

Roe looked to see if his sub officer was joking. It was plain that he was not.

"But aren't you over age, really?" he asked.

"Not more than two years. I'm thirty-five. They'd be glad to 'ave a man of my varied experience."

It came to Richard that Pye must be insane. At that date he was years over age.

THIS INTERESTING DISCUSSION was ended by an Auxiliary, sent over to tell Pye he was wanted on the phone. The sub officer did not see Roe again that night. He fiddled with routine matters over at the substation until after closing time, unable to complete anything. Then the fit came on him. He went into the vast, moonlit night.

He had only meant to go as far as the corner, so he did not book out. But once he was full in it, in the radiance, against which, on the other side, were triangular dark sapphire shadows exactly laid by houses, the urge returned with the memory of his sister's moon draggled crawl, with Prudence's clear cut, neat refusal to have him, the urge came back, driving Pye to try once more to find how much he could recognise by this light in the bright river of the street, and to get a girl for the evening, out of the blue.

He had hopes, as a boy of nine might go feeling he could slay two ravens in flight with a cat's eye on a string.

As he idled along, playing truant, the milk moon stripped deep gentian cracker paper shadows off his uniform. Then the next building, in a line as acute as its angle to the moon, laid these back on as he went.

It was as if the warm air was powdered.

He crossed over to avoid an intermittent glow made on his beat by a policeman. In full moonlight now, Pye crossed once more into the next sharp triangle of soft shadow, as soon as the officer, bobbling the primrose torch, had passed.

Pye grew desperate. "Just such another night," he said in official tones beneath his scented breath, while he rolled a violet cachet against the denture.

At that, so sudden it brought him up sharp, the tart, stood back in a doorway, shone a copper beam, from the torch she carried, full on her left breast she held bared with the other hand. She murmured, "Hulloh love." Longingly he ogled the dark purple nipple, the moon full globe that was red Indian tinted by her bulb, with the whiff of scent. "Jesus," he moaned, but it was too near his substation. "Don't you go hangin' around," he added indistinctly, and shambled off. She laughed into a cough and then, when she snapped down the light, was again, and at once, indigo, and the door against which she stood.

He came to a pub which was not the one he used with Richard, but a house visited when alone, out after a girl. It had gone closing time. The door was barred. He pushed, then rattled the handle he had to grope to find. But it was not until he surprised himself banging on the brass plate, which seemed enamelled, that he realised he had had enough, or rather that the air, the intense impartiality of moonlight, had so stepped up what he had consumed with Richard that he was wavering on the wet verge of drunkenness.

Meantime he was unlucky. While he was out Trant rang him. Chopper, who took the call, had his own pension to consider. Chopper was not going to cover Pye again. It was enough to have been caught once. He did not actually say his sub officer was adrift. What he rang back to tell the District Officer was that Pye could not for the moment be found.

Trant ordered a car, booked himself out, and was on his way down. To give them a drill. Richard was already back from the pub. Chopper, anticipating that Trant would try to catch Pye out, sent Richard across to see if the skipper was up with Prudence. Roe did not like it. He said he would rather not.

"It's long odds the DO will be along to give us a turn out," Chopper said. "We can't let the skipper down."

"Yes, but what if I miss the drill?"

"Trant'll never notice one man not riding."

"But I can't go in and say, 'Have you got Pye in with you, dear?'" said Richard.

"Oh go on up, for Christ's sake, and look sharp about it. That's an order if you like." There were no witnesses. If Roe had been caught, which he was not, Chopper would have denied having given the order.

Trant wasted no time when he arrived. He put the bells down, watched the drill without comment. Then he asked, "Where's the sub officer?"

"I can't make it out, sir," Chopper said. "Why, he was here a moment ago."

"Tell him to phone me the minute he gets back."

With that the DO stepped into his car, his driver winked, and he was driven off to Number Fifteen. A group of men stood in the doorway, watching. Shiner was with them.

One said "What a smashing night."

"It is and all," another answered. "And 'ow about the drill? It was fast I reckon."

"Barrin' the fact we was let down by the skipper. Same old story time and again. Pye puts the bells down as often as three occasions in one day, 'e gives more drills than they get in another substation on the ground, yet when it comes down to brass tacks, when somebody takes a fancy to drill him, he's not even on the bloody premises."

"It's dodgy," Shiner said, "I fancy we're to expect changes in this ship. Why, d'you see what I see? It's Savoury, or my eyes are no better than the skipper's in the moonlight. Hi, cock." Then as Richard came up, "You've missed a drill."

"Did Trant get on to my not being there?" he asked.

"How did you know it was Trant turned us out?"

"Because I was sent to see if I could hunt up the skipper. Chopper thought the drill was coming off."

"So little Peewee's conger eel chasing, eh? Well, I don't blame 'im. At least 'e's a man, not like some in this unnatural dejectipated ship, that's too scared to do more than look over their shoulder."

"That's OK Shiner," one of them said, "but the skipper's let us down bad."

"Don't make me sick. We're all men in this outfit. If 'e likes to go out after a bit of ong dong once in a while I'd be the last to lay the blame."

"Yes, you would."

Shiner took this last remark up, bit it. An argument developed. Richard went to find Chopper. Prudence had not appreciated his calling at the flat for Pye.

Although it was hardly mentioned, each man in this group outside was aghast at the news, for the evacuation of Dunkirk was on. In that deadly moonlight brothers were dying fast, and not so far off. A week's time and it might be anybody's turn. But the moon, fixed in the sky without a cloud, flooded everything with intolerance, made such a cold peace below that it did not seem possible that extermination could be so near, over to the east.

Pye felt menace in the streets such as had not oppressed him since the day war was declared.

He was doubting whether his men would be of much use in the great fires they had to expect if Hitler did come over. He did not think there was one to pull him out of a bad spot, bar Wright. They had no experience. He felt the politicians had left his country at its enemies' mercy, and had given him an inexperienced crew when the whole of fire-fighting was the trust each individual had that the man behind him would get him out if need be. He forgot he had had the training of his men. He said aloud:

"I feel bloody awful."

"You're tellin' me," a voice replied.

Pye almost started out of his pelt. He was standing in shadow near the entrance to that night club he used with Prudence. It seemed then as if every doorway in London held someone looking at the night, the spread of death it was at present. He had thought he was alone with his bad thoughts, unseen, as he watched Richard go over to Prudence's. And leave again. But he was not jealous. He did not think that pansy could stay long. All the same, he had recognised him with ease.

"I never saw you mate," he announced, in the general direction of that depth of indigo shadow from which the voice had spoken. "It's a funny thing, this moon. Would you say you could recognise a individual in it?"

"You're from the fire post around the corner, ain't that right," the unknown pronounced. The man then spat. Pye began to see him. There was a blink from his watch-chain. "I can recognise enough to know you ain't no ruddy parachutist."

"There's always that," Pye agreed. "No, what I 'ad in mind was the days I was a youngster. Maybe it's the night, or something I ate, but I got a fit of rememberin' back."

"Yes," the stranger said, "it's worryin' times these are and no mistake. I wouldn't wonder but you was speculatin' on 'ow soon you'll get action."

"I've a fine lot of lads under me," Pye answered, and then was silent as a taxi drew up outside the club. Richard had been such a short time over at her flat it might be that she was not there. She could drive up any bloody minute for a last drink with that pilot she was always on about.

"Yes, I don't seem able to escape from it," Pye went on, when he thought he saw it wasn't her. "They say that's the gladdest time of a man's life. I'd give anything to 'ave that part back, but not to live."

"I don't follow."

"To know what really occurred," said Pye, dropping his voice. "Of course I know, but I can't be certain, not absolutely. It's interferin' with my sleep."

The stranger was impatient of what, to himself, he termed vapourings.

"It's rotten when a man can't sleep. But did you listen to the twelve o'clock news? It don't seem possible, now, do it? Not on a bloody night like this," he said.

"Anything in this bloody country's possible, mate. Well, I must be moving. Good night."

Stepping out into the light, which made him into a drowned man walking, the sub officer left indignant silence. But he paid no attention. He was taken up at present with a fury for Prudence that he could not put a name to. It was lust. Such had recently been the effect of his worrying about his sister. "I must find a woman," he said to himself, "Oh sod the game." He crossed quickly into that bounded sea of shadow. He grew furtive. He imagined women where none were. He spoke suggestively to gentian hooded doorways.

Then he heard a snivelling gulp of tears in treble.

He hesitated. He stood quiet as a cat, intently listening. Again the snivel. At that Pye darted right in. He came back out into full moonlight holding at arm's length, thrashing with legs, struggling, not the lost girl with flaxen hair he had imagined, crying out for her mother, but a small, rough boy with snot pulsating at his nostrils, skin, hair and eyes all of a colour.

"Lemme go, lemme go, guv'nor," the worm whined and was suddenly quiet, going limp, and who fixed Pye with his crafty eyes.

"Ain't you got a snot rag?" the sub officer asked. "First things first," he added, echoing Piper.

There was no reply. "Come on then, don't be nervous, lad, you've a tongue to your 'ead. 'Ave you got a 'andkerchief, because if so you want to give it a blow."

The boy sawed the back of a hand across his nose, then wiped off on his trouser seat. Immediately the mucus reappeared, almost Eton blue in this brilliant light, and which trembled, weaving with each breath he took, each calculated silent sob.

"You're a scruffy kid, ain't you," the sub officer mentioned, glad to forget sex for the moment. He was beginning to enjoy himself until he noticed the boy was watching.

"'Ere," he said, suspicious, "what's your game?"

Then what he was holding began to twist about again, every part of it moving at once. He had to hold the lad well away from him.

"What's the rush?" he asked.

"You're 'urting," the boy replied through his teeth.

"I'm not lettin' you go in all that hurry," the sub officer said. "Come on now, what's your name and where might you live?"

Once more the struggling collapsed. Again the crafty look. This time, Pye did not notice because he was looking up and down the empty street, the river between banks.

"Would you be a copper, guv'nor?"

"Jesus Christ, no, not on your life. I'm Fire Brigade, I am. I got LFB on my buttons, look."

"Straight up."

"No skylark," Pye assured the boy, using one of Shiner's expressions. He could spot no one about, though that was no certainty in this light, with his eyes. "'Ere," he said, "have I seen you before, let's have a look." He was glad of this. He drew the boy towards him, holding hard with both hands. "For pity's sake blow your nose, lad," he said, "and if you've no snot rag use your fist, again," he said. "No, I don't suppose I ever saw you in my life, even though it is difficult by this bloody moon. Well, it's not as if I'd got all night. Come on now, what do they call you?"

"I'm lost," the boy replied.

That did it.

"That's a diabolical bloody tale," Pye said, bursting out in a murderer's loud voice, thinking of Christopher. The flesh and bones seemed to shrink in his hands. "How old would you be?" he went on, quieter, to cover up.

"Rising nine guv'nor. You're 'urting."

"I'm hurting am I?" Pye announced and did not relax his grip at all, though the sudden rage was dying. "Come on now, where d'you come from?"

"I'm all on me own." The snivelling began again.

"You mean you daren't go back." As he said this it came pathetically over Pye that if he, even at the age he now was, should be living in the country, back with his parents, if he found himself outside he would not dare go back to the cottage, such was his feeling of guilt when the fit was over him. Not on a night like this, in any event. His eyes filled with tears.

He cleared his throat.

"What have you done, boy?" he asked, in his official tones. He got no reply.

"You'd better tell," he said, meaning it was better to have it out and not, like him, be suckling on an ulcer the sickly, sore-covered infant of his fears. But the way he brought the words out made it seem a threat.

"Come on now." He spoke loud, and, in his upset, he shook the boy, who let out a wail.

"For Christ's sake, hush," he said. "You'll have all them Auxiliary bloody Firemen round in a minute."

"Lemme go."

Pye's answer was to shift his grip, and not hold so firm. He thought the bones he had his fingers round, on these two arms, were like sticks, like a girl's. But the fit had passed.

"When was it last you 'ad some grub?" he enquired, calm.

"Day before yesterday," was the lie given him.

"We'd better get something inside yer," Pye said, "you just come along, mate."

"Where're you takin' me?"

"To the Fire station."

"I ain't never been in a Fire station," the boy started. Curiosity won him. He stepped out willingly. Pye kept hold of one elbow.

"Quietly now," said the sub officer, all at once, too late, unsure that it was wise. But he took precautions not to be seen. He got the boy to his room in the billets without anyone knowing he was back. As a consequence he did not learn that Trant had been down until the next day, when it was much too late. For he slept alone, and Chopper never thought to look, assuming that he had taken one more night off. At the crisis of Pye's affair with Prudence he had often not come back till morning.

After getting the lad some bread and cheese, which had been left out in the kitchen for his own supper, and fixing him up on the easy chair in his bedroom with a blanket in which he went to sleep at once, the sub officer hardly considered the boy again. He went to bed himself quite soon, profoundly miserable, allowing the routine business of the station to run riot in his head. He was surprised, when called next morning, to realise he must have gone to sleep at once.

He was called by Piper at seven with his cup of tea. It was one of those little extras the old man undertook in order to keep on the right side, to preserve the privileges won by doing things for Trant.

"Shall I get another for the nipper," he asked, as if it was most natural.

"Yes, do that, will you," Pye said.

He made the boy wash, he had a lavatory to himself as officer in charge. He did not know what to do next. Then he decided the DO had bawled him out enough, he considered, and he would take the lad into breakfast openly with the men. You could not send him away hungry. After all, there was a war on. The old order there used to be about no visitors in stations was out of date. There was nothing to be ashamed of. You could not hand a mere kid over to the police because he was sleeping a night out in these times. But if he, Pye, as officer in charge, tried to get him away unnoticed, the back way in daylight, they would most surely be seen. Besides Hilly would not charge him for the extra meal.

In this way it came about they both had breakfast with the men, who thought the lad must be the new messenger boy. At that time these boys had no uniforms. And Piper was not telling them what he knew, he was keeping that for later, for Trant.

When Pye heard from Chopper that Trant had caught him adrift he was so worried he gave the lad half a dollar to go. He fairly pushed him away, and tried to forget for as long as he was allowed.

He was not allowed to forget for long.

The telephone bell soon rang. Pye answered. The DO was at the other end.

"This is Mr Trant here," he said, "I want sub officer Pye."

"Speaking, sir."

"Oh it's you, is it? I want to speak to you. When I came down last night where were you? There's going to be a charge made out against you. Who d'you think you are? I'm sick and tired of you."

"Listen, sir, I . . ."

"I don't want to hear any more. You've let me down. I've 'ad plenty. You'll be up here sharp at ten fifteen the day after to-morrow, Tuesday, and you'll keep anything you might have to say till then, you . . . well I won't say it, only I'll add this, I'd've seen you now but I've to go to Headquarters. I'm finished with you."

"Yessir," said Pye. When he heard the receiver slammed back he buried a burning face in his hands.

Ten minutes later Pye was comforting himself that Trant

had not said a word about the lad. As to being adrift he made up his mind to explain how anxiety for his sister had driven him out, how loss of sleep due to worry about her had made him not accountable. Even so he was weighed down. He was in dread. Even the men noticed a greater change in him, at once.

SOME MONTHS LATER, after nine weeks of air raids on London, Roe was unlucky one morning. A bomb came too close. It knocked him out. He was sent home, superficially uninjured. They called it nervous debility.

He slept in the train all the way down to Christopher and Dy. He slept in the hired car. He went straight to bed when he arrived. He slept another sixteen hours. Then he got up. He saw the ground was under snow. But this time he felt odd, with an aching emptiness behind the forehead.

Air and light, reflected off snow through the opened window, whipped Roe's face, smacked his eyes. He noticed steam and smoke-drenched grit up his nose, the leavings of one fire after another, night after night. For a few mornings he could still taste the sour debris when he bit his nails. It made him shake. When he blew out a match he got the stench again. Until, after three days, he began to come out of it, although he was worse than he realised.

He went out with his sister-in-law and Christopher. He just put his arm through hers and could not believe the lack of noise. The menace was gone.

The big house was shut up. His parents lived in one of

the lodge gates, Dy in the other. Money was short. He had never felt the need for money less.

Yet he would not let Christopher look in by a blank window at what had been home. The furniture he knew was sheeted, the soot deep in each cold fireplace. He called the boy back, whose reply was to make a snowball off the window ledge, over which this same light had once made cannons for his ship of bricks. Christopher threw it at him with the awkwardness of the very young, and came away.

"It doesn't seem possible," said Richard, expanding.

"I know," she answered.

"He looks wonderfully well."

"Yes," she said, "and hasn't he grown? It's much better for the old chap down here. We've been so excited ever since we got the telegram."

"Were you very worried?" he asked.

"No. We knew you'd be all right." He looked at her. He was irritated to find she was laughing.

"Did you? I wish I had."

"Don't think about it," she said. "You can forget it all now."

"Except about going back," he put in. He shook.

"You aren't," she said, "you're staying here, I've arranged everything," and this white lie, which he swallowed, satisfied him. But he felt awkward. To hide this he called the boy.

"Opher," he called, "what shall we do to-day?"

"I don't mind."

"Shall we have a bonfire like we did that last time?"

"If you like. Look," Christopher said, another snowball in his hand, "I'm a German airman, I'm bombing."

"I'll tell you what, let's have a bonfire, then put it out with stirrup pumps."

This idea was a success. Christopher repeatedly asked, "I say when?" Dy insisted that it should be in the afternoon, for Rosemary was coming over from school.

"You won't call me that when she comes to tea, will you?" Christopher asked. The fact that he did not like being called Opher before his cousin pleased Richard.

"Of course not," he replied, and felt better. But in less than five minutes he was back at it again.

"You must have thought I'd never wake up, asleep all that time?" he asked her.

"No, that's all right, I knew you would."

"I was badly in need, you know."

"Yes. But you mustn't think any more."

He could not stop. "It's extraordinary up there," he went on. Christopher had drifted ahead. She realised she could not prevent Richard trying to get it out of his system. Because she knew him she had planned to take him empty walks, her idea was to keep his mind vacant so that he should have complete rest, and yet not leave him alone. But she understood she could not stop him now.

"The extraordinary thing is," he said, "that one's imagination is so literary. What will go on up there to-night in London, every night, is more like a film, or that's what it seems like at the time. Then afterwards, when you go over it, everything seems unreal, probably because you were so tired, as you begin building again to describe to yourself some experience you've had. It's so difficult. When you heard, what did you imagine the room was like that Christopher was in, I mean before the police brought him back?" He had begun talking to her as though she was her dead sister.

"Oh don't. I couldn't. That's just what was so awful."

"Well, I did. Even to the firelight on the walls. Like the flames did the first night."

"We don't know if they had lit a fire. It's no use that sort of thing, no help," she said.

"I'm sorry," he answered, "I suppose I'm trying to involve you."

"No," she said, "go on."

He started again. "I think I only brought it back to when the old chap was taken away because it must have been so much worse for her," meaning his wife, and forgetting she was dead at the time, "than it was for me. I don't know. But what makes me laugh," and he was not even smiling, "is to think how different the real thing is to what we thought it was going to be. And the way the people have changed, you've no idea. We're absolute heroes now to everyone. Soldiers can't look us in the face, even."

"Quite right too."

"You get so frightfully tired that half the time you're in a fog," he went on, wavering.

"I suppose it's a sort of protection by nature," she said. "I do wish something of the kind was arranged when one was having a baby."

"Yes," he replied. He wanted to go on talking about himself. It was urgent. "This is the first time in weeks I've felt rested and when I get in I'm going to sleep the clock right round again."

"But you won't before the children have their tea, will you?"

He had a surge of rage.

"Why not?" he asked. "You're surely not expecting me to dance attendance on a nursery tea?"

"Well, you see, there's no nursery now. The days of nurseries are over. You'll have to be with them unless I bring you some in bed. But do stay up. Just for them. Please. It makes all the difference for him to have you in front of Rosemary. Besides," she added, and she was not going to give in, "it will be so good for you."

"All right," he said, "I'm sorry I'm being tiresome. Tell me, d'you find it awful without a nanny?"

"No, not a bit, really. You see he's old enough to look after himself. He's no trouble. It's a great relief on the whole. There's not the nanny to think of all the time."

"That's one of the things about the blitz," he said, getting back to himself as soon as possible, "there's not a sub officer within sight. You just get ordered on to an address. I'm usually in charge of our pump, and you're absolutely on your own. I used to wonder in the old days about Peewee, how it would be possible to fight fires and try to spare his feelings."

She said to herself, there he goes, he's back again.

"Who's Peewee?" she asked.

"Why Pye, of course. Didn't you know, that's what Hilly christened him? You remember Hilly," he asked awkwardly, "the driver you met when you brought Christopher along that time?"

"Oh her," Dy said, remembering the girl very well. She had obviously been up to something with Richard. "What's become of her?"

"Hilly? She's about still. Yes," he went on rather fast, "the great idea is to be on your own."

Yes, and to have your wife's sister with your parents not on her own, she thought.

Then he opened the floodgates, really getting down to it.

"The first night," he said, "we were ordered to the docks. As we came over Westminster Bridge it was fantastic, the whole of the left side of London seemed to be alight."

(It had not been like that at all. As they went, not hurrying, but steadily towards the river, the sky in that quarter, which happened to be the east, beginning at the bottom of streets until it spread over the nearest houses, was flooded in a second sunset, orange and rose, turning the pavements pink. Civilians hastened by twos or threes, hushed below the stupendous pall of defeat until, in the business quarter, the streets were deserted.)

(These firemen at last drove out on to the bridge. Here two men and a girl, like grey cartridge paper under this light which stretched with the spread of a fan up the vertical sky, were creeping off, drunkenly, defiantly singing.)

(The firemen saw each other's faces. They saw the water

below a dirty yellow towards the fire; the wharves on that far side low and black, those on the bank they were leaving a pretty rose. They saw the whole fury of that conflagration in which they had to play a part. They sat very still, beneath the immensity. For, against it, warehouses, small towers, puny steeples seemed alive with sparks from the mile high pandemonium of flame reflected in the quaking sky. This fan, a roaring red gold, pulsed rose at the outside edge, the perimeter round which the heavens, set with stars before fading into utter blackness, were for a space a trembling green.)

"I almost wetted my trousers," he said, putting into polite language the phrase current at his substation.

"I had an old crook called Arthur Piper on my crew that first evening," he went on, "he was killed about three hours after. I'll tell you about him some time. He was old, it was his fifth campaign. When he saw the blaze from the bridge all he said was, 'Oh mother.' It sounded so odd coming from inside the taxi. No one else had said a word."

"Don't talk about people being killed."

"Well, he was. So was Shiner Wright, that same night. But what I can't get over is the months we sat waiting. Now it's on us, not nearly as bad as we thought. We were sitting talking one day. Everyone was agreed that it was going to be so noisy, when we did have a raid, that the only thing would be to carry paper and pencil so as to write messages. Shiner was the one man there to say it wouldn't be necessary. Well he was right. Of course, he had had experience already. He had been invalided out of the Navy with a bad arm. But when it did come there was hardly any noise at all. You see there were practically no guns at first."

The anxiety she felt for him did not prevent her, in the other half of her head, thinking how very dull his description was. But she could not get over the great fact. This was how wonderful it was to have him with her. Particularly along this dejected path she had grown to hate in the months she had been down here. And she began to feel confident that he was all right, really. He was just doing his usual, going over everything.

"Did I tell you?" he went on. "We used to have tremendous arguments about whether the Regulars would be any good. Well, of course, it was exactly what might have been expected, which was just what we did not think of at the time. Some were, and some weren't."

Every inch of the path they followed slowly through the wild garden, which was no longer tended, would, at any time before this, have reminded him of so many small events he had forgotten out of his youth, of the wounded starling here, the nightingale there one night, the dog whining across the river one morning, while he stood motionless behind that elm, to watch two cats from the stables. Because it was overgrown, now that the old tidiness had, so to speak, been allowed to ramble, he would once have lingered all the more with what was left him of days when these surroundings were the moist fat skin which covered the skeleton of his adolescence. To-day it was different. In his pre-occupation with air raids he could even let his son run on ahead without sentimentalising over the boy.

He had forgotten his wife.

Even when, twelve months later, he had begun to forget raids, and when, in the substation, they went over their experiences from an unconscious wish to recreate, night after night in the wet canteen, even then he found he could not go back to his old daydreams about this place. It had come to seem out of date.

". . . but when at last we drove through the Dock," he continued, taken up by this urge to explain, "there was not one officer to report to, no one to give orders, we simply drove on up a road towards what seemed to be our blaze. Of course it was half daylight in the glare reflected from the pall of smoke, but we couldn't see our fire, there was a line of sheds three hundred yards in front."

As he gave this inadequate description he was avidly living that moment again. It had been an unwilling ride.

(He was cold as they churned along in the taxi, which was boiling over from the distance it had been driven towing the heavy pump. Part of the steering wheel shone blood red from the sky. The air caught at his wind passage as though briars and their red roses were being dragged up from his lungs. The acrid air was warm, yet he was cold.)

But there was nothing in what he had spoken to catch her imagination. She went along at his side, by this path she hated, and looked up at his face in what he took to be the attention she was paying to the account he gave. In fact, she was thinking of her dead sister and of how she would describe him to her if she had to. She was trying to analyse the extent to which his features had altered. She listened with half her mind as she decided his face was thinner, while his neck had thickened. His shoulders were broader. He was much dirtier than he used to be. Of course, his hands were awful, and then probably he could not get them clean. But his forehead was grey with dirt. Suddenly, with a real pang, she saw grey in the red hairs at his temples. She almost put the fingers of her hand up to them, and then she did not.

". . . no one to report to," he was telling, "just a road leading to what was obviously a gigantic fire and no one knew if it was the right wharf. We had been ordered to Rhodesia Wharf, Surrey Commercial Docks. I never felt so alone in all my life. Our taxi was like a pink beetle drawing a pepper corn. We were specks. Everything is so different always from what you expect, and this was fantastic. Of course, we couldn't hear for the noise of the engine, and we had shut the windows so as to get more inside. There was only the driver, old Knocker, on the front. No one said a word. Yet I suppose it was not like that at all really. One changes everything after by going over it."

"But the real thing," she said, getting her teeth into this, for she liked arguments, and the bit about the beetle had drawn her attention because she thought it vivid, "the real thing is the picture you carry in your eye afterwards, surely? It can't be what you can't remember, can it?"

"I don't know," he said, "only the point about a blitz is this, there's always something you can't describe, and it's not the blitz alone that's true of. Ever since it happened I feel I've been trying to express all sorts of things."

"I expect that's the result of your being blown up."

"No," he said, exasperated suddenly, "there's an old fault of yours, you're always trying to explain difficult things prosaically."

"What's prosaically?" she asked. She did not understand.

"Oh, ordinarily," he said, his exasperation cooling. "But you must let me plough on, Dy. It was so fantastic afterwards, when we were ordered out of the Dock, it was almost like an explanation of the whole of our life in the war, waiting in the substation for just this. I do so want you to get the whole thing."

"I'm sorry."

"Well, when we got round those buildings I told you about, they were great open sheds really, for keeping the weather off the more expensive timber, we were right on top of the blaze. It was acres of timber storage alight about two hundred yards in front, out in the open, like a huge wood fire on a flat hearth, only a thousand times bigger."

(It had not been like that at all. What he had seen was a broken, torn-up dark mosaic aglow with rose where square after square of timber had been burned down to embers, while beyond the distant yellow flames toyed joyfully with the next black stacks which softly merged into the pink of that night.)

"Then an officer did turn up, out of a surface shelter. I was just getting off the step to report to him when he saw us. He yelled out to take cover, as though I'd insulted him by arriving. So I dived off the cement road under some big baulks of wood in the nearest open shed. As I listened to the planes I remember thinking this was the first time I'd lain on the earth in London. Hyde Park doesn't count. Then I saw the crew was lying on the hard road. I'd read somewhere that if a bomb fell on it up to six hundred yards away, they would have their ribs crushed by the vibration. So I yelled out to come where I was. And old Shiner, who'd had some the night before, though not so bad as this, shouted back for me to move instead. D'you know where I'd put myself? Right under a skylight in the roof, quite thirty foot up, just where the broken glass would have cut me to ribbons if a bomb had brought it down. And when the particular plane, which seemed to be searching, searching, searching, when it did drop its load I've never waited so hard. But they didn't drop anywhere near that time."

"Darling," she said, gently malicious, "I thought you wrote and told me you people never take cover, that you work all through the raid." She was not going to take him tragically.

"So we do now," he said, not noticing, "but we know by this time more or less how near the bomb is going to be. And that night being the first, we were strange. All except Piper. He was absolutely true to form. When there seemed to be at least five planes overhead, would you credit it, he got up from where he was lying and went across to the officer who had shouted at me? Believe it or not, the old Pied one stayed with that man all night. I don't suppose they moved nine yards away from the shelter. So Piper was making up to officers till the last, and it killed him, because when a bomb came down, just before we had to evacuate the place, that was where he was killed. The officer was decorated in his coffin for the way he had directed our fire-fighting."

"No!" This time she was shocked.

"Well, what does anything matter?" he replied. "And green as we were, you don't know how good some of us were that night, Regular and Auxiliary. Shiner was superb.

He should have been in charge of our pump. Because I made a Piper mistake almost at once. You see there was no room left to put our suctions down into the water. As soon as that first wave of bombers passed hundreds of men came out of the ground, it was surprising really, and went back through the mounds of burned-out stuff to get back to the fire. There wasn't room to get in among their pumps at the dockside."

(Nearby all had been pink, the small, coughing men had black and rosy faces. The puddles were hot, and rainbow coloured with oil. A barge, overloaded with planks, drifted in flames across the black, green, then mushroom skin river water under an upthrusting mountain of fox-dyed smoke that pushed up towards the green pulsing fringe of heaven.)

"I went up with my crew to the fire, which dried out my rough mouth even more. And a sub asked me to try for some drinking water. Instead of sending one of my mates, I went myself. You see, that was wrong."

"Why?" she asked.

"Because I was number one, I was in charge, and I shouldn't have left the crew."

"But you were told to, surely?"

"Yes," he said, "but I ought to have passed the order on."

"No, I'm sure you were right. No one can disobey orders at a time like that, can they?"

"That's just the moment when you have to disobey if you're any good," he said. "But what a night. Think of the way we'd waited a whole year behind those windows, then suddenly to be pitchforked into chaos. We used to think we'd get some directions. Instead we had about eight acres of flames and sixty pumps with the crews in a line pouring water on, when the bombing did not drive them off. And, because of the size of the whole thing, doing practically no good at all. And no orders whatever."

"But I don't see," she said. "You're telling me that it was

no use giving orders, that there was nothing you could do, really, anyway nothing more than you were all doing."

"Exactly," he said, "that's exactly it. In some fantastic way I'm sure you only get in war, we were suddenly alone and forced to rely on one another entirely. And that after twelve months' bickering. Each crew was thrown upon itself, on its own resources. The only thing to do was to keep together."

"It sounds grim." She shuddered. He had caught her attention properly.

"It wasn't," he replied, "it was like mustard. No, as a matter of fact, we should have been withdrawn to let the timber yard burn out. It was surrounded by water and we couldn't have stopped the shower of sparks flying off in front with the wind if we'd had all the pumps in London. No, what I mean is, we were suddenly face to face with it, as I was with Pye two months before when I pulled him out of the gas oven."

She wondered again, as she had often done, why someone else could not have found that hateful man.

"Well, you were all wonderful. Everywhere, every day I read the most wonderful things about you in the papers."

"You should have seen us evacuating the Dock," he answered, "only that was later. There was nothing wonderful about that. No, somehow, even with old Pye, I always seem to be making up to the Regulars, I'm not able to help it. Can you think of a more ridiculous picture than a number one man going to get water for a sub officer? They're no more than sergeants after all."

"Well anyway," she said, "I think it was very brave. I'm sure carrying water round a place like that was no joke."

He began to get exasperated again. "You don't understand," he replied. "Well, anyway, I got on to one of the big ships tied up to the dock at the rear of us. They fetched a little caretaker out of the Pied Piper's shelter to shew me where I could get water on board. I asked him what Piper was talking about back there, describing the old man carefully, but this caretaker was a Swede, and I could not make him listen. He got me to sit down in the crew's quarters. You've never seen such filth lying about in all your life. He simply would not fetch the water. He went on and on about his own brand of fatalism, making out that when your number was up it was up, you can imagine the sort of thing. And I was nervous to get back. I was afraid Shiner would think I'd gone to ground. Every time they dropped a bomb in the river it shook the ship as though someone had fetched the keel a great welt. Nothing came very close. The ship rocked gently in between. We might have been off to sea down the old Tamese."

She was not listening once more. Their walking up and down was beginning to get on her nerves, and this path, half a mile long through the wild garden under snow, was so wet to the feet. For when they came to the stile, which led out of the garden, he had turned back. She had planned a walk by the road below. He was so deep in his account she did not like to tell him what she wanted. So they had retraced their steps. Now they were coming to that stile again. She wondered if she could get him out of this beastly, decaying place. But he was hot with the breath of his first night in real London. And the old boy, who had found himself a stick, was ranging busily about through undergrowth, to one side or the other, slashing down the snow from overweighted branches.

She decided this was one of those occasions when you could not interfere.

"But when eventually I did get a bucketful, I'd heard some incendiaries fall pretty close, and once I got off the ship I found they'd dropped on a line right across what timber was left, over the yard we'd come through to get at the blaze. Right across our line of retreat. Anyway, everyone had come back to fight this new lot, and I saw Shiner in action for the first time. He was absolutely terrific. You know what a huge man he was. Well, he stood up top of a pile of timber throwing planks off to get down to the seat of the fire, where an incendiary had fallen in a sort of deep pocket. The light from it was that flashlight white, the wood round him brilliant yellow, he had lost his tin hat, his hair was down over his black face, and he was doing more than I'd thought one man could."

(He had said, "Hi, cock. Boy, am I enjoying this." And Richard particularly remembered him some twenty minutes later. The fire, red now, had taken a good hold. The picture was of Shiner right up in it, mouth wide open, snarling, drooling at the flames. The man had been much too close, but that was like him. Richard remembered he tried to explain why he had been under cover on the ship, and not up at the fire. All Shiner caught of what Richard shouted were the two words, "drinking water," at which he had called back, "Let's have some, cocker.")

At this moment Christopher came up.

"I say, dad, what shall we do?" he said.

"Don't call me dad, call me daddy."

"Now run along for a bit, darling, daddy and me are talking. There's a good boy. Isn't it terrible," she said to Richard, "he calls me mum."

Christopher said "Oh lord," and wandered off. In a moment he was happily laying about him, on his own again.

"That awful local school," his father said.

Suddenly, in spite of herself, she spoke about herself.

"I feel so useless down here," she said.

"Darling," he said, pressing her arm. A rather affected look of great tiredness came over his face.

"No, I don't really," she lied, when she saw. "It's quite right, I must be with the old boy. Now, go on, you were just at the most exciting bit." She encouraged him although she could not have told the point he had reached.

"Well, we could not get water, it was hopeless from the

first. You see the blast from the bomb which probably killed Piper, I expect it fell while I was in the ship, because I never heard it, that blast had brought all the remaining skylights down, and the broken glass cut the hose. Each time they turned the pumps on there were just huge spurts of water way back at gashes in the hose, we never got anything at the branch. You should have heard Shiner curse the pump operator, who couldn't catch a syllable, he was too far away even when his pump was not operating. You don't know the noise our pumps make. And that was happening all over, burst lengths I mean. We had to give up. The fire had taken charge. In the end someone came back with a message to say the sub officer was killed, and that we were all to get out as best we could. Because the flames had got across the road, the only one we could escape by.

"Then I did a thing even Piper would not have done. You know the old man hadn't joined the sub officer in that shelter because he was windy. Being as he was, he just couldn't resist it. I never knew the sub from Adam. I'm sure he didn't want the old fool. It was simply that he couldn't have been able to get rid of Piper. Well, when word came for us to clear out, back to the Gate, because our escape was cut off, I was too quick. You see it was no good trying to roll up the hose, which was hopelessly cut about, and ruined. And the pump that had been trying to supply us with water wasn't ours, it was the other crew's job to get it away. But when I did come across Shiner again, at the Dock Gate, I asked him where he had been. And d'you know he'd helped them manhandle that pump right through the flames, though they couldn't possibly have managed it by the road we took when eventually I got a lift out."

"But what are you blaming yourself for?"

"I was too fast in getting away, that's all."

"You don't mean to say you really think you ran away?" As she asked this she put her left arm up over his shoulder. She smiled at him with genuine amusement.

He laughed. But she was beginning to irritate him again. "Well it was awkward. You see it was the second time I'd got separated. But things came out all right afterwards, as you'll see. Anyway Shiner was careful not to lay the blame. It was a nasty moment. I simply went off on my lonesome, trying not to run, to see if I could get hold of our own pump, to get it away. By that time nearly everything left was alight. And great high piles of timber, too. Everyone was clearing out. The smoke came in gusts. I couldn't find the crew. The pump wasn't where we'd left her. I began to run to one abandoned taxi after another. Everything looked deep red and it was getting frightfully hot. There wasn't a sign of my crew, or Shiner. No one answered a question, not that there were many left to ask. So I gave up, and jumped on the step of a taxi that was moving off. Then I saw what we had to drive through. You know, it really was a bit much. The road had those high open sheds on each side, stacked with timber, well alight. The wind was blowing the most enormous swirling flames scything right across the road, which kept on being blotted out by smoke. Each flame would shut off suddenly, disappear, then sweep out red again, quite forty foot long, the bigger ones, sweeping across parallel with the ground, and fiercer than you can imagine. Well, the driver of this old cab didn't seem able to get more than nine miles an hour out of her. And he chucked up the sponge. I'll agree we were still moving, but he opened the little window into the back and said:

"'Jack, I can't do it.'

"At that a small man put his face right through and cursed him completely until he did drive on. It wasn't too bad in the end. Just very hot and a good many flying cinders. It didn't last more than a minute."

"Go on," she said.

"Then rather an amusing thing happened. As soon as we were out of danger I got off. I was till trying to find my pump and taxi. It seemed pitch dark out of the flames. I fell in getting off that step though we can't have been travelling more than five miles an hour. That made me realise how tired I was. There were a few random piles of timber, but nothing alight, and I could see a pink gasholder at the bottom. There was nothing up above. I had my back to the blaze. We must have been the last to get out because I was absolutely alone. Nothing had passed me."

He stopped. He coughed nervously. Then he went on:

"And it was then that I came on a little man behind a low wall of timber, holding a branch, yards out of range of the blaze behind. I asked what he was doing. He said he was waiting for water. I just managed to see he had got a small fire he could have put out with a bucket. So I said I'd follow the hose back to his pump, and give them the order to turn on. I hadn't gone more than two lengths when it ended. They had simply driven the pump off, abandoned him. He was connected to thin air. I went back. I didn't enjoy going even that short way back towards the blaze. So I told him and we walked away together."

"Excuse me a minute, darling," she said. "Christopher," she shouted, "come here. Do be careful. You'll only be getting wet through. That last lot of snow went all over you."

She was really concerned. She forgot Richard.

The boy paid no attention.

"Christopher," she went on, "you heard what I said." She took her arm away from Richard, detached herself. "Come here when I tell you, I mean it." Then when he did trail along back to them, "Why look," she said, before he was close enough to see, "You're absolutely soaked. Oh isn't it vexing."

"I'm not. Really I'm not, mum."

"Let me feel. Well, you're not too bad," she agreed, but thought that, in the nanny's day, he would have had to change everything, right down to his skin. It was difficult to know how particular one ought to be.

"Look," his father interrupted, "haven't you knocked those branches about enough? There's hardly a bird left in the garden since you've been out. You'd do better to put food for them. They starve in this weather you know."

"They're Polish people," Christopher said, "and I'm a German policeman, rootling them about."

"Well, if that's so, hadn't you better carry on the good work where it's drier? Why not go back to the stables and see if you can't kill some more mice with a spoon? You could think they were Czechs," his father said.

"Oh thanks, I say. That's a lovely idea," and he ran off, stumbling in the snow, diminutive.

Dy looked up at Richard. She laughed. "I give you best," she said, adding, "but he wasn't too wet, was he?"

"No, you'd wrapped him up well. Every child in the world is war mad now. I suppose I am. Except that I'm not keen on the war. But I seem to talk of nothing else."

"That's just what I want," she said, patting his arm as you would pat a dog. He warmed to her for a moment, then turned back to himself again.

"It's so marvellous to be here once more." As he said this his eyes filled with tears. The moment she saw these she drew away. "Go on with what you were telling me," she said, brisk.

"You're sure you aren't bored?"

"Of course not, it's wonderful," she lied.

"Well I limped along this road, because I had hurt my foot somehow, I don't know when. We came round a wall. There was a whole collection of pumps drawn up. Almost at once I found the crew, except Piper of course. They were frightfully pleased to see me. Shiner thought I mightn't have been able to get out. He said he'd stayed back and looked everywhere, as well as help get that pump away. I expect he had, but I left long after he did, I'm sure now. Then we noticed Piper was missing. I thought we'd better go back to look. 'Naw,' Shiner said, ''e'll only be crawlin' after the

LFB,' meaning the Regulars. I stuck out, arguing that we couldn't abandon the old man. The others said we should be better off without him. Then another wave of bombers came over. Someone up in front shouted, 'Everyone to abandon the Dock.' We were in a nasty spot if a bomb had fallen, jammed in a mass by the Dock Gate. So all the taxis and tenders began to move off. That rather settled the question. We got in and went. But not far. I wouldn't have that. Not on account of old Piper, mind. Merely because I didn't think we'd been given a proper order."

"Why? You couldn't expect to see the officer in the dark, surely?"

"It wasn't dark remember, but a sort of half daylight, at that distance from the fire just like the last light of day in streets. No, as we drove away it didn't seem right to me, somehow."

"You don't mean a fifth columnist gave a bogus order?"

"Oh no, only that it looked as though we were running from a fire that had got the better of us. I thought the chaps up in front wanted to get away, that one of them had just sung out, and the rest had followed like sheep. So I told old Knocker to draw up for a minute. There was a certain amount of stuff coming down just then. Shiner got almost agitated. He wanted to know what we had stopped for. But I wasn't going to tell him. And I wouldn't tell because I was afraid he'd override me. Thank God the old Pied one wasn't with us. If he had been I think we should have gone back just to get rid of him at the station. Well, I stopped first one and then another pump driving away in the direction we had been going. They didn't know who'd given that order, they said, and drove on. It looked fishy to me."

"You mean it was a sort of panic?"

"Yes, more or less. Then Shiner got down. He began to get angry. This street was dead empty again. 'What are we waiting for, cocker?' he asked. He looked enormous, I remember. So I said I wasn't sure about that order. He said to let us get back to the old substation and be reorganised. It came out he thought the Dock hopeless because there weren't any officers, or any orders. He said we couldn't do any good on our own. I pointed out it seemed like running away, that we'd been driven off for the moment, but when things got quieter we ought to go back. I asked Knocker White, the driver, what he thought. He wasn't having any. He merely said I was the number one, it was my responsibility. So I said, 'Well we're staying.' Shiner said 'OK, mate. If you say so that's all right by me.' A bomb began to come down, close. We flopped.

"You know," he went on, "it was a bit of a moment. We'd had months waiting at the station, quarrelling over Pye, and about whether one man had done more night-guards the week before than another, and whether poor Pye had his uses, or if his running after girls made life harder for us. Also all the Piper trouble. Thinking it over I'm sure the bother with the Pied one was that he stank. He was abominably dirty. There were some who made up to the Regulars almost as much. For the matter of that, I did. The only difference was they did not choose such high officers. No, there it is. After twelve months there we suddenly were men again, or for the first time. In deciding to stay we proved it. I shall always be glad we did, although Shiner was killed. He was so good he would have been killed anyway."

"When was he?"

"Later that night, or rather in the morning. He went off on the prowl to get a drink and almost the last stick of bombs that came down must have killed him, blown him into the water when we were back at the Dock, for we never found a trace. We did make a search for him."

"Was he married?"

"No, he was on his own. Before that he saved my life. Where I'd got down between what I thought was a street sand box and a wall, you know one of those things they spread gravel from when it's wet, just after we'd decided not to go back to the substation, he stopped me, 'Don't lie up against that, cock,' he said, 'it's a distributor box.'"

"What's that?"

"The Electricity Department. Something like ten thousand volts passes through it. I moved out double quick. We found a park behind the wall, with a trench shelter. We went to ground there for a bit."

"How did he save your life, darling?"

"I'm coming to that in a minute. It was incredible in that shelter, absolutely pitch black. A woman was moaning for water in a foreign accent and as we went down the ramp we found it was packed, there were so many people you could not sit down. We hadn't been standing, huddled, for more than three minutes when a drunk came up outside. I could see him against the open doorway. He was raving that he was going to shew a light to the Germans up above. He repeated this when a voice asked what he'd said, and three huge men pushed past me, tearing up the ramp. I thought they were going to kill him. And d'you know what? Shiner and Knocker both followed them up. Although we were in the first real bit of shelter we'd had that night. Anything to be in a row. It was just the same at the substation whenever someone started baiting Piper. He was no more than a silly worn-out old man, yet great hulking fellows like Shiner would get up to encourage him to fight. Someone, whoever it was, would be taunting the old hermit with how often he had been on the Labour Exchange, the Lido, and then Shiner would begin calling him by his Christian name, saying, 'Go on, Arthur, 'ave a go.'"

"So what happened?" she asked. He was beginning to get hoarse, had stopped to eat some ice.

"Nothing. A bomb came down close, with the noise of an express train going through a station, and blew up that distributor box I'd been lying beside. There was a most appalling flash."

"And that man? Had he shone a light?"

"Oh no. He was drunk. I don't know what happened to him. We were all knocked off our feet. In the confusion he got away."

She was really concerned. "Darling," she said, "it must have been too dreadful." Her eyes filled with tears. He did not notice. He was beginning to tail off, as though the impulse which had driven him to tell, like a clockwork spring, was beginning to run down. He felt very tired.

They walked along in silence. "Too dreadful," she murmured, then she asked:

"What are you thinking about?"

"Only the last extraordinary thing in that fantastic night." He spoke as though it was too remote to have any interest.

"Tell me."

"Well I don't know. But cutting a long story short, we stayed in that shelter until we'd had a breather. Then I thought we might get back to the Dock. There was a bit of an argument so I said I'd walk back to the Gate and see if I could get some definite orders. Knocker and Shiner tossed up to see who should come with me. Shiner lost. He followed about twenty paces behind, so that one of us could pick the other up if anything happened. I think he still thought we ought to go back to the substation. But it was all much quieter up above.

"When at last I did get back to the Dock Gate there was not a pump to be seen, only about a dozen Auxiliaries leaning against a wall. The blaze was in full view now, much closer. It was terrific. The Auxiliaries never moved or said a word. They looked as though they'd had all the stuffing knocked out.

"Then I saw a great car coming down that road we'd evacuated the Dock by. It was obviously one of the Chiefs. It drew up in front of us. As two or three minor officers got out a man said in a frantic voice inside, 'What are all these men doing here?' When he got out and came towards us, I saw it must be one of the Chiefs. I think it was the one who is rather a friend of Hilly's.

"Well, you know, I made up my mind at once the only thing I could do was to beard him before he could tackle me. So I went up, saluted, and told him I'd been ordered out, which was more or less true, and been told to stand by a hydrant outside with my pump, which was untrue but an example, you see, of what they call the Fire Brigade mind, and finally I told him I had come back for orders. That was true. He asked me where my pump was. I told him three hundred yards up the street. 'Right,' he said. 'You see that ship over there?' 'Yessir,' I said, noticing for the first time a great ocean-going merchantman ablaze, writhing with flames from end to end. 'Well then take your pump,' and he waved his hand, 'and put it out,' he shouted. Three men with one pump.

"Shiner walked alongside me on the way back.

"'What did he say, cock?' he asked.

"'He said to put that bloody liner out,' I told him.

"'Suffering Jesus,' was all Shiner said.

"But luckily it did not come to that. For just after we'd driven through the Gates a sub appeared who took us off to the left, towards the old gasometer. We had to stop the fire getting round the end of a wall into another, untouched, timber yard. We stayed there, oh, until far into the morning. There was nothing else. Only the pigeons flying about burning. Some were on the ground, walking in circles into the flames, fascinated. And of course Shiner was killed later on."

"Darling, you mustn't let it get you down."

"It doesn't worry me," Richard answered stoutly.

He did not think it did.

She then said a very foolish thing, because it was true.

"I wonder what's the meaning of it all?" she asked.

He felt a flash of anger. It spread.

"I know this," he announced in what, to him, was direct answer, "you've always been most unfair to Pye."

She was astounded.

"Pye?" she asked.

"Yes, to Pye," he said. He stopped, turned away from her. "That's the tragedy."

"What d'you mean?"

He could not look at her. He knew, if he did, that it would break down, that he would not be able to go on, that Pye would be nothing; because he now knew the whole experience was almost over.

"Well," he began, whipping himself up, speaking in a new high, cracked voice, "a man can be responsible, somehow, for his wife, can't he, but never for his sister, never. He'd lived alone with her for years. She was obviously half crazy. Then she took Christopher away. That was hard luck on everyone, but when I was posted to his station it was much worse for him than it was for me. Then what finally ruined him was the authority he got. He didn't do anything to get it. It came with the war, because he was an experienced fireman. He wasn't in the least ready to have men under him. Hardly any of them were. The wonder is that he was as good as he turned out to be. But it was sex finished him off, and sex arising out of his authority. You see there were a couple of enthusiastic amateurs he got in with through being in charge. He just couldn't take it. Well, he used to invite this Prudence woman out, and it's the old story, what she liked was more than he could afford. That is to say a gin and lime in the local wasn't enough. She had to have it in a night club, which came twice or three times as expensive.

"One thing led to another. In the end he got too confident. He was caught out once or twice, absent without leave you know. I'm not sure what he thought about his sister. He told me once he would rather she stayed in the asylum.

But what he could not forgive was that she had been put inside."

Roe was shaking.

Dy stamped. "Richard, dear, you surely wouldn't have her running around?" Her voice was shrill. She chanced a look at him, but all she could see was the back of his head.

She was beginning to lose her temper, as he could tell. When he spoke again it was more in his usual tone of voice.

"Yes," he said, "but why should he pay for her? The asylum people were threatening a writ at the end. Oh, I know he was earning bigger money than he had ever got, but even then it wasn't up to his new standards. And he went and brought back a boy late, and kept him the night in his room."

"Him, too?"

"I don't say it was sexual. I'm sure it wasn't. I don't think it had anything to do with what his sister did. Old Piper made out he'd got to know the parents afterwards, that they'd told him the boy was so mad to see a raid he often stayed out all night in case there was one at last. Piper said, too, that he informed Trant, the District Officer, whose bathroom he was doing, what the parents had told him. I expect this was the first they heard up at Number Fifteen about the boy. He was a snake that man. So Pye was doubly on the mat. And that was the end.

"But I'm sure it was unpremeditated, just like this," and he leant his full weight on the stick he carried. It went six inches into the ground. Resting both hands on the handle he stood, halted, ridiculous.

"Don't be a fool," she said angrily. She thought it was absurd.

He was silent for once. He felt his rage rise.

"So Pye committed suicide?" she asked, although Richard had written to tell her weeks before.

"In the gas oven," he said. "But he had the sense to turn

off the automatic burners in the boiler first. Or we should all have been blown up."

He waited, watching his anger. Then he heard the verdict.

"I can't help it," she said, "I shall always hate him, and his beastly sister."

This was too much for the state he was in. He let go. "God damn you," he shouted, releasing everything, "you get on my bloody nerves, all you bloody women with all your talk."

It was as though he had gone for her with a hatchet. She went off without a word, rigid.

He felt a fool at once and, in spite of it, that he had got away at last. Then his son came up, gravely looked at him.

He said to Christopher, for the first time:

"Get out," and he added,

"Well, anyway, leave me alone till after tea, can't you?"

London, June 1940–*Christmas* 1942

ALSO AVAILABLE IN HARVILL PANTHER

Gerald Kersh

FOWLERS END

With an Introduction by
Michael Moorcock

In the darkest, furthest corner of London is a bustling, squalid, ramshackle community built on deceit and despair: Fowlers End

"One of the best comic novels of the century"
ANTHONY BURGESS

"The book provides the grisly fascination which clings to any dissection of rottenness" *Time Magazine*

ALSO AVAILABLE IN HARVILL PANTHER

Maureen Duffy

CAPITAL

With an Introduction by
Paul Bailey

A lone Londoner maps the city, hearing beneath its surface the urgent whispers of the past. As he listens, he grows convinced they are predicting London's future.

"Louis MacNeice would have relished the fiction. So will all who care for London" C. J. DRIVER, *Guardian*

"Her subject is London, its past and its fate . . . a cabaret of voices from the past cut in and out of her narrative as, firm in her locus, she moves back and forth in time. Her city takes on the dimensions of the City of Man – or Woman: I closed the book intending to reopen it as soon as possible to see what I might have missed"
JULIA O'FAOLAIN, *Observer*

ALSO AVAILABLE IN HARVILL PANTHER

Alexander Baron

THE LOWLIFE

With an Introduction by
Iain Sinclair

East London; home of dog-tracks and boarding houses, winners and losers, but mostly losers.

"A beautifully observed, understated study of an East End Jewish gambler . . . something of an underground cult"
JOHN WILLIAMS, *Guardian*

"No matter how sordid the situation, how depraved the thoughts and ambitions, the reader compulsively goes along with Harry . . . For all its hard and cunning realism this is an exceptionally moving book" ***Books and Bookmen***